C. C. EKEKE

For

Nicole & Jason

Thanks for the crazy acronyms ideas

Short Story Summaries

BOUND
In the weeks leading to the Union-Imperium trade merger, Honaa receives news that further jeopardizes Star Brigade's survival.

GAMBIT
A Kedri mercenary makes a dangerous play in hopes of a better life.

OUTWORLDERS
Four rookies ponder their futures the day before Star Brigade's fate is decided.

TERRITORIAL
V'Korram takes violent measures to force Liliana Cortés out of Star Brigade.

DESCENT
Khrome helps Liliana overcome a longstanding fear.

BELIEVE
Surje's confidence in his abilities is tested after not getting on SB-1.

DISCIPLE
Sam D'Urso gives her protégé a new assignment.

PREY
Two bounty hunters search Bimnorii for a lethal yet lucrative target.

AFTERSHOCK
Sam and Liliana bond over the outcome of the Alorum ambush.

SAMARITAN
A stranger in a strange land discovers the seeds of a conspiracy that could devastate the Galactic Union.

GIFTED
A young Nnaxan child's nightmares reveal his family's bleak future.

FOREWORD

Hey there. I'm really excited to present these brand new short stories to you, but bear with me while I give a little backstory.

When I was first writing Star Brigade: Resurgent over a decade ago, I knew immediately that I wanted to expand this universe. But I wasn't sure if I had more than one book in me.

Fast forward to when I was editing the first edition, and plans for several Star Brigade books were filling up my head. Full-length novels aside, I'm always a fan of the smaller moments that complement the larger universe.

The idea to write short stories came from another sci-fi franchise where collections of tales surrounding important events in that universe. But after a few false starts some years back, I tabled the idea. Chalk it up to laziness.

Then about two years ago after spending months editing a draft of the next Star Brigade novel, I needed a serious recharge for my creative juices.

What I ended up with were several short stories, quite a few occurring during the events of Star Brigade: Resurgent. Even better, writing these stories gave me a greater sense of some of these characters' identities.

Most of these shorts feature POV characters from the first Star Brigade novel, others focus on non-POV supporting characters, while quite a few introduce non-book characters who just could have greater roles to play in future stories. I chose sixteen which complement Star Brigade: Resurgent the best and to give you all a taste of what's to come.

I've also included a few bonuses, like the original opening chapters from the first edition of Star Brigade: Resurgent. Way back when, I figured the best way to introduce the character Marguliese as well as give weight to

Habraum's backstory was via flashback after the infamous Ferronos Sector War.

However, I was never totally happy with how these chapters meshed into the overall story. Neither were critics or book readers. While re-editing the first Star Brigade book, I yanked them out while cherry-picking elements to integrate into Resurgent's overall timeframe.

In this anthology you'll find the original two opening chapters from the first edition of Star Brigade: Resurgent.

There's also one more bonus feature in this collection: an appendix on the Galactic Union, giving some details and backstory on the star-spanning hyperpower that Star Brigade is part of. So kick back and enjoy.

Regards,

CCE

Bound

Captain Honaa Ishliba was in full black and grey Star Brigade captain's uniform when he received the bad news. It was currently nighttime, with only medimechs floating around Hollus Maddrone's main Medcenter and its labs.

Honaa sat across the desk of Dr. Rwynyr Simony in the latter's office, his triangular-snouted jaw hanging agape. Suddenly, the maroon-skinned Rothorid couldn't feel his own legs.

"You're joking, yesss?" he hissed, hoping and *praying* it had been a joke.

The Xyobic doctor's face usually beamed. Yet tonight it was a study in graveness, the paper-thin fronds stick from his forehead limp with sorrow. Simony had his upper arms folded and his lower hands on his hips. "I wish I were joking, old friend."

Honaa shook his head, a vain attempt to fight off the horrifying reality slowly marinating through his brain. Had Dr. Simony gotten better at keeping a straight face, or was this the truth? "Hasss to be a misssstake."

"I'm afraid not. These tests are—"

"Run thossse tessstsss again," Honaa demanded, barely hearing the doctor. "*All* of them."

"Honaa—"

"Run. Them. Again," he repeated slowly, an edge of menace in his voice. Dr. Simony ran the tests again, blood, full body bioscan, DNA mapping.

The test results did not change.

Honaa's mind was reeling. In the midst of the sterile, off-white office, he felt like a stain. The fifteen-year Star Brigade veteran was sick from a disease that struck maximums at random, a spiteful cosmic toss of the dice.

The anger had fled, leaving only fear and shock and questions. "How? *How* did this occur?" Honaa was frantically pacing back and forth in Simony's office, anxiety making his thick tail stand at rigid attention.

"That is the insidious thing about this pestilence. It can strike anyone with maximal abilities. Anyone." Simony stood stock still behind his desk as Honaa paced. The Xyobic's sober, unemotional answers didn't ease Honaa's shock and dread at all, but the Rothorid appreciated the tone regardless. The last thing he needed was to worry about someone else's panic.

"But...I feel fine. Except for the slight fatigue and power fluctuation..." Honaa's voice drifted off at the memory of how this nightmare had started. Last week he'd felt abnormally tired by just generating a phase shift during a group practice with some rookies. At the time, Honaa had written it off as fatigue. These past few weeks he'd been running around Conuropolis, begging UComm higher-ups for support in what felt like an impossible bid to avert Star Brigade's decommissioning. Then, in a solo practice yesterday, Honaa again had trouble maintaining a phase shift. He instantly scheduled a full checkup, three months early.

Now, the Rothorid veteran would have given anything to go back to that point in time where he had no clue what was wrong. The fear had escalated, forming a vise around his chest and squeezing, making breathing a challenge.

"What you've been experiencing," Dr. Simony continued, "are preliminary symptoms of the disease."

"I heard casesss where if caught in time, it can be cured," Honaa ventured, grasping desperately for some lifeline.

Simony shook his head immediately. "I'm sorry, Honaa, but we caught this too late."

Honaa's heart ached, and the fear clenched tighter. So this was permanent, and guaranteed to get worse. He had to know when, to plan and prepare. "How much time do I have?"

"By the looks of it, 2-3 months. You'll have to resign from active field duty, obviously. Not immediately, but soon."

The facts of his dilemma flooded in, drowning his already overwhelmed thoughts. "Sssam and I are the only sssenior officersss left," he realized aloud, feeling the panic squeezing a little tighter, his hissing growing higher and more manic. "Ssshe'ss not even a captain!"

"I know," the Xyobic nodded.

"If I ressssign and word getsss out why, Ssstar Brigade will be finissshed." The gravity of that statement hit like a meteor strike.

The doctor's features spasmed, as if pained. "I can offer a solution to dampen the symptoms—"

The mere suggestion stopped Honaa in his tracks. He whirled on the Xyobic, sharp teeth bared. "I will NOT cover up my affliction!"

The Xyobic jerked back in surprise, but recovered his composure quickly. "Was not suggesting it. I remember the xenotrophin scandal."

The memories that Simony's pointed tone shook loose shuddered through Honaa from head to tail.

Almost nine years had passed since Honaa had stumbled upon a fellow Star Brigadier, a legend within the organization, with the same illness. Yet, in this now-former Brigadier's obsession to remain field active, she had chosen to hide it using illegal xenotrophin boosters and developed quite the addiction. Legend or not, Honaa had felt no remorse for reporting her cover-up to Star Brigade's senior officers. The irony of finding himself in the same position forced a dour hiss of laughter out of Honaa.

By now the illness must have rendered the former Brigadier powerless, the same fate awaiting Honaa. Fear squeezed at his chest once more and the laughter subsided. "I-I am sssorry, friend," he said in a listless voice. Simony deserved none of the vitriol he'd brandished. "Thisss isss all much to take in." Honaa sank into a seat, defeated.

"I'll give you medication to reduce the fluctuations for a time," Simony approached his old friend, "so you can get your Star Brigade affairs in order."

Honaa stared off at nothing. He had pondered his future a lot over the last year, but this new wrinkle changed everything.

The touch of the doctor's upper right hand on his shoulder startled Honaa back into the present. "You have done all you can to save the Brigade," Xyobic said compassionately, staring down at the Rothorid. "Even your fellow Rothorids would not fault you from walking away."

Honaa's answer was an icy stare. As versed as Rwynyr Simony was in the biology of countless species, he was thoroughly oblivious in regards to Rothorid culture, how they would react if he retired, yet left without doing everything possible to save Star Brigade. Honaa swallowed his ire and shook the doctor's hand. "My thanksss. I will let you know what I decide."

After departing the Medcenter, the first place Honaa wanted to go was Memorial Hall, to look upon former Brigadiers and forerunners fallen in battle for answers. Should he leave now or wait until the end? But to look upon those life-like holograms who had served Star Brigade valiantly, incapable of preserving what they had died for? *No, I can't face them. Not when I know that I will fail them.*

Honaa took a less frequented translifter back to his quarters. Before he could step two feet inside his quarters, a chime informed him of a long-distance transmission. After the news he'd received, Honaa had the overpowering urge to ignore it. "Origin of transsssmission?" he wearily asked.

"Rothor IV," the computer voice chirped. Honaa accepted the call without another thought.

In a few moments, the hardlight hologram of another Rothorid appeared; a female shorter than Honaa by half a foot and sinewy in build. Her dark green scales, spiny head crest and stubby two-foot tail indicated a Rothorid subspecies from the wetwoods. Her eyes were blood red, with razor-thin black pupils and a flatter muzzle than Honaa's. Her features were sharp, pointed—the most beautiful face Honaa had ever known.

"Jashee," he addressed her in Wuiroth, the hissing native tongue of the Rothorids. He gave her a nod to the left, the standard show of affection for a Rothorid's one companion. "Thisss sssurprise isss mossst pleasssant."

"Honaa," Jashee Ishliba replied in Wuiroth, doing the sideways head nod to the right. "You are misssssed amongssst usss."

Honaa had not even thought of how to tell Jashee. On instinct he planned to do what he had been doing over the past several months—give a vaguely detailed story under the pretext of classified information. Jashee didn't need to know how he had not been on an official active mission in almost four months. It might come across as whining about doing his duty. The half-formed story was just leaving his lips. The next thing Honaa knew, the words just started to spill out.

Honaa told her *everything*.

The whole time he spoke, Jashee's scaled and muzzled face remained a mask, giving away nothing. After finishing, he felt surprising relief from sharing this, his inner burden unexpectedly lighter.

Jashee regarded him in silence for a long moment before asking one question. "What will you do?"

He wanted to return to Rothor IV and his family. Honaa was sick of the frustration, sick of sitting around being useless, sick of the political games UComm was playing with his and the other Brigadiers, sick of watching the corpse of Star Brigade slowly rot into nothing. Honaa wanted out.

But his selfish wants were not what Star Brigade needed. And that was not what would honor his family on Rothor. Honaa gazed upon his companion's magnificent face, with that unyielding strength shining through.

Honor your duty. Honor your family. The words every Rothorid lived by thundered through his skull. He thought of those that had fallen in battle almost a year ago on Beridaas. He thought of the dozen-and-a-half rookies with no direction and no leadership. He thought of Sam D'Urso, who could have left months ago, but stood by him and Star Brigade. Honaa thought of his offspring, who would be judged by the choices he would make regarding Star Brigade. The choice was easy then.

"I am bound by duty, oath and honor to ssstay and fight for Ssstar Brigade'sss sssurvival," he hissed, remaining as bloodless in face as his companion. "If thisss affliction takesss itsss toll firssst, then I will find another way to ssserve. Either way, this mussst stay sssecret until that day comesss. But if Ssstar Brigade doesssn't sssurvive...then I can return home to you and the offssspring."

Only then did Jashee's mask crack. Sadness, need, pride and love rippled across her muzzle. "Tha-that choice will honor our family greatly," her hiss was whisper-soft, yet sharp as a razor.

The Rothorid male bowed his head, "Assss our family dessservesss."

She smiled, displaying the most radiant sharp teeth Honaa had ever seen. "You alwaysss will be the conssstant ssstar of my exissstence."

"And you, mine...my one, my only," Honaa whispered back, His heart warming. He ached to touch her, caress her. *Not yet,* he reminded himself painfully. *Not until my duty is done.* The Rothorid held up a taloned hand. Jashee held up hers, until the two hands pressed together via hardlight hologram. Honaa closed his eyes and inhaled. He heard his one companion's tail rattle with bliss. Across an ocean of stars, for a brief while, they were one yet again.

When the transmission ended and Jashee's hologram faded, Honaa was alone in his quarters. Then the fear of tomorrow returned.

Gambit

"Stay calm." Those were the words that Norad Gour—former Imperial Officer, present-day mercenary and aspiring arms dealer—chose to live by. But given the Kedri's current predicament, the living part looked rather bleak.

Norad was a towering six-foot-ten-inches of beefy muscle, sporting the characteristic Kedri features: overarched brow, wide-set beady eyes, small bony spikes called *kutaa* jutting from both cheeks, and flat, squashed nose. Even his long, dark blue mane of hair was cut in the infamous shorlong style: spiky short in the front, hairless on the sides, long and flowing down his shoulders in the back.

But Norad's composed temperament was at odds with a Kedri's typical response to such a situation. He currently sat in the premium passenger cabin of a starliner traveling from the non-Union world of Xiliad, to the gas giant Ipsis. Or more accurately *was* heading for Ipsis, until it got caught in a rogue interceptor ship's tractor beam.

The situation wasn't helped by how the passengers sitting opposite Norad, in the premium passenger cabin, had revealed themselves as cheap cravens. There was also this small, coppery sphere, known to many as mindscrambler, floating to his right. Currently, it was scanning his and the other two passengers' retinas, using them to remotely shrike into their various vault accounts. And if he or the two other cabin occupants were to try deactivating said sphere, their brains would all be zapped to mush.

Norad had no doubt that more of these mindscramblers floated around in the starliner's premium passenger and general passenger sections, courtesy of the no-named space pirate gang spacejacking this space flight. Voyages traveling through the Merrivel Nebula to Union Space usually got accosted by space pirates on a semi-regular basis.

"All we want is your vault currency, folks!" a digitally masked, human voice boomed over the starliner's passenger cabin comms, one of their hijackers. "Comply and you might all make it out of here alive." The hijacker stated this as if their safety was a privilege.

"Ssstay calm? How can you sssay that, Kedri?" hissed one of Norad's annoyingly panicked cabin mates, Xuvaal Hoskaraba, a spare and sinewy-built Rothorid with scaly tan skin and diamond-shaped eyes of milk-white coloring. His triangular snout and thin lips peeled back testily to reveal white, needle-like teeth. "We, like most passsssengers, are unarmed."

Idiot. Norad felt a flush of irritation across his thick green hide. It galled him that this borderline fetus called himself a warrior. "You will live to see another day and we will both profit off this relationship," he replied, never letting his ire show above the surface.

"We've agreed to no relationsssship yet, Kedri," snapped Hinaa Gahlakahn, the other Rothorid in the cabin. This Rothorid was shorter, more thickset than his associate and much less amenable, with blackish leathery skin and blood-red eyes.

"Thessse ssspace piratesss plan to rob usss blind!" Xuvaal hissed. His tail stuck straight in the air, vibrating rapidly in fear.

"No they won't," Hinaa scolded. He glanced uneasily at their cabin mate. "We won't get our payment from our lassst job until two days from now."

Norad stared back at the pair in visible disgust. "First off, never tell a prospective supplier how much monies you don't have," he chided through clenched, jagged teeth. "Second. Stay. Calm." The two Rothorids finally took heed of his words and hushed. They were representatives of an upstart, all-Rothorid mercenary group called the 'Wrathorids', one of the few client meets that he'd finally been able to get in Union Space. This once obscure group had suddenly been gaining a sterling reputation in the arenas of gunrunning, drug trafficking, and killing for hire over the past year.

Up until this ill-timed spacejacking, Norad was less than impressed. And the feeling was clearly mutual, despite all the impressive Imperial weaponry holos the Kedri had displayed and the reassurance of his supplier's reliability. Norad had no clue whether these Wrathorids were playing hardball or were just stupid and shortsighted. Despite his contempt, Norad knew he had to impress these two and gain their business. *The Wrathorids can be a stepping stone,* he reminded himself, *to bigger and better clients.* That was, if the Kedri didn't throttle these two cravens with their own tails.

An idea sprang to mind then. He glanced at his clothing: a long, blue-gold Kedri tunic over a skintight obsidian body suit that served as light armor. The latter was a weapon in itself that had passed discreetly through spaceport scanners—Imperium tech, of course. *It was a good idea to wear this,* he mused. Norad eyed the small copper sphere hovering to his right and raised his hands slowly into the air.

Hinaa's eyes nearly popped out of his head. Xuvaal looked ready to have a heart attack.

Norad slapped a hand over his eyes, exposing the back of his hand to the copper sphere. The orb lit up in retaliation, only to violently vibrate, spark, and drop like a stone. It hit the floor with a *clunk*.

"Energy deflector," Norad muttered as the two Rothorids' jaws dropped, "Imperial tech at its simplest and best. Stay in the cabin." He rose from his seat without another word and headed for the door. "Now hopefully those mindscramblers were networked together—"

A glance outside into the premium passenger cabin showed an opulent burgundy and gold-striped aisle. Several mindscrambler spheres lay on its floor, all deactivated and useless. The silvery humanoid-like stewardroids, also serving as travel security, lay motionless on the floor as well. That, at least, explained to Norad why these space pirates' incursion hadn't been stopped. The Kedri heard a loud, expletive-laden shout beyond the egress separating the general passenger section.

Norad marched forward, the door sliding open for him. He strode into the general passengers section, an ovular beige section of three rows, separated by two aisles, coppery mindscrambler spheres strewn everywhere. Each row had groups of terrified passengers from every imaginable Union memberworld, three passengers seated next to each other with thin transparent blue dividers, sixty per row. All of them stared in silent bewilderment at three armed hijackers bickering heatedly. The trio wore light camouflage armor and masks, no emblem indicating their pirate gang affiliation. But a quick look told Norad that two of these pirates were human and the four-armed one was a Nnaxan.

"The mindscramblers went down before we cracked any accounts," cried the Nnaxan in a digital masked voice. "We have to reactivate—"

"Too late for that!" one human demanded, the digital mask not hiding her gender. "Just transmat us back to the ship before UComm…" The female trailed off as she and her cohorts finally noticed the near seven-foot Norad.

Without a word, the human space pirate in the cabin's rear snapped up his pulse rifle menacingly. But the Kedri was too fast, despite his massive size. Combat reflexes honed since childhood kicked in, and the Kedri juked to one side, snapping up his left fist.

Neuronanocytes in his mind synced to the suit, forming a sleek mini-blaster around his wrist gauntlet. With a thought, he shot off three bright bursts on heavy stun. The first hijacker took two in the chest and went flying. Norad dropped to a knee and jerked his head sideways, just missing a white-hot pulse blast from across another aisle. The other two hijackers opposite Norad had their pulse rifles cocked and unloaded blistering volley after volley.

The general passenger cabin erupted. Passengers were screaming, desperate to escape their seats.

Norad ducked for cover between seats in the middle aisle. The Kedri remained calm, a product of one too many battles. He had to end this firefight quickly, before it became a bloodbath. The Kedri picked up a disabled mindscrambler and tossed it at the Nnaxan space pirate. He whipped his pulse rifle around and blasted the sphere to dust motes. More screams erupted as panicked passengers ran for cover, blocking the Kedri's line of fire. But instead of becoming useless cannon fodder, several swarmed the Nnaxan and dragged him down, their fists rising and falling.

Seeing that made Norad smirk. The last pirate standing looked on from her corner, panicked as she spoke desperately into an earcom. The Kedri rose like a viper and aimed his gauntlet blaster at her just as she spun around to defend herself.

Both their weapons barked. One missed.

A heartbeat later, the space pirate's body shimmered and vanished. By the shocked noises from the other passengers, so did her two felled cohorts. Norad rose to his full towering height, breathing hard. That felt good, though battle was no longer as addictive as he once remembered. The Kedri was greeted by stares and gasps from his fellow passengers. Most had obviously never encountered an actual Kedri before.

Fortunately, most were unharmed, though some sported minor burns from stray hits during the blistering firefight. A gaggle of passengers gathered by the viewports on the right-hand side, some spouting in Standard Speak, "UComm scout ships just arrived! We're safe!"

As if on cue, the autopiloted starliner lurched suddenly. Norad guessed that the space pirates' interceptor tractor beam holding the vessel in place receded. As soon as it was free, the starliner made an emergency hyperspace jump, continuing for Ipsis. Immediately, Norad felt his heart leap with triumph, right as applause and gratitude from his fellow passengers engulfed the Kedri.

"Have you two decided?" Norad asked casually after returning to the cabin a little while later.

Xuvaal bristled. "We'll confer with our council and—"

"Abssssolutely not," Hinaa cut him off. "Your weaponsss are impressive and you ssssaved our vault accountsss. How ssssoon can you begin sssupplying usss?"

It worked. Norad resisted a victorious smile. As many of his species believed, pride was a poison that could route any near-victory. "Once you sign our agreement and make your initial payment, which I hope won't be a recurring issue," was his stoic reply.

Xuvaal opened his mouth to respond, but Hinaa silenced his counterpart with bared needle-like teeth. "You'll have both by midday tomorrow."

"Did I not say that we would profit from this relationship?" Norad brought his fists together and bowed. And to his surprise, the two Rothorids returned the Kedri greeting.

Thirty macroms later, the ship arrived at Ipsis Commerce Station, which orbited the enormous ivory and gold gas giant Ipsis. ICOM was a massive tree-like structure, larger than most military starbases Norad had seen. Its four interconnected tube-like sections were dark green and gold in coloring, encircled by various rings and sported branch-offs to accommodate new stores, hotels and megabistro centers.

ICOM was Norad's preferred accommodation when visiting Union Space. The commerce station boasted a vast selection of Kedri cuisine and accoutrements, as well as proximity to an old contact whose presence...and body...he enjoyed.

But being the largest, most diversified commerce station in the Rhyne System meant being the most heavily visited. The spacelane traffic around ICOM, always an eyesore to Norad, would worsen in six weeks once this absurd Union-Imperium Trade Merge was finalized. That might jeopardize some of the Kedri's current business ventures, which was why this trip held such importance. Norad needed to lock down potential clients now, before Union Space was flooded with Kedri technology and weaponry. And there were other engagements that required his attention. But he'd worry about those after he'd taken care of his business ventures.

Officials from Union Command Security Services were waiting once the starliner arrived at one of ICOM's civilian spaceports. All 101 passengers were meticulously questioned about the spacejacking incident, including Norad. He answered any questions with as much accuracy as he could provide. Apparently the space pirates had escaped in their unmarked interceptor ship, and UComm AeroFleet had yet to track down their whereabouts. The Kedri couldn't say that he was surprised...or disappointed.

"I shot to kill, so no doubt two of their numbers are dead," Norad replied to one question. And since they hadn't analyzed a weaponized body suit like his before, the authorities had to take his word as fact.

After the fifteen macroms of questioning, the Kedri received a mild scolding for bringing his weaponized bodysuit onboard the flight, but sincere gratitude from UComm officials for protecting the other passengers. Apparently the injuries of those attacked were minor at best.

Well, the spacejacking had to look somewhat believable, Norad mulled to himself while his more recognizable weaponry was returned.

Once he'd cleared customs, a formality due to being a visitor from a foreign hyperpower, Norad exited the ICOM spaceport and took a gravlev tram to his hotel in the Miracle Sector. Only when safe and alone in a translifter heading for his room did Norad finally exhale in relief. The Kedri then made an encrypted call via his earcom. "I heard your mission was successful?"

His question was met with booming laughter. "Like those Union *chutiyas* could ever catch us. You close the deal?"

Norad allowed himself that victorious smile. "Indeed, Parsec. Your assistance, and that of Kashmere and Eikoh's, was much appreciated."

"Hey," said the human he knew as Parsec Ishibashi, "you're M24 for life, even if you leave us."

"We miss you, Norad!" a Nnaxan voice bellowed in the background. *Eikoh.*

The Kedri missed those friends he still had at M24, but getting overly sentimental in public over emotional bonds was not the Kedri way. "Your methods were…unexpected."

"Rothorids aren't idiots," Parsec stated. "We had to ensure they suspected no deception from you."

"No doubt. How is Eikoh?" Norad recalled how badly those passengers had worked him over.

"Just some bumps and bruises," the female human named Kashmere replied. "He's a big boy."

That relieved Norad greatly. "I'll send over your percentages once I receive the Wrathorids's first payment. And please be discreet with your commission." Norad knew he played a dangerous game selling Imperium weaponry to a competing mercenary group, no matter how small. If any of the Kedri within M24 found out, it could mean his death, as well as those of his three long-time comrades.

"We know, we know," Parsec laughed. "Discretion is our middle names, Norad!"

"Of course. Till next time." Trickery was not a dish the Kedri served often or willingly. But given the plethora of known suppliers out there, his plunge into gunrunning hadn't come without challenges.

Before his days as a soldier of fortune, Norad Gour had served in the Imperium Armed Forces with all the stereotypical wants of any battle-hungry Kedri: fight for the Imperium, reach the rank of Warmaster, a good clean death by way of combat, and a progeny to continue their bloodline. But events and politics beyond Norad's control disrupted all of those goals. And once the Ferronos Sector War had concluded, it grew increasingly obvious that the Kedri Imperium's glory days of conquering others with impunity were over.

After leaving the Imperial military, Norad spent seven profitable years with M24. The large and renowned mercenary group was known for its blend of Nnaxan, earthborn and Kedri members, as well as its ruthless effectiveness. Norad had gotten to war and whore to his heart's content and rose quickly in the group's ranks, only to finally tire of the constant battle a few months ago. That was a near-blasphemous sentiment amongst most Kedri and did not go over well with his Imperium brethren. Norad didn't care. He needed a different path, one that could give him more than fleeting glory from battle, leading him to his current profession as an arms dealer. *And hopefully it leads me to the one I want to spend my life with.*

He finally reached his suite, on the 816th floor of the 2500-story Miracle Living Sector, located within the second of ICOM's massive cylinder superstructures. A retina and thumb scan granted the Kedri access to his room. The massive suite's halolights brightened upon entry, revealing gunmetal grey walls, an open door that peeked into a massive bedroom with wall-sized viewports, and a dining area. Something on the floor caught Norad's eye.

He took a few steps into the foyer, spotting a pile of clothing far too small and feminine to be his. The Kedri jerked his head up, noticing then the steady jets of the shower from his bathroom.

An uninvited guest.

Norad whipped out a dull grey H-4 Quickshot pulse pistol that looked small in his large hands and crept toward the bathroom with practiced stealth.

In the ceiling-high cylindrical bathing chamber was where Norad found his intruder: a petite female human, as naked as the stars were bright, earthborn by her sun-kissed complexion and the spun-gold hair spilling past her shoulders in sodden swaths. She stood with her head tilted back, eyes closed in relish as the chamber's multiple hydrojets sprayed her clean.

Frowning, Norad crept closer. The human seemed unaware of his approach or the pulse pistol he had aimed at her. The Kedri was close enough now to identify two of her tattoos: a Voton emblem of interlocked angled lines on the lower back, and a small, Earth-based icon on the upper left shoulder.

Norad's heart stuttered. *"You?"* he blurted out, shock freezing him in place.

"Seven months and *that's* the pulse pistol you greet me with?" the woman scolded in flawless Kedri Common Tongue.

This meeting was happening sooner than Norad had planned. He didn't bother asking how she'd found his hotel or knew of his arrival on Ipsis. Espionage was her trade, her world. From the doorway, Norad could sense the shower water was near freezing, ideal for a Kedri but not remotely suitable for her species. Then again, the Kedri's shock-addled brain recalled how extreme temperatures didn't bother her like they did 'normal' earthborns. And she was anything but normal.

"Visiting Union Space *without* telling me?" the human asked with an air of mock offense. "Thought I meant something to you, Norad." She still had her back to him, rubbing along the lush curves of her shapely yet fit body, concealing a tattoo encircling the appendage called a 'belly button'—the Kedri Common Tongue symbol for hope. That was Norad's favorite of her tattoos.

"More than you know," the Kedri insisted, unable to ignore the stirring in his loins. "I planned on contacting you," he cleared his throat, "after…securing new business."

"Ah," she shrugged, unconcerned. As icy water splashed down her in steady rivulets, she threaded her fingers leisurely through sopping blonde locks. "Soooo, you gonna stand there and shoot me?" The human finally turned toward Norad, with a gaze that teased and titillated. "Or come here and join me?"

Those words and that longing gaze scorched through Norad. He'd lost count of how many times he'd feasted on the wonders of this human's body. Norad regained his carriage, realizing then that he was still pointing his pulse pistol at the human. Biting back a curse, he let the weapon drop to the floor in a clatter and began hurriedly peeling off his clothing. *The perfect reward after a victorious battle.*

Sometime later, Norad lounged naked across the wide bed, watching his guest through the curtains on the suite's outer balcony. A call had come in for her, important enough that the human took it while they were in the throes. Now she paced back and forth on the balcony, in an unlaced silky black robe and an earcom, jabbering animatedly in Union Standard Speak. One might think she was angry, the way her voice rose, save for how she laughed loudly and often with whomever she spoke with.

"And whose fault is that? Give me a time and place." A brief silence followed. Her big brown eyes widened with amusement. "Corowood Zoo again? Of course," she sighed. "*Christ*, I miss him." Her husky voice grew thick with a longing she'd never displayed for Norad. "You? Eh. Not so much." The human threw her head back with another loud and throaty laugh.

Jealousy stabbed Norad's chest like a white-hot knife. For a heartbeat the Kedri wanted—no, *needed*—to snap the neck of whoever was on the other end of that transmission.

Stay calm. The words rang in his head, and Norad of House Gour felt ashamed. He sucked in a breath, swallowed his wounded Kedri pride and unclenched his fists. Norad had no actual claim to her, nor had he made one after their unceremonious split eight years ago. The woman had built a new life for herself within Union Space in the ashes of her previous one, working now for some military spec ops group called Star Brigade. Though from what she'd divulged to Norad, which was predictably not much, that group's days of usefulness were at an end.

Almost ten years they'd known each other, yet Norad didn't truly *know* her. She'd claimed her name was 'Malyn Rossi,' but Norad knew this to be an alias. She'd given him only scraps and half-truths about the dark and dangerous past she'd been running from when they'd first met, but never the full story.

"Yep, I can make today work," she said happily to her friend. "Alright, see you and Jerm later today." After the transmission ended, the human called Malyn plucked the earcom out and stashed it in her robe pocket. She then leaned over the balcony railing and zoned out on the suite's outer view, idly playing with tangled blonde tresses spilling over her right shoulder. And what a marvelous view this suite had. One could see all of IPCOM's Miracle Living Sector: a colossal tube of vast width ringed from top to bottom by the lights of a million or more inhabitants in their abodes. The concentric rings of civilian light kept going on forever in both directions, bookended by dark and seemingly bottomless holes. Of course, Norad had a privacy screen erected to obscure and mute what went on in his suite.

The Kedri rose and walked through the curtains, coming up from behind and slipping an arm around her waist. His six-foot-ten height to her five-foot-six at times was decidedly pronounced, so much so that the Kedri had to lean down as he searched the back of her neck with his tongue. She arched her back cat-like and made a contented noise.

Their rendezvouses, though brief and infrequent, took Norad back to their time together in Imperium Space. For a time they had been happy, beginning to plan a future—until she left without a trace and returned to Union Space. Over the past eight years, their paths had intersected every so often whenever he'd venture to Union Space. Yet even as his profession veered into murkier territory, and his travels had found him sharing another's bed, Norad's feelings remained unchanged.

"Who was that?" he finally murmured.

"Old friend," Malyn replied without further explanation, speaking again in Common Tongue.

Norad, expecting that non-answer, tried a different approach. "Not Nereyo, I'm guessing?"

She laughed loudly. "Haven't spoken to Rey in months. She's too busy playing 'fashion magnate.'"

Thinking of the legend Imperium operative, Nereyo Kyr, and the disgraceful parody she had become twisted Norad's innards with rage. He pulled back, shaking his head. "Appalling," the Kedri spat.

The human twisted in his grasp. Now he had a close-up of her heart-shaped face, its high cheekbones, large chocolate brown eyes and smooth olive skin bearing few signs of age. The sight was enough to cool Norad's anger.

She reached up to grasp his kutaa-studded cheeks. "Hey you," she purred, wearing her sexiest lopsided grin. The Kedri loved that grin, even the fleshy human lips that formed it. Norad had learned to accept and enjoy Malyn's soft, unscaled body parts, mainly the pillowy pair of breasts he now fondled.

"Hello." Norad's tongue met hers and rubbed around for a bit, until she abruptly threw her little self at him. Surprised, the Kedri stumbled back inside the suite as he caught her, only to trip onto the bed. She howled with laughter, a mischievous look in her eyes as she straddled him. Norad spiritedly ripped off her robe and the twosome picked up right where they'd left off earlier.

After they finished, both were on the floor entwined in each other's arms, her head nuzzled on his massive chest. The bed had more or less been destroyed half an orv ago.

"How long are you in Union Space this time?" Malyn whispered, as if afraid someone was listening.

Norad ran his fingers up and down the silky skin of her back. "Until next week." Interest in Imperium weaponry had risen, one of the few benefits this trade merger offered Norad. "I'm meeting with a few mercenary outfits to offer my services as a weapons supplier, including the Crimson Suns…"

The human jerked up from his chest and eyed him sternly. "Sure about that? The Crimsons Suns are one of M24's biggest competitors, Norad."

"And I am no longer part of M24," he met Malyn's gaze with unflinching confidence that wasn't just empty posturing. Granted, his meeting was with a cadet branch of the Suns, but it was still an opportunity.

Malyn tilted her head, wearing her playfully crooked grin. "Look at you, all risk-taking." She ran greedy hands down his torso, toward his loins. "The Kedri Royal Military Service has no clue what they're missing."

Norad's eyes narrowed beneath his overarched brow. *Was that a joke?* Sometimes he couldn't tell with Malyn. He pulled himself up to a sitting position against the bed. "Even if they offered me the honor of becoming a Warprime, I would decline. It's a political firestorm over in Imperial Space. The ultra-imperialists are riling up the masses again over the Imperium-Union Trade Merger…"

The woman rolled her eyes. "Christ. Those 'Warsworn' half-wits again? Can't your Imperium send them all on a long voyage into deep space?" *Without a spaceship*, her scowl suggested.

Norad chuckled in agreement. "Most of those 'idiots' are from the Warrior Caste, the majority of whom strongly want the Imperium to return to its conquering ways."

"What, that stupid ass Eternal War doesn't cut it anymore?" Malyn snarked, tossing her hair defiantly.

Norad's reaction this time was a cold, angry look. Any other Kedri would have killed Malyn on the spot for such a profane remark. "I enjoy you, human, but do not presume this enjoyment permits you to slight the Imperium's noble struggle against those cybernetic abominations."

Malyn's olive skin paled. "Sorry!" she raised her hands regretfully. "Didn't mean to offend your imperialistic pride."

Her contrition satisfied Norad enough, so he continued, "Many within the Imperium see your Galactic Union as a foe ripe for conquest. You wouldn't believe the lengths Sovereign Kel has taken to keep them pacified."

Malyn draped her arms around his bull-sized neck. "Tell me." Her throaty purr oozed with want.

Norad inclined his head toward hers. "Give me a reason." And so she pumped him for information, while he pumped her until she screamed. The former Imperial Military warrior in Norad felt rather soiled for spilling Imperium secrets to an outsider, especially a Union spy. But the fragrance of the human's flesh was inebriating, the taste of her tongue on his addicting, the heat of Malyn's body muddying his logic as he drove into her one ferocious thrust after another. She nibbled her way down his neck; Norad buried his face in her mass of disheveled blonde hair. They went two more times like a pair of feral beasts, and by then wrong or right no longer mattered, only her. After they'd finished, both were thoroughly satiated in more ways than one.

"Whether or not this trade merger actually happens," Norad said, pulling on a blood-red tunic, "right now, the Imperium is a star ready to go nova. I plan to stay clear until everything settles."

"What does that mean?" Malyn asked, pulling back on her figure-hugging dark blue pants.

"When my business is concluded in Union Space," the Kedri pulled his longish hair back in a sleek plait with a round metal clip, "I won't return to Imperium Space. Not for a while."

"Where are you going?"

"Lawless Space, perhaps," Norad said. "Take some bounty hunting jobs, while finding clients in need of Kedri weaponry."

Malyn shrugged on a white short-sleeved shirt. "And Union Space?"

Norad turned and looked down at his human lover. "I do not know when I will return."

That answer didn't agree with the woman, judging by her soured expression. "Huh."

The Kedri suddenly grew nervous, like an Imperial Legionary before his very first battle. But what he had to ask was one of the main reasons he had visited the Union this time. "Come with me."

Now it was Malyn's turn to be totally stunned. "Saywhatnow?"

Norad, seeing the opening, pressed on. "It can be like when we were together in Imperium Space."

The human adjusted her shirt, shock giving way to scorn. "*Now* who's living in the past?"

"Says the one desperate to save a dying organization," Norad threw back.

Malyn's nostrils flared. "Star Brigade *isn't* dead yet!"

Careful, he told himself. "Not yet, but eventually." Norad took measured strides toward Malyn. He knew that this beseeching was a risk to his pride and to their relationship. But the Kedri wanted Malyn at his side permanently. "See how this government disrespects you again? You deserve better."

She folded her arms and scoffed. "And life on the fringe with you *is?*"

"All these years in Union Space, wearing this veneer of civility has spayed you. Come with me and I'll remind you how to live again." Norad stood before Malyn, dwarfing her. "What is truly keeping you here?"

That question struck home. She looked away, locks of golden blonde tumbling down her shoulders. The conflict on her features grew more pronounced. "There are members of Star Brigade that need me," she disputed, sadness edging her words. "Who will care for them?"

"Who will care for you?" Norad retorted, his cavernous voice soft but firm. The Malyn Rossi he'd known eight years ago wouldn't have hesitated to up and leave her current life. But back then, Norad hadn't been ready to ask what he was asking now. Clearly, both parties had changed. He traced a thick thumb along Malyn's jaw, feeling her shiver with pleasure. "We can travel the stars together and build the life that we should have years ago." The Kedri's two hearts thudded so hard within his chest that he feared Malyn would hear them. Exposing his inner wants like this felt so odd. But in Norad's eyes, she was worth it.

A reluctant smile tugged at the corner of Malyn's lips. She was much more intrigued by Norad's offer than she was letting on. "There's one more thing I have to try to save Star Brigade," she insisted, her stubbornness as admirable as it was exasperating.

"And if that fails," Norad grabbed onto Malyn's hips, drawing her close, "and Star Brigade dies?"

"Then," she gazed up at him through her lashes, a wicked glimmer in her eyes, "and *only* then, will I strongly consider the prospect of joining you."

Outworlders

2nd Lt. Tyris Iecen always enjoyed a good game of Planet Master.

Planet Master, aka PlaMa, needed at least two players, but worked better with three or more.

The strategy behind this hologame involved each player commanding some faction that strove to either defend their land or conquer the entire planet. Player options ranged from primitive tribal to post-hyperdrive society to extraterrestrial invaders, each which were customized to a player's preferences. Many players preferred the virtual world network version, allowing for gameplay with beings on entirely different worlds. But since Tyris and his friends were all stationed on Hollus Maddrone starbase, they stuck strictly to the version of PlaMa utilizing a massive hologram planet.

Fun times and deep conversations about life had happened during many a Planet Master game. It was how Tyris had bonded with his three best friends, when they were all Star Brigade recruits.

But tonight, the Tanoeen Brigadier was late. Not his fault. He had Bevrolor of Azelten, the senior field operative in charge of Star Brigade's ordnance division, to blame. That blockheaded of a Nubrideen had called a pointless meeting to discuss tomorrow's mysterious all-hands meeting. Tyris had doubted that she'd provide some useful insight to him or Star Brigade's two remaining quartermasters. And Bevrolor didn't fail to disappoint. She had stood in the small conference room, her three eyes wide with outrage, griping over how much better she could run Star Brigade. In short, it was the same deluded, ultra-matriarchal monologue Bevrolor gave about everything.

No wonder you never got onto a combat team, Tyris mused as he had suffered through the rest of the Nubrideen's pointless rant. Lucky for Bevrolor, the only visible features on his face were two beady pits of cobalt blue with shiny-white pupils. Since arriving in Union Space years ago, too many staring bystanders and so many stupid questions had forced the Tanoeen to hide his fluid-like maw under a mask of crystalline ice.

After an orv of his life had been wasted, Tyris raced to Hollus Maddrone's Living Quarters. The six-foot-three-inch sculpture of chiseled, crystalline ice strode through the empty corridors at top speed. Despite cursing his own tardiness, Tyris knew the others would be forgiving. And all of them had undoubtedly heard about tomorrow's all-hands meeting.

Soon Tyris arrived at Jan'Hax's quarters, where everyone agreed to meet. Before entering, the Tanoeen reminded himself to avoid mentioning tomorrow's all-hands, unless someone else did first. He had decided to worry about tomorrow's meeting...tomorrow.

Tonight was all about PlaMa and hanging with his friends. The door slid open and the Tanoeen stepped through.

Tyris took in the room setup as soon as he entered. The small common room had been cleared out to accommodate four chairs, three of them occupied and surrounding a massive floating globe. The holo planet's land-to-sea ratio eerily resembled the Union memberworld of Kheldoroth. Its glow spilled out into all corners of the room, but was still overpowered by the common room's halolights.

Tyris's trio of friends and colleagues stopped talking and turned as he entered the room. Jan'Hax sat opposite the door on the other side of the globe. His physique was tall, rangy and overly spare. He had a duck-billed snout of a mouth and leathery green skin covered in warts, typical of most Ciphereens. Khrome, of the biomechanical race called the Thulicans, was the shortest of the group at five-foot-seven. But his hulking, silvery physique more than made up for any height shortcomings.

Surje looked more humanoid than the rest, despite the dim glow of his red skin and the three rounded, mohawk-like bony crests atop his bald head. The Voton was just under six feet in height, with a lean and wiry build.

Khrome, Surje and Jan'Hax immediately responded with a boisterous "HEEEEEEY!"

"Sure, sure," Tyris waved it off with a sharp hand chop, taking the one unoccupied seat. "Apologies for being late! We set up?"

"Yes," Jan'Hax nodded. He kept fiddling with something on the massive transparent planet holo between them. "Everyone's schedule is unoccupied for the next few orvs, I gather?"

Khrome made a rude noise that sounded like metal scrapping against gravel. "I'll only need one orv, after my invasion brings you all to your knees."

"Playing extraterrestrial invaders again, Khrome?" Tyris asked wearily.

The Thulican smiled as wide as his noseless, cobalt-blue face would allow. "It's the best role. I got aerospace superiority."

"We'll see about that," Tyris challenged, fingering one of the large icicle-like spikes jutting backwards atop his head. Innovative as Khrome was, his PlaMa faction choices were as old-fashioned as a backwater planet dweller's.

"Who am I?" The Tanoeen ran his fingers over his side of the globe, accessing his player data. After realizing how late Bevrolor's rant was running, he had asked his friends to choose his faction. At a glance, Tyris instantly regretted that decision. His faction was a pre-hyperdrive culture, still using *gas-powered* automobiles. The Tanoeen's annoyed expression must've been telling, as his three friends chuckled fiendishly.

"That's what happens when you're late, Ty," Surje giggled, only to visibly fret over not clarifying what he meant, which always made the Voton over-clarify. "Late to play. The game, I mean—"

"Can we begin already?" Khrome cut in before the Voton over-clarified them all into semi-unconsciousness.

"Let's," Tyris rubbed his hands together. Everyone put on their thin gameplay visors, syncing with the PlaMa holo globe before them to access their resources, player options and characters.

Once all four players brought up their massive 7'x7' holoscreens, the latest Planet Master game commenced.

Jan'Hax played as a post-hyperdrive civilization, hell-bent on unifying all nations on this fictional planet into one world government. Surje, always up for a challenge, chose a consolidated faction of moon and space station colonists, rebelling against Jan'Hax's aspiring global empire.

Each player's massive holoscreen displayed whatever aspect of their faction they were currently maneuvering. Several smaller screens appeared in the corner of the larger screen, ready to be accessed at a player's discretion. The mood was light and fun, with the usual competitive jabs being flung back and forth. Just another regular PlaMa game, like when they were Star Brigade recruits.

Back then Tyris had roomed with Surje, and the two hit it off instantly. During their first month on Hollus Maddrone, Surje had introduced Tyris to Khrome, a huge PlaMa dork already who had gotten their mutual Ciphereen friend hooked. The trio became inseparable, even outside their twice-a-week PlaMa games. A short while later, Khrome had befriended another recruit in the form of Jan'Hax, bringing the young Ciphereen into their circle. Despite a grating penchant for long and fancily worded explanations, Jan'Hax ended up using a pre-hyperdrive society to win his first ever PlaMa game. In short, he fit into their group like a missing puzzle piece.

Of the quartet, Tyris was the only one not from a Union memberworld, colony or territory. Being a legal alien from a non-Union world had earned Tyris the informal classification of 'outworlder'. The Tanoeen wore the label without shame, but Khrome forbid him from using it on just himself.

"Why do you care what I'm called?" Tyris had asked in confusion.

"Because," the Thulican had replied blithely, wearing that trademark sparkly grin. "We're all stationed somewhere that's not a homeworld for any of us. Technically we're all outworlders." Hence, how their group's informal name came about over a year ago. Since then the group had enjoyed a recurring cast of satellite members, many who made guest appearances during PlaMa game nights. But the core four members of the 'Outworlders' remained unchanged.

As expected, the PlaMa game was a seesaw of action, suspense, twists, and strategic genius between four experienced players who knew each other too well. But in time, certain mistakes revealed player weaknesses. Jan'Hax surprised no one by dismissing Tyris's tribal faction and attempting to subjugate Surje's spacestation/moon colonies by force instead of negotiation. This, along with the Ciphereen's overextended forces that were uniting the planet, left him open to Khrome's space invaders. Surje's faction, which could have provided much needed defense against the space invaders, ended up tag-teaming against Jan'Hax, leading to a massive global war.

Meanwhile, Tyris made stealthy moves with his ignored faction via guerilla-style attacks on Jan'Hax's forces. The Tanoeen then kept acquiring more and more technology in hopes of reverse engineering it. That drew the attention from a small cadre of Khrome's factions, looking to team up against Jan'Hax's crumbling empire.

"No fair!" Jan'Hax whined. "Everyone's ganging up on me!"

"Only because you suck at ruling a world government,' Khrome threw back gleefully. "Now you're gonna get crushed."

After over three full orvs, the quartet took a break from gameplay. Everyone shut down their holoscreens and took off their gameplay visors.

It was Surje who finally broached what everyone had avoided. "Are we going to talk about it? The all-hands meeting? Tomorrow? For Star Brigade?"

"Not sure which Star Brigade all-hands you mean, since we've had so many recently," Tyris snapped, with more bite than intended. The Tanoeen just wanted to spend time with his friends and not dig into Star Brigade's fate.

"Easy," Khrome told Tyris before addressing the group. "You think Star Brigade's toast?"

"Yeah, pretty much," Surje answered quickly.

"No clue," Jan'Hax gave a stiff shrug. "Honaa and Sam aren't talking."

"Maybe," Tyris finally admitted, a hard thing to say after almost two years. But with so little movement or communication from their remaining superiors, what other conclusion could he draw?

"What are we going to do now?" Surje asked the group.

Tyris had given his future post-Star Brigade a lot of thought over the past few months, so he answered first. "Think I'll hook up a merc company. Remember what actual combat feels like."

"Ah. Combat…" both Khrome and Jan'Hax cooed nostalgically.

The thrill of combat, the taste of a hard-fought victory, danger around every nook and cranny of a battlefield. Tyris had expected that when joining Star Brigade. But other than a few sparse side missions from months past, the Tanoeen had found nothing but disappointment. "All the boom-boom and ka-BANG of a skirmish. Starting to think I imagined it from another life."

Surje fixed on Tyris with one of his intense, unblinking stares when something bothered him. "What about heading back to your homeworld?"

Tyris responded with a stony frown. "And do what?" Titanoa hadn't felt like home since the 'Temporal Incident' many years ago. Now Titanoa had become infested with Imperium military bases and research stations. Other than the occasional visit every few years, Tyris had no plans on returning.

"Might head back to the Twin Spheres for a while," Khrome sighed, "figure out my next move." Unlike Tyris, the Thulican actually missed home.

"Me too," Surje nodded hastily. "Head back to Aurealis, not the Twins. See the parents and take a breather."

Tyris exchanged a look with both Khrome and Jan'Hax at this news. "You better not turn all Joiner celebrant on us when you go home—"

Surje rolled his colorless eyes. This wasn't the first time his friends had expressed such concern on this particular matter. "*Lights be gone*, I won't! My parents know that's not the life I want."

"Until they try talking you into it for the zillionth time," the Tanoeen retorted, unconvinced. He'd known Surje to talk tough about defying his parents…when they were light years away.

Surje glowered, his complexion darkening. "Not this time."

"Like how they didn't talk you out of dating a human?"

"Oh, go fall in a black hole," Surje snapped, the glow of his red skin as angry as his expression.

Taking the hint, Tyris leaned away. "Point made. You're inconvincible."

A tense lull landed in the banter, during which Jan'Hax cleared his throat. "Isn't anyone going to inquire about my post-Brigade activities?" he complained.

"Does it involve heading to Fortuna to waste your currency on gambling?" Khrome asked flatly.

The length of Jan'Hax's pause spoke volumes. He raised a webbed finger defensively. "Wasting is such a harsh word."

"Then why ask?" Khrome decided, drawing laughs from Surje and Tyris. "Really feels like UComm plutoed us. All that training and time, wasted."

"Wasn't entirely wasted," Tyris countered. "Met some great sentients, got some invaluable training. And…we all became better friends."

"We don't know if tomorrow's a death knell for Star Brigade," Khrome insisted. Clearly his hopefulness was undimmed.

"Then explain to me why this is the first all-hands we've had in months," Tyris threw back, throwing cold water over Khrome's optimism.

"Not just the field operators," Surje chimed in. "Analysts, pilots, astroengineers. Anyone with any part in Star Brigade." The Voton suddenly turned a shade of heated red. "Even the reserve Brigadiers. In one room."

Jan'Hax's eyes narrowed. Tyris began clenching and unclenching his fists. If the mention of Star Brigade's decommissioning had ruined the quartet's jovial mood, talk of reserve Brigadiers detonated it entirely. Everyone in the room knew who Surje so subtly referred to—a former earthborn friend, who had ducked out of active Star Brigade service after completing a xenobiology fellowship. The memory still stung.

"Oh, come ON you guys!" Khrome groaned with annoyance. "Lily never had any contractual obligation to become an active Star Brigadier after her fellowship ended. Stop punishing her already."

Only Khrome remained on the Liliana Cortés bandwagon. But in Tyris's opinion, the Thulican forgave others way too easily.

"Khrome's got a point," Jan'Hax conceded after a long and loaded silence. "And it's not like Lily went and pulled an Addison Raichoudry."

The memory of Addison Raichoudry and her unceremonious departure sent a collective cringe through the group, Surje more than most.

The Voton leaned forward, staring at nothing. "Earthborn women are strange," he muttered.

"No joke," Tyris agreed with a rude noise. Of all the odd species he had encountered in Union Space, humans offered both a surprising adaptability and a volatility that could be troubling.

"The meeting could be good news," said Khrome, not accepting defeat.

"Or that the Brigade's getting decommissioned."

Khrome gave Tyris a reproachful look. "You're just a comet full of sunshine, you know that?"

If the Tanoeen had a visible mouth, it would reveal a broad and toothy smile. "Comes with the sparkling package." He always knew how to push the Thulican's buttons.

"If the Brigade ends tomorrow," Jan'Hax cast a sweeping gaze over his three friends, "it's been fun serving with you all."

Khrome's grin stretched ear to ear. "Truth."

"Likewise," Tyris added with genuine enthusiasm.

"Hear, hear!" Surje raised a fist in the air, for no apparent reason other than to show his agreement.

Jan'Hax wasn't finished. He waved his webbed hands to get everyone's attention. "How about this post-Brigade idea? And no, it does not involve Fortuna or gambling, so save me the sermon, celebrant!" Jan'Hax countered as Surje opened his mouth angrily.

"Alright, humor us," Khrome allowed, arms spread wide.

"Us four, traveling through Union Space, taking in all the sights."

Tyris perked up. "Like a space tour?"

"Yes," Jan'Hax continued. The Ciphereen smacked his duck-billed mouth with excitement. "We pick some planets to visit, no set time table on how long we stay on any of them."

Tyris considered the proposal. He had been curious to see more of Union Space since arriving here over five years ago. And who better to take in the sights than with his best friends? He nodded with cool acceptance. "You've had worse ideas."

Surje agreed, lighting up with a warm red shine. "I like it. Jan'Hax's idea. Seeing more would be fun. Of Union Space, that is."

"Let's do it…if Star Brigade get decommissioned," Khrome added.

"Which it will," the Tanoeen insisted.

Khrome ignored him. "Now, can we finish the game? I'm not done conquering this world."

Surje scoffed, putting back on his gameplay visor. "Not going to happen. My faction may be a bunch of colonies, but I'll still win. The planet, that is. I'll rebel against you."

"Which I'll be ready for, now that you've told me," Khrome crowed, reactivating his holoscreen.

Surje swore in loud Votonese, his skin flashing bright red at his misstep.

Jan'Hax snorted. "Worst. Intel Operative. Ever—OW." The Ciphereen jumped in his seat. Surje had given him a hard, electric-charged poke to the ribs.

Khrome and Tyris both guffawed. "You asked for that," said the Tanoeen between squally-like bursts of laughter.

Territorial

V'Korram Pryderi-Ravlek's victory roar rang across the unremarkable rolling plains long after he had finished, again and again, each echo growing more distant.

Every nerve ending tingled with triumph. His senses felt heightened and alive from the high of killing something.

Or in his case, killing several things.

The Kintarian stood at his full six-foot-nine-inch height, massive chest heaving, exerted but not exhausted. Through curtains of stringy ginger hair, he stared at the dark blood soaking the length of his tawny fur-covered frame and dripping from his clawed fingers—blood that wasn't his own.

V'Korram smiled in satisfaction. Glancing around to appreciate his handiwork made the smile broaden to display razor-sharp teeth.

A small slice of the short bluegrass plains surrounding him was torn up and littered with bleeding, mangled corpses—Kintarian corpses. The sinking sun cast a warm red glow over the grasslands, adding a macabre glow to the scene many would called gruesome.

V'Korram, however, reveled in its beauty.

Some of these carcasses had their throats ripped open; others were missing limbs or heads, while a number had their innards spilling out of shredded abdomens.

Every Kintarian lying dead at V'Korram's feet were members of his clan or immediate family, which was precisely why he had slaughtered them. This was how he had spent the afternoon of his day off.

The Kintarian's three litter brothers, his two litter sisters, numerous siblings from his parents' other litters, both mother and father—V'Korram had taken his sweet time with those two in particular before killing them.

These clan members had once been his everything, only to abandon him at his lowest moment, believing others' lies, disowning him from the Pryderi clan and the greater Ravlek pride.

The Kintarian turned a dispassionate eye down at the face of his father, which resembled juicy shredded meat. V'Korram hocked deep in his throat and spat on it. Family only meant that they eviscerated you with a reassuring smile.

If only you were real, V'Korram noted sullenly.

And the smile began to fade, as did the euphoria. Just like every time before.

Any time the anger and self-loathing threatened to devour him, and even the sweetness between Bevrolor's thighs wasn't enough to satiate him, V'Korram 'killed' hardlight holograms of his disloyal clan to unwind.

He planned to keep slaughtering his former clan as long as it took, until they were utterly dead to him. And when every member of his clan was actually dead, they would mean nothing to him.

Given Star Brigade's current state, he had absolutely needed to—how did earthborns phrase it—'blow off steam.'

The field operative training sessions with his alleged teammates had been an embarrassment. And this legendary Habraum Nwosu that Sam brought back to 'save' Star Brigade, had been less than encouraging thus far. 'Out of his depth' would be the understatement of the millennium. V'Korram wasn't sorry about what he'd said to Nwosu the other day. How could any Brigadier trust in the crimsonborn's commitment, after he'd left when times grew tough?

However, the Cercidalean didn't have much to work with in terms of seasoned Brigadiers. Sam and Captain Ishliba had more experience between the two of them than any of the remaining Brigadiers on the roster—literally.

And something smelled off about the Rothorid. The onset of some disease, possibly. Whatever the issue, V'Korram had respect enough not to say anything to Honaa. As long as this illness didn't compromise Star Brigade's 'progress'.

And the euphoria had vanished completely. V'Korram bristled.

The Kintarian contemplated running his personal HLHG program again, but decided against it. Twice in one day was enough.

"End program," he ordered in a brusque growl.

The rolling plains of bluegrass, the deep-red sunset, the bodies of his clan, even the rivers of blood staining his body —all of it vanished. Now the only things covering the towering Kintarian were tight black athletic shorts and sweat. The latter saturated V'Korram's tawny body fur and the long ginger mane he tossed back from his face. Neon blue walls surrounded him now, pulsing slowly with energy.

The Kintarian strode from the HLHG suite, his swift yet graceful footfall never making a sound. He had passed through the suite's rotund atrium and headed for the exit of the HLHG Sector.

And that was when V'Korram's attention got drawn to his right.

Down the gunmetal grey corridor he saw HLHG-1 occupied, as indicated by the deep red square at the top of its rectangular door console. V'Korram's ever-present scowl deepened. "Who?"

Curious, the Kintarian turned on his heel and strode for the very first of the six Hollus Maddrone HLHG suites. As he approached, V'Korram took a quick whiff of the air, catching the lingering scent of whoever had last entered the HLHG suite—recognizing its fragrant, human softness.

Her. V'Korram's pointy ears flattened, his already sour mood turning pitch-black.

'Her' being Dr. Liliana Cortés, that feeble, undertrained weakling of an earthborn underserving of her maximal powers. Frail, skinny and *weak,* even for a human.

One lucky shot during an organization all-hands had Captain Nwosu convinced this Cortés had field active potential. The notion was laughable, and further proof of Nwosu's questionable leadership. Cortés had no business as a field operator, let alone stepping foot on Hollus Maddrone. V'Korram knew that the moment he'd met her at Bilbao Interplanetary Spaceport. Cortés had gotten nauseous on the trip to Hollus…from being inside a spacefaring craft. What *Star Brigadier* got nauseous on a spacecraft? And the training sessions during which she'd frozen or just curled up and shrieked her nonsensical head off?

The memories quickly filled V'Korram with near explosive rage.

He almost spun around and stalked off…almost. But a wickedly curious part of him couldn't resist. The Kintarian just had to see this earthborn's attempts to better her nonexistent skills.

Cortés must have expected everyone to be off-base today. *Probably why she didn't make her training session private.* One optical scan from the side console, and the doors slid open for V'Korram.

She crouched in the dead center of the neon-blue room. The black tank top and tight grey active nanoclothe ¾ pants she wore overtly emphasized how the doctor's body was mostly legs, topped off by a slim built torso with spare arms.

Her usually light honey complexion was flushed from exertion, the cropped boyish black hair lank from perspiration, her delicate features a mask of unthreatening determination. The air was awash with her scent, which V'Korram found gallingly aromatic. At first, the Kintarian couldn't tell which program the doctor was running, until he followed her gaze up toward the globe-shaped mechanoid circling several feet overhead.

The target practice mech, V'Korram recalled, remembering with a cringe how much those low-level blasts stung when one didn't dodge in time. Either Nwosu or Sam must have suggested this for Cortés's training.

The doctor, focused on her robotic opponent, hadn't noticed V'Korram entering. *She should've sensed me the moment I arrived,* the Kintarian critiqued. *A good soldier is mindful of their surroundings.*

Cortés remained crouched and waiting, eyes tracking her aerial target, hands clasped like a pistol. The sound of her heart pitter-pattering with dread filled the Kintarian's heightened hearing.

The mechanoid fired. Cortés dove to the left, barely dodging the *put-put* of pulse blasts striking her last location.

She twisted her slender frame quickly…almost *expertly*, firing off white rings of sonic energy in a sweeping blast. A high-pitched whine that most species wouldn't have heard stabbed at V'Korram's eardrums. He flinched only for a moment, until the sonic blast ended.

The sphere-like mechanoid tried zipping away, only to fly into the full force of Cortés's sonic burst. It dropped like a stone, hitting the floor with a loud *clank!*

The doctor stood up, more surprised than V'Korram that she'd struck her target without getting struck. "Yes!" she pumped her fists in genuine triumph.

At least she's working hard to improve, a voice in V'Korram's head considered. But he refused to accept such little steps. On his supply runs to Korvenite internment camps with Sam, she had cryptically alluded to how the Brigade didn't have several months to train new field operatives. Several weeks felt more accurate.

V'Korram snorted, folding his arms and leaning casually against the wall near the entrance. From what he'd seen of Cortés, the Kintarian doubted she'd last a month. It behooved him and Star Brigade to expedite that eventual departure.

At that moment, Cortés turned, saw V'Korram and recoiled. Her ovular features ran the gamut of shock, embarrassment, fear and anger in a heartbeat. "What are you doing in here?" she demanded, keeping as much trembling panic out of her voice as possible.

V'Korram tossed back his long, stringy mane again, his green-flecked eyes trained on Cortés. "Watching you."

By her peevish glare and the way the nostrils of her long nose flared, Cortés clearly had no interest in an audience. She pointed a dainty finger at the exit. Gods, those hands looked like a hydrospray spurt could break them. "Then watch in the ObDeck."

The Kintarian almost laughed. Her fury was as threatening as a kitten's. "View's better here. Or should I say…more entertaining." He fought back laughter, barely. *Don't laugh, that will do you no favors.*

"Fine." The doctor stuck her nose up in the air huffily. "I'll leave." She then marched all graceful and stiff-shouldered toward the HLHG suite exit.

V'Korram's smile became a scowl. That wasn't the reaction he'd hoped for. *Need another approach to show her why she doesn't belong.* She had almost passed the Kintarian, when he stepped in Cortés's path with one stride. He stood almost a foot taller than the doctor. Compared to her willowy frame, V'Korram was a solid wall of lithe muscle. "Want real practice? Try a living target."

She backpedaled immediately, staring up at him in disbelief. "You?"

The Kintarian bristled at the dumb question. "See any other living sentients in here?"

The doctor looked skeptical, pursing her lips in that peculiar way of hers. So V'Korram sweetened the pot. "You get the chance to try hitting me."

And Cortés was sold.

The Kintarian went a considerable distance from her, dropping to a crouch. "Begin," he growled out.

The doctor quickly raised her pointed fingers to chest level and fired. V'Korram effortlessly leapt and somersaulted over the first blast. Sharp contempt filled him while casually sidestepping the second attack.

The Kintarian juked left then right, zigzagging his massive self with practiced ease around the barrage of bright white sonic bursts. The doctor's uncertain aim did nothing to stop him from getting closer and closer, until V'Korram was right in front of her.

Too easy. His left hand swept upward, breaking apart her clasped fingers, his right hand catching her by the throat. V'Korram stood up, holding a gasping Cortés off the ground one-handed, her long legs flailing uselessly in the air. His fingers wrapped around her whole neck.

"Dead," the Kintarian sneered, showing sharp teeth. He opened his hand and dropped her to the ground on her behind. She sat there staring off at nothing, the color drained from her face.

"Again," V'Korram snapped, jolting the doctor out of her shock.

He took the same crouched stance as before, albeit a little closer. Cortés took a deep breath, trying and failing to steady herself. She then settled into a less stiff posture…

V'Korram pounced, not giving her time to prepare. *Conflict waits for no one.*

To his surprise and chagrin, Liliana hurriedly snapped up her pointed fingers and fired right as he reached her.

The Kintarian danced away just in time, and had to backflip over a pair of wide sonic bursts. The doctor pressed him much faster now and with more confidence, shooting off sound blast after white ringed sound blast.

V'Korram weaved and bobbed from side to side, pounced and slid, *barely* avoiding each rattling burst of white sonic rings. This time he couldn't get close enough. Cortés had created a perimeter around her person from all angles, effectively keeping V'Korram at bay.

Not bad, he had to admit, split jumping over another blast. On a positive note, the Kintarian realized her attacks weren't needling his ears so much.

And then he spotted the doctor's attack pattern. Cortés never fired lower than waist level—his waist level. *Which means…*

V'Korram went low on all fours and charged. Cortés dropped her aim to compensate… an instant too late.

The Kintarian rammed his shoulder, full-speed, into her stomach.

The slight and slender doctor was folded in half and lifted clean off her feet. V'Korram *felt* Cortés's ribs creak on impact, heard her cry out as they both hit the HLHG suite floor. The momentum sent the pair skidding.

A heartbeat later, V'Korram had Cortés pinned and completely powerless. One hand clenched around her throat, another hand held down her right arm, while his knee trapped her left arm.

He glared down to see her gaping up at him in wide-eyed terror. By the pained way she sucked in breaths, his tackle had left a mark.

She didn't struggle. Good. The doctor knew when she was beaten. Without her fingers clasped together to emit her sonic blasts, Cortés was helpless…and they both knew it.

"Dead…dead…DEAD," V'Korram spared no ounce of disdain in his deep-throated growl. "Were this a real fight, I'd have gutted you from head to heel already."

The threat sent a shudder through Cortés's body. Seeing a potential teammate so helpless and breakable, it thoroughly sickened V'Korram. In what universe would Cortés ever be on a Star Brigade team? What were Nwosu and Sam thinking?

"Know what I believe? I believe you are weak, that you are a liability." V'Korram tightened his grip around her neck, pressed his thumb into the juncture between her chin and windpipe. He considered Cortés's slender throat and how easily his claws could slice open its delicate flesh. One pop of his thumb nail and she'd bleed out right here in the HLHG Suite. The doctor's lips parted and out came a choked *yip*. The sound of her quickening heartbeat was the only sound in V'Korram's world.

"You have no combat experience, pitiful hand-to-hand skills, and not one iota of fortitude outside a Medcenter."

After that truth, V'Korram felt every muscle in the doctor's willowy frame stiffen beneath him. Just like in the training sessions, Cortés's terror had paralyzed her completely. V'Korram fought the urge to shrink back in disgust. *Why am I wasting time on this useless creature?* But the Kintarian already knew the answer. He did this not just for the Brigade, but for Cortés's safety. Despite her incompetence, she was innocent. She didn't deserve to die, or worse, have that innocence ruined. Star Brigade could spell the end of her, and vice versa given the unit's weakened state. He should have let Cortés up at this point, but she needed to learn her place. And it wasn't with Star Brigade.

"The smartest thing you can do is leave," V'Korram continued, his voice growing harsher and darker. "Return to whatever overpaid medcenter job you left and *never* look back."

The human's short, shallow breaths grew shorter still with V'Korram's grip on her throat. Her eyes were squeezed shut. V'Korram leaned in close, like a lover, until their lips were almost brushing each other's. At this proximity, her scent flooded his nose, a bizarrely dizzying scent, fueled by body heat and fear. Despite his overwhelming need to be rid of this weakling, a delicious jolt ran through him.

Not victory or hatred, but a sensation that no human had ever triggered in him.

The Kintarian grimaced, forcing himself to ignore whatever that was, and dropped his growl to a whisper. "Stay with Star Brigade, and at best you'll get only yourself killed on a live op. At worst...other Brigadiers will die breaking formation to rescue you."

Cortés's heartbeat hitched, or was that V'Korram's own, as he finally seemed to be getting through to her? Maybe the Kintarian could save Cortés from ruin or death, if she had brains enough to listen. "Is that what you want? To have others die because of your incompetence?" The Kintarian stopped and frowned in unsettled confusion. Needles pricked at his ears, growing in size and discomfort...

The noise started at a barely audible vibration, climbing sharply up to a skull-splitting whine that drowned out everything and anything.

V'Korram roared and jerked his whole body back in agony, slamming both hands over his ears. Yet the whine cut through his fingers, a million white-hot blades slicing into his brain.

The Kintarian didn't remember falling onto his side, but there he lay, curled up in fetal position, unable to hear anything but the ear-piercing drone…powerless to think or move. The pain was everywhere, obliterating V'Korram utterly.

Suddenly Liliana Cortés stood over him, eyes wide and trembling all over, but not with fear. That high-pitched sound radiated *off* the slender doctor in waves—hostile, hateful vibrations. How did she do this without using her hands? V'Korram couldn't figure it out, since thinking had become such an agony.

The ear-splitting whine abruptly cut out. After a long moment, V'Korram uncurled his long body slowly and dropped both hands from his ears, wincing as he tried rising up on all fours. His ears were still ringing, the world still spinning round and round in crooked circles. He staggered sideways and looked up at Cortés, only to freeze.

She was pointing her clasped fingers at him, like a gun. Her oval-shaped face was an unforgiving mask as she uttered, "Dead."

White rings of concentrated sonic energy hammered V'Korram in the chest, sending him flying. The ground quickly rushed up to smack him hard on the back. He lay there for a time, back smarting, ears ringing, bones rattling, muscles trembling. Everything except breathing hurt. He dared to lift his head up, no matter how much his neck muscles burned in protest. Cortés was favoring her abdomen as she limped away with long, hasty strides.

"*Stupid* human," he snarled after her. "You're making a mistake not listening to me."

Cortés stopped in her tracks, but didn't turn around. She inhaled a labored breath. "If I leave Star Brigade, it won't be because you told me to," the doctor replied, the false firmness in her tone unable to mask an undercurrent of panic. She resumed her retreat without looking back.

As soon as the door hissed shut behind her, V'Korram let his head fall back, unable to hold it up any longer.

Under much different settings, V'Korram might've respected her perseverance. But he had too much fury, too much physical pain.

Hollus had become his home, and Star Brigade his calling. After losing everything on Kintare, V'Korram didn't think he'd ever know either again. And now some weak-willed, untested doctor was set to ruin it all. V'Korram gazed up at the neon blue ceiling, heart racing at light speed, and released a pained sigh. "Star Brigade is doomed."

Disciple

"Now what does that mean?" Khal asked in a voice sounding like melted butter. He was stroking the cheek of the female companion sitting across from him.

The slender, high-breasted beauty tittered and glanced at the floor. "That means, me like your kiss," she cooed the Standard Tongue, with the staccato drawl of a Hommodus native. The Nnaxan referred to the movements of the two thick, worm-like craniowhisks that jutted out of her forehead and spilled down past her chest. Right now they were trembling with visible arousal. Under the rose-colored illuminations of the bar they were in, the absurdly named *Red Bar*, the Nnaxan's sky-blue skin took on a lavender complexion. She held a half-empty drink in her upper left hand and caressed Khal's forearm with her lower hands. Their table resided on the second tier of *Red Bar*, away from tonight's large and boisterous crowd.

Red Bar, stupid name notwithstanding, was one of the most upscale and popular bars on Jefferson, a gas mining city-station that neighbored Hollus Maddrone within Zeid. The emerald gas giant was a Terra Sollus/Earth colony, hence why all of its thirteen city-stations bore names of renowned leaders from long-dead Old Earth. Khal only visited any of the city-stations for their healthy array of casinos and bars. *Red Bar* was Khal's favorite. He always killed it here with the ladies. Tonight was no exception. The Nahraini had no clue what his current companion's name was, but figured he'd ask after bedding her.

Khal wasn't much of a drinker, having only consumed one shot of black dwarf tonight. He did, however, feel drunk on the presence of his current company, a Nnaxan stunner he'd struck gold with not ten macroms ago. She couldn't have been older than early to mid-twenties. Girls that age were never much of a challenge for Khal, which allowed him to get creative in his pickup tactics. His angle for getting between her long and lovely legs was to feign curiosity on reading the subtle movements of her craniowhisks—by way of tactile stimulation. Nnaxan always communicated both verbally and with their craniowhisks, usually saying much more with the latter than with words.

So far, so good. Khal ran a hand through his well-coifed mop of black hair and snuck in a quick kiss to her throat. The Nnaxan giggled again, her craniowhisks rippling like slithering snakes.

"And that?" Khal asked, his voice teasing.

The Hommodus native eyed him with an exquisite, shy smile. "Me thinking you are sly too much."

That made them both laugh.

On *Red Bar*'s sprawling first floor, patrons from all over the Union collided in a swaying and shimmying throng of discordant rhythm. The one thing these beings shared was an enslavement to the catchy astropop dance tunes blaring in the foreground. *Red Bar's* second-floor balcony slowly rotated like a planet orbiting a sun, ringed by floating tabletops similar to the one where he and his Nnaxan companion stood. Each tabletop came above stomach-level, surrounded by parties of two or more patrons deep in raucous celebration. Khal drank in the scenery with a smile.

Every Brigadier had gotten the day off. It would have been too easy for Khal to stay on Hollus and hit up his pet analyst Genesis Delgado for a quickie. But he needed a break from the sterile walls of Hollus Maddrone and all those irritating would-be Brigadiers. Hollus and Zeid's woodsy forest moon, Atlas, were all Khal had seen for the past three and a half weeks.

During that stretch of time, Khal's life had been nothing but endurance drills, hand-to-hand combat workouts, offensive ability exercises, environmental survival training, and team field simulations. Wake up, run that gauntlet while finding time to keep in shape and perform his duties in Brigade Intelligence. Day after day, week after week he had pushed himself harder than everyone. Khal was certain his spot on the new Star Brigade combat team was a lock, not just because of his amazing performance during training.

His superior officer had dangled the combat team carrot in front of Khal since his Brigade tenure began. That was the major reason why Khal had helped her oust Lt. Col. Nyell and Major Azohl'ozyma, both gutless turncoats planning to dismantle Star Brigade in exchange for promotions in other UComm divisions.

Since then, Khal had spent the last year at his superior's beck and call, keeping her secrets and assisting in many of her off-the-books side missions. And while Khal knew his boss already had informants all over Hollus Maddrone and its satellite outpost Cobalt Waystation, his own harem of contacts kept feeding him additional intel on the non-Star Brigade inner workings which she continued to find useful.

Khal's actions had produced benefits far too amazing for words, but his true goal was placement on a Star Brigade combat team. His superior had promised that and more, cunningly nurturing those ambitions for the past year. *She lied to me, again*, Khal seethed. And he fell for it. Again.

No, he told himself firmly. Khal refused to let that injustice poison his current mood, not when he was doing so well with this scrumptious Nnaxan.

"Are you troubled, sir?" Khal, realizing he had zoned out, turned to see the Nnaxan girl watching him warily. Her craniowhisks wavered in a slow, concerned manner.

"No," Khal smirked, "it's nothing that'll take my mind off you." He leaned in again and nibbled on one of her tiny ears, earning a delighted squeal out of the Nnaxan. Her fleshy craniowhisks began to ripple from root to tip in a slow, pulsing manner.

Got her. "Now what's that mean?" Khal whispered in his sexiest voice.

"There you are!" an angry human voice demanded before the Nnaxan could answer.

Khal frowned and turned slowly. His eyes nearly popped out.

Under the red-tinted lights, he glimpsed an earthborn female about average height standing behind him. Her dress—short-sleeved, black and button down with chest pockets and a thigh-length skirt—honestly looked like someone had poured her into it with that insane body of hers. Her complexion looked sun-kissed and smooth as silk, her hair butter-blonde and tumbling past her shoulders in glossy sheets. And that stunning face, those big russet eyes... Khal knew her at a glance.

His superior officer, Sam D'Urso.

It took him back to the first time they'd met over two years ago during his time at the Union Intelligence Bureau Training Academy. Sam had sashayed into his life with that naughty lopsided grin and more curves than a winding river, offering him a better outlet for his abilities than the UIB could ever provide. Khal had been mesmerized from the start.

Yet tonight, Sam was the last being Khal wanted to see.

"What are you doing here?" he hissed through gritted teeth.

"I should ask you the same thing, 'sweetie,'" his superior officer snapped. "Is *this* what a night out with the boys entails?"

Khal straightened up, alarmed. He didn't bother wondering how Sam had found him. More troubled was her jealous girlfriend act. And they hadn't even spoken before he came to Red Bar tonight. *What the hell is she playing at?*

"Me sorry?" The Nnaxan girl looked from Sam to Khal, confused and with her lower set of hands on her hips. "But you are who?"

"His betrothed!" Sam angled an accusing glare at Khal. "Whom he proposed to last week."

"What? *No!*" Khal gaped at his boss in horror. Bad enough that she didn't place him on the new combat team. Now she had to mess with his easily-earned prospect? The Nahraini turned to the now enraged Nnaxan with desperate pleas. "No, she's not my fiancée. She's lying. Look, I—"

The Nnaxan girl hauled off and slapped him, with both right hands. Khal staggered back, the left side of his face stinging fiercely.

Disgust quickly surmounted desire, and both the Nnaxan's craniowhisks rippled in a threatening way that made Khal cringe.

The girl stormed off through the crowd, and Sam openly guffawed. "My understanding of Nnaxanese is a bit rusty, but I think that meant something like 'die by way of meteor strike.'"

Khal held his still-smarting cheek tenderly and moved to pursue the Nnaxan, but Sam placed a hand on his shoulder to stop him. "Sorry for the cock-block. We need to talk."

Khal shrugged her off and rounded the table. "What do you *want?*"

"Sex," Sam purred huskily, as if the answer were obvious. She leaned over the table, lips perfectly pouted, giving Khal an unhindered view of her abundant cleavage.

Khal gaped back in a daze, pulse quickening, loins stiffening, that Nnaxan girl already forgotten. Sam's gaze had scorched away the fog of his anger. Khal recalled his last 'reward' for an off-the-books task. *She's never pity-fucked me before,* he considered, leaning in closer. *Oh well.*

Sam threw her head back and laughed loudly…mockingly.

That wiped the sex-glazed look right off Khal's face. A flush of embarrassment crept up his neck and he jerked back furiously.

"Not tonight," Sam straightened up and grinned suggestively grin, beckoning him toward Red Bar's exit. "Let's go talk."

Khal stayed put and kept the table between them, partly to wait for his 'excitement' to go down. "About what?" he asked, not caring how rude he sounded.

Sam arched an eyebrow. "You *know* what." Clearly an open discussion about Star Brigade amongst civilians wasn't an option.

"You and Nwosu made your decision," Khal countered stubbornly. He cast an uninterested stare over Red Bar's swelling patronage. "What's there to talk about?"

"Plenty," Sam ran both hands through her hair. "Like your future."

"You mean the lack thereof?"

Sam's smile withered like a leaf kissed by frost. "Christ on a *goddamn* comet. Get over your man-period and come here!" She grabbed her subordinate by the arm and marched him toward the bar's exit. Khal would not have taken this humiliation from anyone else. Yet even though he had half a foot on Sam in height, her wrath was a terrifying force when roused. So Khal held his tongue and let himself be led away.

Once they were safely inside Khal's personal shuttlecraft cargo bay, in one of Jefferson's parking structures, he finally unloaded on Sam.

"Why?" he demanded curtly. Khal was past caring that she outranked him. "*Why* wasn't I selected for the new combat team?"

Sam had seated herself in a booth taking up most of the cargo hold's right-side wall. "You're not ready," she said without hesitation.

The blunt reply stung worse than that Nnaxan bimbo's slap. Khal sat down heavily next to her. "After all the shit I've done for you. The side missions, helping you oust Azohl'ozyma and Nyell, yet you have the gall to tell me I'm not ready?"

"Yes," Sam twirled locks of blonde between her fingers, as casual as if discussing the weather. "You've mastered the basics of your telekinesis, but you're lazy about moving beyond that. And you don't support your teammates well on the field with your abilities. *And* your bragging is pissing off the other recruits."

"It's not bragging if it's the truth," Khal scowled. "Besides, Khrome brags all the time."

"Khrome's funny," Sam made a face. "You're *not*, pretty boy."

Khal clenched his teeth, intensely disliking when she called him that. He couldn't let this injustice stand, not after hedging all his bets on becoming an important player in Star Brigade. And it all started with snagging his spot on a combat team. "Khrome and Tyris getting spots, I understand. Even that psycho Kintarian of yours makes some twisted degree of sense. But you and Nwosu have a really skewed view of combat-ready to pick that useless doctor chick over me."

"Lily is green, yes," Sam nodded coolly, not remotely perturbed by his critique. "She also possesses a special set of skills that you don't. Does it make sense to bring two intel officers on the same team, when we needed a full-fledged doctor?"

"No." Khal remembered this Dr. Cortés, the one with the killer aim who passed that little test Nwosu set up during last month's all-hands. During the weeks of training, Khal had caught Cortés stealing looks at him more than a few times. *She wants me, not that I blame her.* He was used to females from all different species gazing at him. The doctor was cute enough, but nothing extraordinary. Her legs, though, were amazing, going on for light years.

Legs or no legs, everyone knew how terrible Cortés was. Khal had heard about her freak-out during a field mission simulation two days ago. And rumor had it Cortés also was terrified of space travel. *Yet she lucked her way onto the combat team because she's a doctor.* Knowing that irked Khal even more.

"I should have never left the UIB for this waste of time," he spat, folding his arms and turning away from Sam sullenly. "I could've been an active field agent by now, if I'd stayed with the agency—"

"Let me tell you what your future would be with UIB," Sam cut in sharply. She didn't yell, but her voice and face conveyed a cold, petrifying rage. "You *might* be a desk jockey or you may even be an active field agent in a few months. But most likely, they trot you out for a few high-profile missions only. But the majority of the time, you're probably a lab rat, poked and prodded, testing your abilities to the point of agony, never seeing daylight again. They'd even deny you sex," she added pointedly, making Khal flinch. "All because of your maximal powers.

"Or worse," Sam continued, insolently tossing her hair, "you'd be picked up by some black ops outfit. Would there be missions? Absolutely. But after six months," her russet-brown eyes narrowed, looking like chips of burnt auburn under the cargo bay's halo lighting. "Maybe a year of that, and all the immoral shit you'd be forced to do for this 'great' Union would eat you up inside and make you want to kill yourself."

Khal was so stunned he briefly couldn't speak. "Y-you can't know that," he finally said, but with no confidence backing his retort.

Sam crossed her arms and studied him contemptuously. "I know it for a fact, young man. But hey, if either of those options appeals to you, I'll have Captain Nwosu get the transfer order signed tonight."

A protracted silence followed while Khal digested Sam's words. *You're valuable, but not invaluable*, she all but said. More than once, she had been less than forthcoming with him, but in this instance Khal knew Sam was shooting straight from the hip.

"I'll stay," he shook his head and sighed, defeated. "I just...I want to be out in the field. I haven't done much with my life, but I feel I can do this well if given the chance."

His frustration reached Sam, and her hard edges melted away. "I know," she said in a husky whisper. "And you will." She caressed his cheek tenderly, like a lover would. Her warm touch made Khal's skin tingle, soothing away his unease, distracting him. Just for a moment.

Sam only displayed this type of affection with Khal when it suited her.

"When?" he asked peevishly, pulling back. "It's been almost a year."

Sam leaned in closer, eyes alight with fiendish mischief. "I've got big plans for you, pretty boy," she declared, suddenly playful again. "And it all starts tonight."

She wants something, Khal realized. Of course, another task that brought him no closer to combat-team placement than before. Instead, he hid his suspicions behind a mask of calm. "What do you need from me?" Maybe the task might be interesting, and she'd reward him like all the other times.

Sam pulled out a 5-inch datapad as slim as a paper sheet from her belt. She keyed in a code across its typepad. Instantly, the viewscreen was filled by a squid-faced Rhomeran with maggot-white skin. "Meet Glu Zlliosho."

Khal stared at the holoimage blankly, not recognizing this 'Glu Zlliosho.' "Who is he?"

Sam made a rude noise. "That's for *you* to find out." She flicked off the holoimage and slid the datapad back in her belt. "I sent the image and the name to your Union TriTran account."

"You want me to find dirt on this guy?" asked Khal.

"Find out everything you can about him," Sam nodded. "What does he do for a living? Where does he live? Does Glu have family? What's his favorite food? What's his political affiliation? Who's his favorite polymaero player? Does he even like polymaero? Everything, anything, and then some."

"What for?" Khal scrutinized Sam as she stood up. He wasn't sure how spying on some Rhomeran would get him on a CT.

Sam leaned near the shuttlecraft's side exit. Khal could not deny the suggestive way that she carried herself: relaxed in posture yet oozing confidence and an irresistible feminine allure. "Get me all that and be patient," Sam kept her husky voice at almost a whisper. "Keep improving and follow my lead these next few months. You *will* be placed on a Star Brigade combat team."

The phrasing confused Khal. "But we only have one Star Brigade combat te—" The import of Sam's words sank in then.

She gave him a barbed smile. "Still mad at me?"

A combat team. Meaning that this first combat team would be Nwosu's…and then Captain Ishiliba would get his own. Khal shook his head, and felt a smirk pull at his lips.

"Good," Sam sassed, like a teacher giving a student a pat on the head. She whirled around and out of the cargo bay with a mesmerizing sashay. "You got till the day after tomorrow," she called over her shoulder. "And tell *no one.*" Her departure was marked by the hissing open and shut of the shuttlecraft door.

Half an orv later, Khal was on a return course to Hollus. As his ship hurtled through Zeid's roiling emerald clouds, he had already started a detailed search through official and unofficial databases on this Glu Zlliosho. So far, nothing. Was he a covert agent of some sort? Working for the Rhomeran AcuNet maybe?

Searching for a needle in an asteroid field, Khal considered with a smile. Not unlike the test Sam had tasked him with after their first meeting, to ensure he was worth poaching from UIB's grasp.

Khal had no complaints then or now. He always excelled at cracking the challenging mysteries. Meanwhile, he sent a transmission to a data analyst friend posted on Star Brigade's nearby Cobalt Waystation. After almost a month of training and no sex, Khal needed some action tonight.

"Hello?" answered a young human female with a faint Martianborn lilt.

"Hey Gigi."

"Hi, sunshine," Genesis Delgado's voice instantly brightened.

"Still on your shift?"

"Just got off," she replied blithely. "About to fly up to Hollus for dinner with the girls. What's up?"

She's coming to Hollus, Khal perked up. That saved him the trouble of flying down to Cobalt. He recollected the wonders Gigi could perform with her sweet little mouth and smiled wolfishly. "Come over after dinner."

A sharp intake of breath could be heard on the other end. "Sure," Gigi replied after a charged moment, barely hiding her eagerness.

"Luminal! See ya soon."

"Bye handsome," she whispered.

Khal ended the transmission, still smirking. He'd gone through his share of extracurriculars amongst Hollus's female personnel, but Khal enjoyed Gigi's company the most. While plainer and plumper than his usual type, Khal couldn't get enough of her unflappable positive outlook of the universe. Plus Gigi always came whenever he called, had zero complaints about their arrangement, always made time to help him on intelligence tasks, and could keep her mouth shut. In short, Gigi was perfect.

Khal glanced at his ETA to Hollus: 10 macroms. He expected Gigi in about two orvs, more than enough time to get some headway on this task.

Right then, data from his Glu Zlliosho search began to appear—the boring personal minutiae, of course. Then he spotted Glu's connection to Bhoryus Corp, a renowned military defense contractor.

"Okay, this just got interesting,' Khal murmured, pointing and clicking to access the data packet.

Believe

Surje could no longer feel his arms, his legs, or even his head. Not in the physical sense, at least.

That's because at the present time, he had no arms. Or legs. Or head. In the physical sense.

Having shifted from his solid humanoid form into plasma form, the Voton had no need for corporeal extremities. Surje felt disembodied, as if floating in zero-G, yet connected to everything—the metallic tang in the air, the dim luminosity from the halolights above overpowered by the light leaping off his now shapeless body. All of Surje's senses amplified tenfold, even though he had no physical means to touch anything.

This never gets old, he mused. Surje's thoughts were shared by the Voton couple joined with him.

You both ready?

More than ready, Jabei thought.

Qarm's joy was like an actual sunrise. *I've been waiting for this since the moment I met her.*

Let's proceed then.

Right now the Star Brigadier was a fluid mass of glowing red, joined with two other Voton, also in plasma state. Qarm burned bright orange and Jabei throbbed with pale blue shimmer. Together the trio formed a sizeable floating sphere of brilliant plasma energy, flooding the small quarters they were in with blinding light. Surje, Qarm and Jabei were joined in mind, body and soul.

On its own, a joining transcended tactile sensation or individualism. But a joining under the radiance of the Living Light, allowing that hallowed glow to fill them up and guide them… Surje could find no words in any dialect to describe how that nourished his soul.

Even though I walked away from that life.

His mother was a Sun Matriarch, his father a high-ranking Joiner celebrant. They had taught their son everything he knew about the Living Light, pushing him into becoming a certified celebrant in hopes that he would one day take over their ministry. Surje remembered the training, getting the certifications, yet feeling no passion for that path. He wanted to contribute his gifts to a more active calling. A long, difficult stretch of time passed before his parents accepted his choice to enlist in UComm and then become a Star Brigadier.

Correction—*attempted* to become a Star Brigadier. Surje's father had come around first, seeing his son's maximal gifts as bestowed by the Living Light itself. For all the good that did. A pang of resentment twisted his insides. *Lights be gone.*

Excuse me, Pleiad? Jabei's bafflement bled into Surje's past memories.

Apologies, Surje stammered. He'd let his private thoughts taint into the Joining. With a thought, he steeled away that part of himself from the Joined sphere.

Despite his refusal to become a Joiner celebrant, in times of doubt or fear or sadness, the Shining Faith remained Surje's refuge. Like it was tonight, after finding out he hadn't made the new Star Brigade combat team. At least Sam D'Urso, his superior officer, had told him herself. For a human, D'Urso was at times unorthodox, but her frankness was appreciated.

Still, Surje needed time to clear his head. So he was spending his evening at Roosevelt, one of many gas mining cities floating inside of Zeid. Roosevelt also had a number of Living Light sources which he'd grown familiar with since being stationed on Hollus Maddrone Starbase.

But right now, he brushed aside his needs and failures. Surje focused on Qarm and Jabei, the young Voton couple he'd just met at a modest Shining Faith source, not two orvs ago. They were missionaries, about to start a new journey on Kheldoroth. The two, so dutiful to the Living Light, so drunk with love for each other, were desperate to become merged before their mission started. Surje had officiated Mergings before. How could he refuse them?

Qarm and Jabei had already exchanged fragments of life energy with one another, then interweaved their senses. Now was time for the bright words.

Do you Qarm, Surje began, *pledge to join your life with this female, protect her from the Infinite Darkness, guide her down the path of radiance until she leaves this plane and joins the Shining Host?*

Qarm beamed, showering the sphere and the room with his love. *I do.*

Do you Jabei, pledge to join your life with this male, protect him from the Infinite Darkness, guide him down the path of radiance until he leaves this plane and joins the Shining Host?

I so do, Jabei replied eagerly, her inner light as luminous as her partner's.

Through the illumination bestowed in me by the Living Light, I now pronounce you Merged.

The ensuing light flooded the room entirely, chasing away all shadows. Little by little, Surje separated himself and felt the Joined sphere lose its cohesion.

Moments later, the multi-colored radiance faded. The three Voton stood in their solid, naked humanoid forms where the Joined sphere once floated.

Surje returned to his reddish wiry and trim physique, three roundish crests jutting proudly from his skull. Jabei was a lithe and lovely sight, bearing only two round greyish crests atop her head. Her glow burned deep blue with love for her new Merger partner and gratitude to Surje. The male Voton had a strong-jawed face and three blockier gold crests atop his head. He was a bit doughy in physique but carried his weight well. Qarm shone as deeply with love and gratitude as his wife. "Thank you, Pleiad Surje for doing this," he gushed. "We wanted to start our mission together on Kheldoroth the right way."

"It was my honor," Surje smiled with genuine happiness. "We are all One with the Living Light."

"We are all One with the Living Light," Qarm and Jabei repeated.

Jabei slipped into white robes matching those of her partner, though more form-fitting than Qarm's. Surje pulled on a blue button down shirt and grey slacks, all of fine nanoclothe crafted specifically for a Voton.

After Qarm and Jabei left the source, Surje stepped outside the place of worship and onto the preceding walkway. It was night time according to Surje's chronometer. He placed his hands on a rail, leaning forward, and began zoning out on the foot traffic of beings bustling through Roosevelt's Teddy District. The ring-like and multi-tiered locality had been crafted with angular high-tech artsy elegance to resemble an actual city-state downtown. An odd location to have a Living Light source, but the contrast always fascinated Surje.

"I knew it!" The sharp, metallic voice from Surje's right snapped him out of his reverie.

Can't be. He whipped around and gaped. Two very non-Voton figures approached him. The short, burly being was clearly Thulican, his skin a silvery casing of living metal that few weapons could pierce. The taller and lankier being, a Cryonite, resembled a sculpture of ice crystalline with large spikes jutting backward atop his head. Even in their night-black UComm jumpers, Surje knew them both at a glance.

"Khrome? Tyris?" he realized how annoyed he sounded, how angry his body glow came across, and tempered his voice. "What are you doing here?"

"Looking for you, Sparky," Khrome replied with his typical broad and easy smile. "Figured you'd be here since this is the Living Light source you frequent the most."

Tyris looked less amused, though with no visible mouth or nose, the Cryonite's mood was always a cause of speculation. "You vanished on us, WHOOSH!" he said, his voice a high, crisp breeze.

Both Tyris and Khrome had been placed on the new Star Brigade combat team. Even Liliana Cortés, away from Star Brigade for over a year, made the cut.

Surje hadn't. He just needed a night without Star Brigade, to figure out his next move.

"Been so immersed in training," he sighed, planning to go faith heavy to ward off any suspicion of bitterness. "I needed a reconnect with the Shining Faith…" He realized only two of his best friends were present. "Where's Jan'Hax?"

"Keeping the shuttle warm while we get you." Khrome's smirk grew obnoxiously large, which Surje thought was impossible. "Us four are going out to relax and reprieve."

"Not tonight!" Going out to rabble rouse was the last thing Surje wanted. "I'm not in the mood for any…" Surje's frustration and fatigue had left him tongue-tied.

Tyris arched a non-existent eyebrow. "Chicanery?"

"Yes, that," Surje gestured at Tyris's apt word choice. "I'm taking part in a Joining ceremony, then it's back to Hollus for some sleep."

"Except that you're NOT," Khrome countered merrily. He sidestepped a gaggle of clucking Galdorian girls either heading to or returning from a fun evening. "We're all hanging out away from Zeid for a spell." A nearby musical concert must have just ended, as the wide walkway Surje and his friends were on had suddenly flooded with beings of all species. The three friends moved their conversation away from the traffic stream and into the Living Light source's foyer.

"We deserve a night out," Tyris's enthusiasm resembled wind chimes. "Star Brigade is operational again! We'll finally go on live field missions!"

Their jollity sent a stab through the Voton, darkening his body glow. And the bitterness boiled through. "Easy for you both to say, since you got on SB-1."

To their credit, Khrome and Tyris didn't appear surprised by his reaction. "Not everyone could get on one team," Tyris stated with breezy firmness. The halolights above twinkled off his ice crystalline body. "And it's not like you bottomed out like Bevrolor. You really stepped up during these last training sessions."

"Good," the word tasted like ash in the Voton's mouth. "But not good enough to get on a combat team." He shook his head, recalling the dialogue he'd had with his mother not two weeks ago. Maybe she was right. "This may be a sign that Star Brigade might not be where the Living Light is guiding me."

"Wait. A. Macrom!" Khrome cut him off, his deep blue face no longer smiling. "You don't actually believe that, do you?"

"What I believe doesn't really matter, if the Living Light illuminates a different path for—"

"Surje," Tyris's approach was calmer than Khrome's, but just as blunt. "What do *you* think?"

For an instant Surje hated them both. Not for making SB-1 when he didn't. Both were talented and deserved their placement. He hated them for knowing him so well and realizing he was using platitudes to hide from unpleasant truths. The Voton sighed. "I don't know. I really want to be a Star Brigadier. But..."

"You're not thinking about becoming a full-time Joiner celebrant, are you?" asked Khrome. This idea clearly bothered him.

"Well…" Surje really wished they had not come. He didn't have the headspace for this conversation right now. "Being a celebrant is what I'm good at. I'd be doing something worthwhile. What is so bad about that?"

Khrome choked back disbelief. "How about *a lot?*"

Those words drew disapproving looks from Voton coming and going from the Shining Faith source, so the trio wisely strolled away from the place of worship. They finally found a nook of space not far from the source and pedestrian traffic.

"Weren't you telling us that life was too restrictive?" Tyris continued his interrogation.

"And that your maximal abilities should be used for something good instead?" added Khrome.

Throwing my own words back at me. The Darkness swallow you both! "No, I just…I guess I expected something after being a year of almost nothing," he admitted. Nwosu coming back had been the first gasp of anything good for Star Brigade in months. To be so close, and drop the ball. He failed. "What if I never make a combat team?"

"You will, Sparky," Khrome made a face. "For someone with such staunch faith in the Living Light, you really don't believe enough in yourself."

Surje turned away in shame. Again, his friends' words struck home.

"At least Khal didn't get on a combat team either," Tyris chided as they began to walk.

That made Surje laugh. "True," he agreed through his chuckles. Khal Al Abdullah was the other intelligence field operative under Sam D'Urso. Thank the Radiance that arrogant, self-absorbed worm didn't get on SB-1. *What about the next combat team?* And just like that, the Voton's good mood sobered. "Khal will probably get on a combat team sooner than me."

Khrome shook his head stubbornly. "Only if you let that happen."

"Are you going to let that happen?" Tyris asked, leaning so close that Surje could feel the cold air wafting off him.

Surje had no faith in what he was about to say, but said it anyway. "No."

"Can't hear you."

"*No*," the Voton barked.

Khrome's massive hand covered Surje's shoulder when he grasped it. "We will all be field active and on a combat team someday. Say it with me."

"Khrome—okay, fine," Surje grumbled in annoyance. His friends would never let him lose confidence. "We will all be field active and on a combat team someday."

"Someday," Tyris waved a finger in the air. "But tonight, we head to the Peloponnesian and marinate."

Khrome's round yellow eyes sparkled with mockery. "You mean 'celebrate'?"

"Just realized that, so shut up," Tyris snapped.

Surje rolled his eyes. "Lights be gone! The Peloponnesian *again*? Jan'Hax went two nights ago!"

Tyris and Khrome exchanged a knowing glance. "Apparently, he's got a good feeling about tonight," the Thulican snarked.

That answer didn't satisfy Surje, not after seeing Jan'Hax already lose so much currency to gambling. "Why do we keep encouraging him?"

Tyris rolled his dark, beady eyes. "We're letting it slide tonight, since he didn't get onto a combat team, and you're a nanoclic away from joining the Shining Way."

"Okay, okay!" Surje raised his hands in surrender, laughing. Tyris and Khrome were right, as usual. The Voton was worrying too much again. Not believing in himself again. He'd worry about Star Brigade tomorrow. "Point taken and driven home. Let's go already!" The trio began to walk away from the Living Light source. "Wait," a realization hit Surje then, annoying him more than enlightening. "Did Jan'Hax not show up because he knew how I'd react to us hitting up a casino?"

"He may have suggested we mollify your anger before we reach the shuttle," Khrome admitted with exaggerated innocence.

Surje shook his head and smiled. He knew his friends as well as they knew him. "So are we going to watch and ridicule as Jan'Hax loses his currency, or what?"

Descent

Right now Liliana Cortés wanted to scream in frustration.

If only she had the strength to do so. The doctor lay gasping urgently for breath after having been knocked flat on her back for the umpteenth time. Every inch of her svelte body ached. The clingy workout suit she had on was soaked to the skin in sweat.

As she lay sprawled on the floor of a hardlight hologram suite, a floating spherical mechanoid—her unconquerable foe—hovered overhead. For a moment, Liliana could have sworn that the mechanoid hovered back and forth in a victorious fashion.

The doctor knew becoming a field active Star Brigadier was a mistake. But two weeks ago, she hadn't realize how large of a mistake. There had been a reason why Liliana staunchly declined to active field duty after her fellowship finished.

But this time around, Sam D'Urso and Captain Habraum Nwosu had been so hard to refuse.

Regardless, the past two weeks only confirmed her massive mistake. She had Pluto-ed nearly every practice session, and almost gotten killed on her first live op.

Anyone else she told about her career change wholeheartedly agreed, especially her mother, during their last Transnet conversation. "I don't care what trivial need you have to use those cursed powers. For Union's sakes, quit now," Dr. Marimar Cortés had snapped.

"You said you were done with that Star Brigade nonsense after your fellowship. Do you actually think you have the stomach to do what they do, míja?" Her mother, ever the great motivator.

Which had led to the past two orvs of Liliana being continuously knocked on her ass. She had been trying to better hone her sonic abilities when it came to aiming and shooting them. It was a simple HLHG program, designed for maximals with energy expulsion-based powers like herself. A small, spherical mechanoid, equipped with a low-level pulse blaster, would float around the room shooting at the young doctor. Her goal was to not only evade the mechanoid's blasts, but also strike it as well.

The digitized *putt-putt* of the mechanoid's blaster became the bane of Liliana's existence. Despite her improvement in dodging, she would get tagged more often than not. The first time Liliana got tagged this session she squealed at the top of her lungs. It basically stung like a supercharged mosquito bite on the tip of a mule kick.

Captain Nwosu had once told her, "You howl bloody murder at first, but after a while it'll feel like wee pinpricks." Liliana reminded herself that this came from a Brigadier who could battle three floating mechanoids at once without getting hit.

She tried sitting up, and her body angrily protested. "Still waiting for those pinpricks!" she shouted.

Her problem wasn't dodging the blaster shots. Liliana used to run six miles a day before joining Star Brigade, so she had the conditioning. Moreover, these past few days the doctor had progressed to where she could shoot down the mechanoid without getting hit.

But today's unexpected mission had Liliana second-guessing again, putting too much thought into how she would shoot the mechanoid or which direction to dodge a pulse blast. By the time she made up her mind, *BLAM*, she'd get drilled.

Liliana couldn't help it. She was a xenobiologist who analyzed the tattshi out of situations. But life-and-death combat situations were decided on instinct. A Star Brigadier needed good instincts to survive live missions.

"I can't even survive this training program," Liliana finally winced her way up to a seated position. After limping back to her quarters, the doctor treated herself to a hydrobathe. Streams of hot water cascaded from the ceiling, washing away the grime and easing the many aches troubling Liliana's slender body.

Mentally, Liliana remained overwhelmed with doubts. Should she continue struggling as a field-active Brigadier, or work solely in the Medcenter?

Or just resign? She had planned to, after today's disastrous mission.

But Marguliese's suggestion, which clearly *wasn't* a suggestion, had stayed Liliana's decision…for now.

The Cybernarr's appeal still hadn't given Liliana any idea on how to overcome her hyperspace sickness. Once aboard any spacefaring vessel, she began overanalyzing the reality of being trapped in an enclosed metal tube, hurtling through space at stupefying speeds. At any moment, those speeds could rip the ship into a million pieces. And outside of that ship was space, an infinite everything…and *nothing*.

Liliana shuddered, continuing pondering her choices as she dried off and threw on greyish pajama pants and a snug burgundy t-shirt with the circular Star Brigade logo. She was still drying her pixie-cut hair when an urgent beeping caught her ear.

Liliana turned. *Who in the cosmos is calling me this late?* Across the room, her TransNet console with its wall viewscreen lit up with the bold text.

Secure Incoming Call. Section M: Cuende Facility.

Liliana's eyes widened. Cuende, a small town in northeastern Navarre she was unfortunately familiar with. It could only be one being. Liliana's professional impasse became background noise as she hurried over to the TransNet console.

"Liliana Cortés. Display caller with TriTran," she said. Moments later, the 3D image of a human male appeared right in front of Liliana, seated on the floor.

The earthborn human bore a conspicuous resemblance to Liliana. Their hair and eyes were both dark brown; even their faces seemed sculpted of the same oval shape. His skin was much paler—akin to someone who hadn't seen much natural sunlight. Through his white t-shirt and shapeless pants, he looked a bit doughy from lack of physical activity. And his hair had recently been shorn off.

He saw Liliana and his face lit up. "Ana! Hola!"

Liliana's heart sang. *He's having a good day.* She sat on the floor opposite him, even if he was actually on Terra Sollus and she on a starbase floating within the gas giant. "Tommy, mi amor. ¿Cómo estas?"

Tomás shrugged. "As good as can be in this prisión!"

Her older brother always called her 'Ana' or 'Ana Lucia' like most family members did, while she preferred to call him 'Tommy' instead of his full name, Tomás Carlos.

At least once a week they spoke, either face to face or via TransNet. Yet even when catching her brother on a good day, Liliana still remembered the terrifying fury that had distorted his face years ago. That memory was always a knife thrust to her heart.

The two Cortéses sat and talked about everything and anything happening all over the Galactic Union in their usual rapid-fire Spanish banter. Things felt normal, which Liliana needed in her life right now.

"Still no word from Elena?" Liliana asked, referring to one of their first cousins.

"Aunt Flor spoke to her a week ago. Said she was okay, but that's it."

Liliana gasped, surprised and a little hurt. "You heard about Ella and didn't tell me?"

"Hey!" Tomás threw back. "You were too busy with your Star Brigade thingamajig job."

The fact that he knew stunned Liliana. "Who told you?"

"Papá. Other than you, who else would've told me?"

"Okay," Liliana straightened, taking note of the sudden bite in Tomás's voice. She resolved to stay on topic. "I really can't say too much about what I'm doing—."

"Thirteen years, Ana," Tomás interrupted, his face twisting in anger. "Thirteen years and she won't even call me on the TransNet."

"Tomás," Liliana said calmly, knowing what was coming, "let's talk about something else."

Tommy rose up, seething. "It was an accident! *Why can't she forgive me?*"

"Please," Liliana struggled to stay firm. These outbursts weren't unusual, even on his good days. "You know what happens when you get mad like this—"

"I DON'T CARE!" Her brother's anger tasted of torment. "She doesn't hate you!"

"Tomás, bastante!" cried Liliana. Suddenly the doctor was twelve years old again, cowering before her brother's blind rage. She could feel tears welling up.

"*Cállate* Liliana!!" Tomás roared. "STOP COVERING FOR HER!!" Tomás's TriTran image became staticky just then.

He tried to speak again. But something seemed to constrict his voice. The image of him normalized and Liliana, through watery vision, noticed his wide eyes loosing their crazed glow. Tomás began to focus on her again, blind rage giving way to regret. And a wave of gratitude washed over Liliana.

A nanochip at the base of Tomás's brain constantly monitored his med levels. Should Tomás start losing control, like now, the chip immediately released a payload of depressants into his bloodstream.

Finally Tomás sank to his knees, head lolling forward. "Lo siento, Ana. I got…carried away," he murmured in a languid voice. "My drug cocktail is kicking in now."

Liliana nodded in silence, wiping her tears away with long fingers and staring despondently at the floor. She mentally checked off the long list of inhibitor drugs in Tomás's bracelet, which suppressed his Zenitrophin levels and regulated Tomás's mental state—Zenitrophin being the neurohormone produced exclusively by humanoid maximals.

Tomás, a maximum like Liliana, had manifested at fourteen years of age, four years earlier than she. But unlike Liliana, Tomás had difficulty controlling those abilities, as his body produced too much Zenitrophin. No doctor or solution had been able to help, and the problem worsened with age. Then, three days before his eighteenth birthday, one of Tomás's outbursts on a space shuttle almost killed their whole family.

From then on, his home had been a secure Section M facility in Cuende, explicitly for maximums with uncontrollable and dangerous abilities. Since that horrible day thirteen years ago, Liliana couldn't ride any spacefaring vessel without extreme bouts of terror and nausea. And from that day forward, their mother hadn't visited or spoken to Tomás once.

He straightened up with a deep breath and eyed his younger sister. "Muy bueno," he said snidely.

Liliana's tears finally stopped, but the pain of seeing her brother like this didn't, even after thirteen years. "I will find a way to make you better, Tommy."

Tomás chuckled. "You always say that, Ana."

"Because I mean it," Liliana insisted, meeting her brother's gaze.

"I know." Tomás smiled affectionately. Something off-screen caught his gaze and sobered him up. "Looks like my little tantrum cut our call time. So I'll be quick." The elder Cortés sibling leaned forward. "Were you truly happy at your previous job with San Ysidro Medcenter?"

Liliana sniffed and shook her head. "I was bored."

"And is this Star Brigade outfit the answer?"

"That's what I keep hoping," Liliana looked away. If only she could answer 'Yes' with complete certainty.

Tomás leaned back as he studied his sister's ambivalence. "Even if this Brigade thing doesn't work out, I know you'd have given it your all. You wouldn't be *you* if you didn't, Ana."

A comforting warmth filled Liliana's heart. She opened her mouth to respond, but then Tomás's TriTran image began to flicker. Their time was almost up. So she blurted out the first thing that came to mind. "Gracias, hermano mio! Te quiero!"

"Yo te quiero también, Ana." Immediately after that, Tomás's image vanished. Liliana now sat alone staring at the spot where her brother had just been.

She remembered when first manifesting, how Tomás's condition had dissuaded Liliana from even trying to gain mastery of her maximal abilities.

Tomás had been the one who persuaded her to learn the fundamentals of her abilities. That was why she had chosen an accelerated medical residency on the military starbase that housed Star Brigade.

Tomás had been as right then as he was now. "I have to try harder," she murmured. That meant overcoming her space phobia. And not by way of drugs or neuronanocyte enhancement. With that goal in mind, she changed into military-issue cargo pants and a long-sleeved black tee. She dashed out of her quarters in the middle of the night, knowing exactly who to ask for help.

With help from Hollus's computer system, Liliana found herself in a launch bay between two long rows of Shadowlancers fighter jets. This launch bay had a more diminutive and sparse appearance than Hollus's other bays that Liliana had dared to peek into. Dim, monotone halolights splashed down from the ceiling, accentuating the bleak ambiance. But that hardly bothered Liliana. Seeing so many spacecrafts, despite their smaller size, almost turned the doctor's legs to spaghetti beneath her.

Small metal tubes…stupefying speeds! Liliana's stomach began to churn. She stopped and shut her eyes. "Khrome?" she called out, the echo of her voice bouncing off the surrounding walls.

"*What?*" came a computerized and curt reply. Liliana's eyes popped open. The short, stocky Thulican stepped from behind the last Shadowlancer on her right and kept walking until he stood right in front of Liliana.

The doctor had three inches on Khrome. But his burly wall of armored muscle made her slim build look like a toothpick. The Thulican cut quite an intimidating pose, especially with the irritated look on his noseless, blue face. Liliana couldn't believe this was the same playful, devil-may-care Khrome who cheered her up the moment she stepped foot on Hollus two weeks ago.

"What is it, Liliana?" he asked with less bile. Usually Khrome called her 'Lily' or some random nickname he'd make up on the fly. But with the newest Brigadier that Captain Nwosu just recruited, Liliana understood completely.

"Hi," Liliana realized that her stiff tone matched her current posture. Focusing solely on Khrome helped the doctor relax a bit. "How are you?"

He looked taken aback. "Captain Nwosu just recruited a member of the species that had my race enslaved for five decades. And when I should have resigned outright, somehow our fearless leader convinced me to stay."

"Yeah, he has a way of doing that," Liliana forced on a smile, which Khrome didn't return.

Marguliese, the Cybernarr. Friend of Captain Nwosu's or not, the Cybernarr species was no friend of the Galactic Union. Which meant no one outside of Star Brigade could know, per Nwosu's orders.

Liliana had been actively trying to forget about Star Brigade's newest recruit. But how could she after Marguliese had saved her life today? Or how Marguliese had later stopped Liliana from calling San Ysidro to beg for her old job back. Liliana shuddered.

"Even worse, we're stuck with her until this stupid-ass Maelstrom crisis is handled," the Thulican raged. "How do you *think* I feel, Liliana?"

Liliana, expecting this response, offered a shrug. "Probably pissed."

"You guessed right," Khrome grumbled. "Been tweaking these 'lancers."

"Wait—what?" Liliana turned her head to take in the numerous spacecrafts around her. Though it was universally known how technologically gifted Thulicans were, their capabilities still continued to amaze her. "You serviced all these crafts tonight??"

"Yeah," Khrome shrugged nonchalantly. It was easier to forget that he was probably smarter than almost every sentient on Hollus Maddrone. "I started after that meeting about Maelstrom's comeback speech. Fixing stuff usually helps me think. But after *Marguliese*," Khrome looked like he'd swallowed acid saying her name. "Part of me doesn't want to report for training tomorrow."

Liliana stared down at the floor. All these spacecrafts were beginning to make her head swim. "This whole Brigade experience seems to be throwing everyone's routine off kilter."

Khrome didn't respond. In the awkward silence that ensued, Liliana decided to get to her point. "Hey," she began, still looking down—avoiding any view of the Starlancers. "Let's help each other with our respective hangups?"

Khrome snorted, "Khrome-Tastic has no 'hang-ups.'"

The doctor looked up incredulously. "Cybernarr?"

The Thulican's glare turned murderous.

Liliana shrank back. "Riiiight."

Khrome caught himself and sighed. "What would you suggest?"

"Let's go somewhere and talk."

Khrome rubbed his chin thoughtfully. "Like Hollusphere or Pilot Pub?"

Liliana cleared her throat. "I was thinking somewhere off starbase."

The Thulican's round, yellow eyes grew wider in dawning recognition. "I know just the place."

Half an orv later, Dr. Liliana Cortés wanted to kick herself—hard. *Off starbase*, she fretted. She should've suggested Pilot Pub. Yes, it reeked of liquor and seedy pilots, but anything trumped sitting on a flying shuttlecraft.

The Unionjack flew on autopilot as they put more distance between themselves and Hollus. All the while the stocky Thulican paced back and forth, ranting about his deep loathing for Marguliese and the Cybernarr race.

Liliana remained seated and listened, nodding when necessary. But her queasiness grew with each small bump of turbulence in Zeid's atmosphere. The shuttle, traveling at sublight speed on stellar drives, was about to breach Zeid's atmosphere and head for open space. Liliana dared a few glances out the shuttle's front viewport, catching the unexciting sight of Zeid's green gases. That, at least, didn't make her feel worse.

Abruptly, the Unionjack shot forward into a slingshot hyperspace jump, rocketing out of Zeid's atmosphere. Liliana got slammed against the wall behind her, but this time she was strapped in. Instinctively shutting her eyes as the vivid green faded into white, her stomach lurched. Before she knew it, the jump ended. The shuttlecraft slowed to stellar speeds, hyperspace breaking back into tiny twinkling stars separated by gaps of inky black.

Liliana waited a moment to let her stomach settle, her anger boiling over. She shot to her feet and directed all that fury at Khrome. "You programmed in a slingshot jump…and DIDN'T TELL ME?"

The Thulican had the gall to smile. "I did." His smile stretched obnoxiously to either end of his shiny blue face. He folded his burly arms across a broad chest. "How do you feel?"

"Like punching in your teeth…if it wouldn't shatter my hand!"

Khrome snorted despite his lack of a nose, his round yellow eyes alight with mirth. "No doubt. How do you feel?"

Liliana bristled. "I just told you—" She stopped. Aside from seriously wanting to hurt him, Liliana actually felt little nausea—if any. "Jittery," she began. "But not too queasy."

"Thought so," Khrome chuckled.

Now Liliana just felt quite confused. "But how was this different from all the other hyperspace jumps?" the doctor pressed.

"For starters, you didn't think a slingshot jump was coming," Khrome turned towards a long side closet to the left-hand side of the shuttle. "And, aside from the fact that we weren't on a mission, you actually enjoyed your traveling companion this time."

Liliana arched an eyebrow. "Huh." The Thulican was right, mainly with the latter reason. Anyone with two working brain cells could agree that Khrome was far more enjoyable company than V'Korram Prydyri-Ravlek. Still, the duplicity bothered her. "I don't like you!" she blurted out.

Khrome tooted skeptically, "You loooove the Khrome-Daddy." Then he began to rummage through the closet he opened.

"Oh, so *now* we're back to the jolly third-person references?" Liliana quipped.

"What can I say? Helping out buddies always hits my happy button."

"But what if my space sickness comes back?" Liliana's shoulders slumped miserably. The whole 'small tube flying at stupefying speeds' dread started to worm back into her thoughts. "I mean, that could have just been a fluke that I didn't feel like yakking all over this—"

"Hey, we're not done yet. My helping hands have only begun to work." Khrome now produced a helmet and manila spacesuit far too slender-fitting for his burly self. This was obviously why he handed them both to Liliana. "Here."

Liliana stared blankly at both objects in his mitt-like hands.

"This is the point where you take both items and put them on." Khrome thrust said items in her face again.

The doctor continued to stare with a puzzled frown. "Why would I do that?" Her brain, for all its xenobiology smarts, seemed incapable of grasping any reason for donning such garb—*ever.*

Khrome shrugged. "Since we're going sub-orbital diving on Terra Sollus, ya might need some protection."

Liliana's small brown eyes slowly drifted up to Khrome. Then she broke into a nervous titter. "Good one, Khrome. Almost had me there!"

"Actually, that slingshot jump took us about three and a half orvs in realtime away from Zeid," Khrome said, completely serious. "And we still got another orv to go. You still haven't taken your spacesuit and helmet."

Liliana opened her mouth to retort, a whole new wave of fear ramming her in the gut. Khrome beat her to the punch. "I'll be with you the whole time. It's quite safe!"

Liliana folded her arms and struck an obstinate pose. "This isn't funny anymore, Khrome. Take me back to Hollus *now*."

"Can't do that."

Liliana's annoyance spiked. "You absconded with me under false pretenses."

"Because you'd have freaked if I told you what we were doing. And because you aren't ready to be a Star Brigadier yet."

"You don't know that," Liliana snapped back. "And you have no right to hold me on this...shuttle prison."

"Well then," Khrome withdrew the helmet and spacesuit from her reach. "What I do know is that you came to me for help." The Thulican's voice took a serious tone. "How can I count on you on a field mission if you haven't dealt with this problem?"

Liliana tore her gaze away. They both already knew that answer. The only sound in this shuttlecraft was the steadfast hum of stellar drives propelling them toward Terra Sollus.

"Give me those." She snatched away the articles in Khrome's hands. Liliana stepped into the shuttlecraft's lavatory and came out ten macroms later in the manila spacesuit, with the helmet held under her arm. It fit her svelte body perfectly. But she walked forward with stiff and utterly graceless steps, clearly not used to wearing a spacesuit.

"Shut up," she growled at Khrome as he stood shaking with barely suppressed laughter. Liliana plopped herself down miserably in a passenger seat. The journey didn't disquiet her nerves anymore, probably because she was so mad at Khrome.

"We're here," Khrome announced. Another bout of turbulence shook the Unionjack back and forth for a few macroms, merely the shuttle breaking through Terra Sollus's atmosphere. This made Liliana shoot straight up to her feet with helmet in hand. But the spacesuit was a bit stiff and the ship still shuddered from the outer turbulence, so she had to stutter step so she wouldn't fall forward. The rattling subsided, and Liliana's gaze caught something beyond Khrome.

Terra Sollus's endless blue flooded the entirety of the front viewport. The shuttle now soared just underneath Terra Sollus's atmosphere. White, cloudy billows had a dreamlike fuzziness as they floated past the viewport, revealing the green and brown chunks of landmass several thousand miles below. That was enough for Liliana to avert her eyes away. She took several deep breaths to calm her nerves, which didn't help. "This sub-orbital jumping will only make my phobias worse!" Liliana whined.

"Put on your helmet and you'll see that it won't," Khrome appeared next to her. To her surprise, he wore a strictly encouraging expression on his noseless blue face. "Now, your suit has about twenty-two orvs of oxygen in it, but I doubt you'll need that much." The usual jokiness in his tone was nowhere to be found. Liliana put on the helmet, after which Khrome dotingly made sure all the latches and air pressure seals were secured. Now wearing her helmet, she sucked in another deep breath. Nothing out of the ordinary, save the tang of processed air on her tongue.

"What about your suit?" Liliana asked, and realized the stupidity of that question. Khrome was courteous enough to just silently sneer. He didn't need a spacesuit or helmet.

"Okay," Khrome began. "We're currently about 50,000 feet over Nahrain, somewhere around the Arabian Desert—*away* from spacelane traffic. We'll jump out and be free-falling at a terminal velocity of about 140 mph. Then your suit's gravity repulsors will kick in at around 5500 feet. I'll slow down my descent around the same time. Liliana?"

The doctor just nodded idly in blank-faced terror. "Okay," she whispered tersely to everything he said. "Okay, okay."

"Alright," Khrome turned her towards the wall they had their backs to. "Navcom, open left side door with the barometric forcefield in place." Immediately, a sizeable portion of the Unionjack's sidewall slid away, replaced by Terra Sollus's vast sapphire skies. Adding to this view was the roar of strong winds buffeting the shuttle's outer hull. Liliana's stomach roiled.

Khrome began moving toward the shuttlecraft opening, clearly expectant that Liliana would do the same. But she didn't. She couldn't. Thoughts of open space, randomly smashing into a passing shuttlecraft or worse, the grav repulsors on her spacesuit malfunctioning, ran rampant through her mind. The realization that an endless gulf of everything and nothing awaited her sent stabs of panic and nausea through her. "I'm...not sure…I can." Her breaths were too shallow, too quick, a precursor to hyperventilation.

"Liliana," she heard Khrome's calm, mechanized voice. "Take deep breaths." She did as she was told, gulping in slower breaths of air. "Now look at me."

Slowly she opened her eyes and saw Khrome standing before her. He placed both hands reassuringly on her arms, which covered up a good portion of them. "I'll be there the whole time. Remember how Captain Nwosu said there was no 'I' in team. Even though there is a 'me.'"

That won a panicky laugh out of Liliana. Suddenly, her legs felt a little less lead-like.

"This is about more than prepping for Star Brigade." The Thulican pulled Liliana in close. "I've known beings who've been alive for a thousand and one years, but have never *lived* a moment. Want that to be you?"

"I don't want to live a thousand and one years!" Liliana blurted out. Khrome glared at her. "Sorry, my mind overanalyzes *and* fills up with bad puns when I'm nervous."

The doctor turned and looked out at the measureless sprawl of white billows and crystal blue oceans beneath them. Beyond that, inky space was dotted with diamond-bright stars.

Everything and nothing. Another wave of nausea hit her. She didn't want to be a prisoner of that anymore. Liliana turned back to Khrome. "You jump, I jump."

The Thulican broke into a huge smile. "On 3." He turned toward the open shuttle hatch. "And don't worry about the shuttle, Liliana," he said right as Liliana opened her mouth. "The autopilot will close the door once we jump, and the craft will be waiting for us after our jump." That quelled some of Liliana's nausea as she faced the open hatch. She squeezed her eyes shut and inhaled as Khrome began his count.

"3!" he shouted.

Liliana's eyes snapped open. Khrome crouched down and leaped out the shuttle. And to her own surprise, she followed right after—eyes closed, of course. The doctor floated, like in a zero-gravity chamber. But she knew better. Around 50,000 feet of sky separated her and the surface of Terra Sollus. That number plummeted fast as she dropped at 140 mph. Her eyes stayed closed. Again she could see that viewscreen from years past, the unending, sickening, sparkling expanse of inky black. *Everything and nothing.*

An all-encompassing terror seized the doctor by the throat like it had fifteen years ago. And the memories came rushing back at gale-force intensity.

Tomás crazed and shimmering and shrieking…

Mama choking and gasping for air…

Papa trying desperately to right their spiraling shuttlecraft…

Liliana screamed loudly. No Khrome, no Star Brigade existed in her closed-off sight. Nothing save a weightless nose-dive that she had willingly agreed to. Her spacesuit *would* malfunction. And the last thing she heard would be her own cowardly scream.

"LILY!"

Liliana stopped screaming. Khrome's voice shouted into her helmet's speaker, piercing through the fog of fear. *I'm not on that shuttle,* she told herself.

"OPEN YOUR EYES!" Liliana hesitantly complied. Khrome floated right in front of her, falling at the same speed. The Thulican's stocky physique was silhouetted beautifully against a golden sky of cottony clouds, silvery skin gleaming. Under different circumstances Liliana might have laughed at how his burly limbs splayed out clumsily to accommodate their rapid descent.

Seeing Khrome beside her like he had promised, wearing his big, goofy grin—Liliana felt safe as she plummeted.

He reached out. "Take my hands!" Liliana fought against the pummeling winds and put her dainty gloved hands in the Thulican's giant ones.

Focusing on Khrome, Liliana began to regain more of her faculties. The Thulican watched her with round yellow eyes, still smiling. Knowing Khrome wouldn't let go, her fear faded slowly. It gave way to a sensation that the doctor had experienced when either solving a patient's malady or making a discovery by way of research.

The euphoria jolted her from head to toes and back again.

Suddenly, everything went white. Khrome disappeared from sight. Liliana shrieked, but his hands still firmly held hers. She tightened her grip just in case. In no time, the Thulican reappeared, shimmering under the sunlight.

"We just passed through Terra Sollus's main cloud layer at 34,000 feet up," Khrome orated. "I'll let you know once we're about to land."

Liliana tensed up, not knowing what to suspect.

"Look down!"

Underneath the helmet her eyes narrowed. Just when she had gotten comfortable with plunging from 50,000 feet up, Khrome has the gall to ask her to look straight down.

Sensing her hesitation, Khrome smiled more broadly. "Trust me, Lily. As a scientist, you'll hate yourself for not looking down."

Liliana whispered a prayer to the Trinitarian God for strength, and then glanced down. Her body flinched away for an instant. Before long, Liliana could not look away.

Below lay Terra Sollus, her place of birth. The oceans appeared so blue, so undisturbed. Liliana peered down at the continents she had studied on 3D globes as a youngster, all of them a mix of verdant green and brownish rock just like she remembered. Intermingled with those colors were ferroment and metal patches of extensive city-states visible from even this far up. A polygonal stretch of sandy country, landlocked on all sides save its western coast caught the doctor's eye. Once she saw two rivers intersecting before reaching that coast, Liliana easily recognized the country, Nahrain, where they planned to land. Looking west gave view to the curve of the globe, its whole side dressed in a patchwork blanket of clouds.

Lifting her head slightly, Liliana could see the southernmost tip of New Europe on Terra Sollus's northern horizon, juxtaposed against the massive fiery blaze of Rynn. Even though she couldn't get a solid look at her home country of Navarre due to the glare, just knowing where it lay was enough. This was Terra Sollus, her homeworld, in a way she had never experienced before. Liliana looked up at Khrome, full of wonder.

The Thulican guffawed. "Told ya!"

At around 11,000 feet, Nahrain grew larger and vaster. Liliana now recognized the Persian Republic at its northern borders and the nation of Kaladdea at its southern borders. The sky around them brightened into a cloudless baby blue, as now they were far beneath Terra Sollus's atmosphere on its dayside.

At around 6,000 feet up, she clearly spotted the unending crisscrossing hovercar lanes above Nahrain, but Khrome and she were nowhere near them. Khrome called out, "Your spacesuit's gravity repulsors are about to kick in. I'm gonna let go of you soon." The doctor stared back at her Thulican teammate, utterly confused. Holding onto Khrome had given her courage, so she didn't immediately release his mitt-sized hands. But knowing she had to for safety reasons, Liliana breathed in deeply and let go, waiting for the fear and nausea.

Nothing happened. Liliana blinked in shock. Khrome guffawed, right before shooting straight up into the air. Upon triggering his flight abilities, the Thulican floated the rest of the way down. Liliana, all alone, looked beneath her. Nahrain's cities, deserts and rivers were growing larger and larger—no longer the size of kiddy toys. Before she could process it all, an invisible wall of jarring force hit Liliana, forcing her into an upright position. In short order, her plummet slowed considerably. Liliana smiled, recognizing the work of her spacesuit's gravity repulsors.

"Say it," shouted Khrome. He floated down into view, arms spread out in typical swaggering fashion. "When you got problems you want fixed, who do you call?"

"I am NOT calling you Khrome-Daddy!" Liliana laughed, adjusting herself to this new, slower descent. Several macroms later, the duo floated onto a rolling expanse of reddish sand—Nahrain's Arabian Desert. Khrome landed expertly at the base of a steep sand dune. He righted himself and looked up towards Liliana, who of course landed at the top of said sand dune. After losing her footing, she tumbled the whole way down. Clouds of red dust marked her long topple, as did Khrome's boisterous laughter.

She finally came to a halt at the bottom of the dune and lay still for several moments. Khrome walked up and gently yanked Liliana to her feet.

"You okay?" he asked, still giggling. The doctor stared back, speechless. She quickly unlatched her helmet, yanking it off. Her skin tingled at the breeze of Terra Sollus's fresh and unprocessed air.

"That was AMAZING!" she shrieked, her words echoing across the Arabian Desert. Then Liliana began laughing and crying at once, all the while hopping around with glee. She felt invincible, as if she could take on the entire galaxy. "Can we do it again?"

Khrome guffawed. "Unfortunately, not today. Practice is in like six orvs. Sometime soon, if you want."

"*I want!*" she said in a hoarse voice. "Thank you!" Liliana threw her arms around Khrome's thick neck.

"No problem," the Thulican chuckled. When she pulled away, the Thulican looked up at her with his large, round yellow eyes. "After we finish training, let's hit up one of Zeid's moons."

Liliana nodded vigorously. "You're a good friend, Khrome."

"Yeah, I know," he shrugged leisurely. Liliana giggled. The Khrome that Liliana knew and adored was back. She spun about and took in the windswept landscape around her. "We should get back to Hollus." In the far east, just beyond a rolling sea of dunes, she spotted the sparkling spacescrapers of Bayn, Nahrain's capital city-state. Then she looked skyward and felt a stab of confusion. "Is the Unionjack going to land anytime soon?" she asked. "I don't see it approaching."

"That's because we're going to it," she heard Khrome say.

Liliana whirled on him and saw an impish grin. "You're kidding!!"

"Nope," he replied. "Strap that helmet back on. We're going for a ride!"

When she attached and pressurized the helmet, Khrome scooped her up in his arms as easily as sheet paper. Liliana wrapped her arms around Khrome's neck, heartbeat thundering. Only this time, it wasn't from fear. "Let's go already!"

Khrome smirked at her right before squatting down. For an instant Liliana could sense a building rumble beneath the Thulican, an upsurge of power building.

And suddenly he rocketed skyward. Liliana whooped loudly, holding on tightly to Khrome. As they ascended, Liliana swiveled her head all around, taking in as much as the helmet visor would allow. Nahrain's immense dune sea below quickly shrank into a modest stretch of lesser ripples. And those ripples rapidly shrank into numerous tiny creases across the country's blocky expanse. Khrome rose further up, and now the curve of Terra Sollus's dayside came into Liliana's line of sight again—magnificent and dazzling.

Right now Liliana Cortés wanted to cry, this time for joy.

Prey

"This is a terrible idea," Ella Valdés grumbled under her breath. She sat alone, at a puny corner booth in the putrid and crammed Hugrask's Hostellaris. To a casual observer, Ella was just another human prospector nursing a drink after a long day of unsuccessful mining beneath Bimnorii's sand dunes. That's how Ella preferred it, or else her job would become much harder.

As usual, Bimnorii was an ungodly oven, even at the end of the day. Noriida Major's sunset cast a deep crimson glow over the mishmash of buildings that made up Rimhara, Bimnorii's largest city-state.

Tonight, Ella had opted to wear only a snug, black armorweave vest over a dark tank top, a sleek khaki utility belt over kurthahide and obsidian nanoclothe pants, along with dark, knee-high buckle combat boots. She carried a smaller pulse pistol tucked in her pants underneath the vest. A larger, more visible firearm would draw the worst kind of heat in a place as dangerous as Rimhara, which was why she prepped hidden weapons in each slim forearm-length gauntlet.

Ella wiped away the sweat beading on her brow, silently cursing Bimnorii's dry heat. Even with a temperature controller embedded in her clothes and coolers positioned all over this hostellaris, she could feel her light olive skin desiccating in protest. The human patted down her neck with a sodden napkin for probably the fortieth time in the past orv, observing any potential threats with beady, dark eyes.

As small as Hugrask's Hostellaris looked on the outside, this place really packed in a crowd. Under the dim blue lights, yellowish clouds pumped incessantly from the long pipes of patrons getting high on bimweed, coalescing into a greenish miasma. That made Ella nauseous when she focused on it too long.

The haze did little to obscure such a disreputable gathering of smugglers, space pirates and overall lowlifes from every ass end of the known cosmos. Three hulking Kedri mercenaries, obvious by their scaly blue hides, bright mohawk-mullet manes and heavy, overarched brows sat in a bigger corner booth next to hers. They spoke in the raucous Kedri Common Tongue, downing hard syrupy liquor in pails the size of Ella's head.

Numerous mercenaries and bounty hunters swaggered through the crowd like kings of the universe, making sure their weapons were visible enough to ward off would-be troublemakers. Somewhere else, a verbal argument between a Cressonish and a Kintarian kept fading in and out of the general roar.

A pair of Nnaxan females, their craniowhisks trembling lustily and tumbling down to their asses, weaved through the dense crowd with what they considered their sexiest sashays, catching the attention of many drunk and lonely males. Phrynes were the Nnaxans' official titles, but to Ella they were straight up prostitutes. The whores purposely avoided the far left of the hostellaris, where many rowdy patrons hollered at a performance Ella couldn't see.

Searing melodies of string instruments reached above the noisy tumult, a total contradiction to the grimy watering hole with its heaving press of patrons. The ugly clash of yowling and gargled dialects always seemed to teeter dangerously toward physical conflict. Ella could taste the constant threat of violence beneath the surface just waiting to erupt. But she knew the simmering menace was endemic on Bimnorii, no matter which part of this hellhole she'd been on. Ella had heard cryptic asides and angry snippets of some gruesome bloodbath in Rimhara's sister city-state, Ymedes. As soon as Ella confirmed whatever happened in Ymedes didn't mess with her job, she tuned out the gruesome specifics.

Dangerous surroundings aside, Ella wasn't afraid, just alert...and angry. She hated Bimnorii and its never-ending fucking desert. But since taking up the bounty hunter trade, Ella kept finding herself back on this dried-out *tattshi* ball. It was like some sand-covered magnet that kept drawing her back no matter how far she traveled away from it.

The reason for her latest visit was the same as always—a job.

This latest one involved hunting quarry from a seldom seen species. After Ella and Jaellyn's fruitless two weeks of searching several worlds in the Lawless Regions, a reliable, yet very expensive contact had tipped them off to a member of this elusive species surfacing on Bimnorii. She scanned the crowd more times than she could count, toying idly with wavy, raven-black hair pulled into a sleek ponytail at the nape of her neck. According to their contact, the quarry frequented this hostellaris. Yet, in the past two orvs, Ella had seen nothing resembling the beast in the holoimage she and her partner had received.

"You've said how bad my idea is three times already," snapped a clipped voice on Ella's concealed earcom. That would be Jaellyn, her bounty-hunting partner, waiting somewhere outside of Hugrask's for Ella to lure their target into the open.

"I'm repeating that to make sure you know," Ella hissed under her breath, but the hostellaris music and uproar was so loud, no one would hear her anyway. "We could get nothing, or I could get killed."

"I *won't* let that happen," Jaellyn stated with sternness that Ella found comforting. The Tarkathian continued, "Unless you have a better idea on luring out our mark, then by all means, state it."

Ella had no comeback for that. She could almost picture Jaellyn's smug look. "That's what I thought, silly human," the Tarkathian stated. "And *stop* rolling your eyes."

Ella, in mid-eye roll, scowled and continued to nurse her reddish Rimhara Bitter Sour, wishing for a stronger drink. Now was one of those times that Ella almost forgot her partner was much younger than her—as in thirteen years old, and trained since birth to hunt in a culture deeming that acceptable.

There was a parting in the crowd, and at the main bar sat the target—an osvowraith. It was a mirror image of the hologram she and Jaellyn had seen before taking this job: rail-thin humanoid, seemingly composed of all sharp angles. Its lengthy nose, pointed like a blunt sword edge, with a deathly pallor obvious even under the dim lights. Oily black dreadlocks from the rear of its head fell down to its lower back. Ella still couldn't believe that *this* being could pose a threat to anyone. According to their contact, male and female osvowraiths look pretty much the same, so Ella referred to the target as 'It.'

The osvowraith sat hunched over on a floating stool, coiled like a snake. Its entire attention was fixated on the performance happening to Ella's far left. In its clawed fingers was a round cup of an untouched fizzy, yellow-orange, a tongue-burning Solar Scorcher by the look of it.

After finding out that osvowraiths weren't just nightmarish bedtime stories, Ella had almost fallen over with laughter. Apparently, osvowraiths were energy parasites that drain the life out of other sentient beings for sustenance. Even when seeing graphic images of osvowraith victims, all pallid and speckled from head to toe with eerie glowing suck marks, Ella just couldn't see this scrawny thing as a threat. Now she noted the osvowraith's laser-like focus on whatever was on the stage—a hunter tracking its prey.

"I see him," muttered Ella, tossing her ponytail over her shoulder. The bounty hunter seriously had doubts about taking this job, especially when their data broker, Xubes, said the client was some human supremacist paramilitary group. "Why the hell do they need us?" a baffled Ella had asked.

"You two, even though you've done quite well recently, are much lower profile than the more known bounty hunters," Xubes had explained. "And you come cheap."

As low-priced as Ella and Jaellyn's services were, the compensation had been way too good to pass up. If the first half of the payment was any indication, this job was triple their usual take for a grab 'n' bag based on the target's rarity. Plus Ella and Jaellyn were in serious need of some real currency for better weapons, foodstuff with actual taste, and, of course, new ship parts. Ella had been able to patch up lots of nagging issues and leaks with their ship thanks to her techie knowhow. But it was only a matter of time before one such issue became serious enough to leave her and Jaellyn stranded in the middle of the Black.

Ella downed the last of her drink and rose from her seat. Amidst the dim and stifling atmosphere, quite a few heads turned when she weaved through the crowd. Ella owed that interest to her near five-foot-ten inches in height. She had always been on the more full-figured side—unlike her skinny-like-a-stick cousin, Ana Lucia. But a subtle sway of the hips here, a sensual half-smirk there and Ella could draw her fair share of male attention.

As she neared her quarry, Ella noticed where the concentration of Hugrask's crowd resided. One look told her why the hostellaris was so packed.

The stage on the far left belonged to a scantily clad near-human girl, her long, violet hair done up in intricate and elegant braids. The chalk-white humanoid was a petite little thing. Her heart-shaped face remained focused and blissful, despite the audience's lewd catcalls and whistles. On that stage, she danced a slow and seductive dance, waving her arms hypnotically to the song's alien string-heavy tempo. Her hips shook and shivered to the melodies, as if independent of her body. Gliding across the stage like an ice-skater in slow motion, the girl's presence filled the entire hostellaris.

Ella stopped and stared, mesmerized. The music, like the dancer, was Korvenite in origin, wreathing her every movement flawlessly, a beautiful fiery union between song and dance. Ella had never heard or seen Korvenite music performed when she lived on Terra Sollus. It had been forbidden in the Valdés household. Clearly, she had been missing out. The performance was like nothing Ella had ever seen. Yet the passion…the fire of this Korvenite's seductive dance, felt so like an old dance style Ella's home country of Navarre had inherited from a long-dead Old Earth country. The Korvenite's eyes, black sclera housing gold irises, lanced into Ella's brain, blotting out every coherent thought…

"Has the osvowraith exited yet?" Jaellyn interjected, a welcome stab of daylight through Ella's mental fog.

"Not yet," Ella murmured clumsily. *Whoa!* She tore her eyes away from the performance, shaking her head to clear it. That Korvenite was putting out some serious psychic…*something*. No wonder the girl had the osvowraith's undivided attention. All her telepathic mojo must look like an all-you-can-eat buffet sign. Ella, now clearheaded, took a good look.

Under layers of makeup and barely there clothing, this Korvenite was a child writhing and dancing for unruly adults, some old enough to be grandparents.

"*Gods*, how old is that Korvie?" Ella mumbled, rather unsettled. The *tattshi* she'd witnessed since leaving Galactic Union borders never ceased to shock her.

"I made my first kill when I turned seven," Jaellyn remarked in a disdainful tone. "The Korvenite can dance at any age she chooses."

Ella snorted and kept moving. "Excuse me for not being raised 'Tarkathian-style,' Jae."

Jaellyn muttered something in her native Tarkathian that sounded distinctly like an expletive.

Ella glanced again at the Korvenite and then at the osvowraith, whose unblinking gaze never wavered once.

All-you-can-eat buffet…

A queer dread chilled Ella. The Korvie was its next victim.

"MOVE." A towering Nubrideen hulk of muscle shouldered forward past Ella, almost knocking the human off her feet. Too rattled to be angry, Ella quickly regained her footing and line of sight. The string instrumental music had stopped, replaced by boisterous applause from the packed-in crowd. The Korvenite smiled glowingly and took a deep bow. Was the performance over? Ella turned to the bar.

The osvowraith looked ready to spring from its seat, the Solar Scorcher drink still untouched. From a strategic outlook, this actually worked in her favor; while the osvowraith found its evening meal, Ella and Jaellyn would catch it off guard. Boom. Easy grab. Easy pay.

Any other coldblooded bounty hunter would have killed for such an easy scenario. Jaellyn definitely wouldn't hesitate using the Korvie as bait, but that was Jaellyn. On many a time in previous jobs Ella had followed her head instead of her heart, sticking with a cardinal rule in bounty hunting: innocents killed during a job are collateral damage and nothing more.

Besides, it's a fucking Korvenite. Why should I care? Still, Ella couldn't wrap her head around the sight of that Korvenite kid spasming as the osvowraith drained her dry...a life ending before it even had a chance to be lived....

And in that moment, Ella made her choice. She pushed her way urgently toward the osvowraith.

"Ella?" Jaellyn asked in the earcom. "What's happening?"

"Confirming target. Standby." Ella ignored the irate objections and forcefully closed the distance between her prey. Now Ella's fear began to rise, not for the Korvie, but for herself. Other patrons were chatting and drinking and arguing over mining sites, totally oblivious to the osvowraith's true nature. Ella reached into a pouch on her utility belt, rubbing her fingers in the fine nanotech powder inside.

The osvowraith moved to get up, raising the Solar Scorcher to its lipless mouth...

...until Ella snatched the drink from the beast's hand and drained it in one long pull. She almost gagged. The liquid seared down her throat like liquid fire. Ella sucked in a needed breath to cool her mouth. "Couldn't let such a fine drink go to waste," she winked sassily, shoving the empty glass back in the stunned osvowraith's hand. With a quick brush of her thumb, the powder was spread across the osvowraith's bony knuckles. She dared a glance at her prey.

The beast was even more oily-looking up close, its narrow and pallid face housing a pair of eyes that resembled dark, cavernous slits of blood-red, but without warmth. "Better down that Solar Scorcher while it's hot next time," Ella teased, suddenly feeling soiled under the beast's unpleasant glare.

She sauntered away, her eyes returning to the hostellaris's left-hand stage. The Korvenite was gone, safely backstage. *Thank God.* Now, if only the osvowraith could find a new target....

Ella cut through the crowded space of Hugrask's, tingling from head to toe from that Solar Scorcher in her system. It kept the panic at bay, but not the wicked glee. Ella glanced periodically over her shoulder. She saw the osvowraith slowly standing up, eyes trained on her.

That's it, sucker. Come to mama. A victorious smile brightened Ella's full and youthful face, making the Terra Sollan native look younger than her twenty-eight years.

"Ella?" Jaellyn said curiously on the comlink. "I'm getting a bio-reading of some bizarre organism from the nanocyte trackers."

"Because I tagged our target," Ella gloated, pleased with herself. "It's heading my way."

"Heading your wa—WHAT?" Jaellyn's shock quickly turned to anger, as usual. "What did you do?"

"Nothing too dramatic," Ella shrugged, eyeing a Nnaxan Phryne with disgust as she squeezed past. "I simply motivated our target to follow me so we could keep track of it."

Jaellyn's fury nearly blew out Ella's earcom, "*You were supposed to—*"

"Calm the fuck down," Ella scoffed, the nonchalance in her voice belying fear as she glanced back. Yep, the tall and gaunt osvowraith pushed through the heaving crowd, its blood-red eyes only on her. Ella quickened her pace, almost colliding with a rotund balloon of a sentient. "Who knows how long it would have taken? This speeds things up."

"*Stupid* human!" her Tarkathian partner spat in impotent fury. "You always take these stupid risks."

Ella smiled. Adding an insulting adjective before the word 'human' was the Tarkathian's way of showing she was worried. Plus, Jaellyn's Standard noticeably devolved the angrier she got. "Love ya too, Jae." The human had finally muscled her way out the hostellaris exit.

The vicious smack of triple-digit heat almost knocked Ella back into the hostellaris. Noriida Major was a blistering crimson ball, leisurely beginning to set. But due to Bimnorii's odd orbit, its sunsets lasted for orvs. Ella gritted her teeth and forced herself out into the early evening furnace. She made a sharp left with brisk, long strides, putting some distance between her and the hostellaris.

Rimhara's streets were swarming with alien beings, some milling around street vendors, while others were returning from futilely mining for desert treasures that had dried up centuries ago. Ella slowed her gait to not be obvious, keeping pace with the crowd for cover. Up above, several hovercrafts soared past, most of them decades out of date even compared to the poorest Union memberworlds. The vehicles' worn and rusted metal all glinted against the harsh radiance of Noriida Major, now a crimson half-sphere, unhurriedly dipping behind the horizon.

"I see him," Jaellyn stated within macroms, "tailing you from afar. I can drop him right here."

Ella frowned sharply, remembering the last time the Tarkathian teen pursued this option on a recent job. "Leaving me to clean up the mess, like on Embrose? No fucking thanks. Wait till I'm clear of any bystanders." Before long, she found a narrow, winding alley right at her left. Ella dodged around a massive Aengerian, its bowling-pin-like body taking up most of the walkway, then slipped into the alley entrance.

She looked back. No sign of the osvowraith—only the normal sounds and sights of pedestrian traffic pouring through the narrow alleyway egress. *It's coming,* Ella assured herself. She continued striding past a scattered bevy of human and Nnaxan beggars looking for more currency to mine their fortune, or the street vendors too poor to pay for 'protection' out on the main streets. Ella ignored them all and turned right, into a more desolate part of the alleyway, narrower than the last one. This path appeared empty. Other than the far-off echoes of sentients and zipping hovercrafts on the main streets, Ella could only hear her thudding heartbeat. *Perfect.* Bounty hunter rules or not, Ella saw no need for innocents to die.

"Jae? Where are you?" she whispered, trying to keep the nerves out of her voice.

"Almost there." Jaellyn sounded oddly frantic.

"And our mutual friend?" the human asked. Glancing warily at the roofs of the rundown, stumpy buildings surrounding her, Ella slowly reached for the pulse pistol under her vest.

"*Ella*," the young Tarkathian cried, "it's almost on you!"

The bounty hunter whipped her head around, but saw nothing. Just a sand-covered pathway and the fading smolder of sunset peeking in from both ends of the alley. "Where—"

Something in the shadows caught Ella's eye. She spun toward it as a blur of motion plowed into her. The bounty hunter felt her feet leave the ground, and then the beast's entire weight landed on her.

Ella grunted. Her ribs screamed in protest, even through the armorweave vest. The sissing continued as a pair of sinewy arms bearhugged her waist like a vise. But by pure luck, the osvowraith didn't have the bear hug fully cinched, allowing Ella to roll through and fight out of the hold. The osvowraith hissed and spat like a wild animal, trying to pin Ella to the ground. And she fought by thrashing and twisting her body every which way with a panicked ferocity. As they tumbled and wrestled across the alleyway, Ella knew in her bones this defensive flurry wouldn't last. Already the beast's iron-limbed strength had her wheezing, and those aching ribs made breathing increasingly difficult.

Survival instincts learned from living on the galaxy's fringe flipped on like a switch. She jerked her torso violently to one side, finally creating just enough distance between her and the beast, and kicked out with both feet as hard as she could.

Ella struck something solid and heard a surprised hiss. Suddenly she was free. The human tumbled backwards into a three-point stance. Across the alleyway, her prey coiled on all fours, ready to spring. The osvowraith glowered, those unforgiving crimson eyes focusing on her with an intense, feral hunger.

Ella shuddered. No way could she outrun her prey. The bounty hunter struggled back to her feet, but a fork of agony skewered her midsection, leaving the woman gasping. Fucking ribs…

"Jae, *where* are you?" she murmured crossly, almost doubled over.

No answer, which either meant the Tarkathian was nearby and didn't want to blow her cover, or had decided to cut her losses and leave. Ella actually wouldn't have blamed Jaellyn if she had chosen the latter. Either way, Ella would not go down without a fight. She reached for the pulse pistol in the back of her belt…and felt nothing. *Shit!*

"Looking for this?" the osvowraith said in a venomous, otherworldly hiss. It raised a clawed hand, which held her cobalt blue, snub-nosed pulse pistol. The beast tossed it aside with a slow smile, displaying long, needle-like teeth. As the firearm clattered far out of her reach, Ella could no longer hide her panic. She backed away, looking for a way out. The osvowraith edged forward, matching her step for step.

What I wouldn't give for my RR-5 pulse rifle right now. She fought her unraveling nerves with a quick mental inventory of the weapons on her person: a dozen sonic marble explosives and three mini thermogrenades in her utility belt, both weapon types which would kill her and the quarry at such close range. Everything else was either for tracking prey or fixing her ship. There was the dagger hidden in her right boot—not much good against this type of quarry—and the mini blaster in her right gauntlet—also no good, since the setting was on Kill.

Ella smirked, remembering the loaded shock dart shooter in her left gauntlet. Perfect. "Seems like I don't need my pistol." Ella pressed the arming mechanism underneath her utility belt and snapped her left arm up, aiming at the osvowraith's chest.

The beast didn't move, responding with a disturbing sissing noise that Ella could only compare to laughter. Something flashed in its narrowed eyes, a third eyelid perhaps.

A baffling breeze began cooling away the oven-like heat in the alleyway, flowing through Ella's skin, seeping into her very bones. *Tattshi!*

She had read about this in Xubes' sparse data on osvowraiths, some type of psychic attack that literally crushed one's willpower. At the time, Ella had found such a thing preposterous.

Not so much now. Her limbs had just gone weak all of a sudden.

She swayed and staggered about to stay upright, only for her knees to buckle. Ella couldn't get back up. *What's the point?* Both arms hung at her sides, leaden and useless. The biting chill made Ella feel like her brain had been plunged into a frozen lake, sapping away her strength. Her soul had suddenly grown so miserable…as if happiness was a half-remembered dream she would never know again.

The osvowraith sprang forward too fast, catching Ella by the throat. It lifted her high up with one hand—slamming her back down hard. The air rushed out of Ella in a loud grunt. Lances of pain stabbed through her spine, neck and ribs.

The osvowraith picked Ella up again, driving her ragdoll body down even harder. The back of her head bounced off the ground, almost knocking her out. Twinkly little stars danced along the edge of Ella's vision. She looked up through blurred vision at the blood-red slits in that blank and sallow face—the last face she would ever see. The long-limbed beast straddled the bounty hunter, tightened its grip on her throat. Ella choked, pinned and helpless.

"You stole a drink from me, frail," the osvowraith hissed with a casual menace. "Only fair that I return the favor."

The osvowraith opened its mouth impossibly wide. The lower jaw separated down the middle into two halves. Out of that gap slid several shining tentacles, writhing like tapered worms as they inexorably slithered down to Ella's prone form.

With the osvowraith clutching her throat, Ella couldn't scream, even if she had the motivation to. Doing that seemed so...meaningless. As she stared upward at the shiny tentacles slithering toward her face, Ella's last thought was, *God, I should've let that fucking Korvie die.*

And then...Ella felt a whistling wind as the tentacles whipped away from her face and into the air. She heard the crackle of electricity on flesh, followed by the most horrendous shriek ever issued from a living creature.

Suddenly Ella could move again, the icy draft scorched away by Bimnorii's evening furnace. She gasped at the vitality rushing back into her limbs and mind. Not questioning what happened, Ella heaved the osvowraith off with a sharp twist of her hips.

The osvowraith tumbled aside in a heap, the smoke of charred flesh trailing off its upper back. Ella sat bolt upright, and immediately regretted it. Blinding pain in her abdomen made the world spin. But what stood before her made the human forget that pain momentarily.

A hooded, elfin humanoid stood in battle stance and twirled a golden shock pike almost as tall as her five-foot-one-inch frame. Her obsidian black eyes gleamed intently, fixated on the fallen osvowraith with the callousness of a hunter moving in for the kill. Jaellyn.

Their eyes met. The Tarkathian's eyes told a story of anger at Ella's recklessness and relief to find the human still alive. Ella afforded Jaellyn a quick smile in return and gestured at their target.

The dazed beast stumbled to its feet and found itself outnumbered. The osvowraith quickly sobered up and jerked its head back and forth, mutely assessing its new circumstances.

Choosing the newer threat, the osvowraith lunged at Jaellyn.

Ella yelped. The beast's wild slash should've skewered Jaellyn through the belly.

But she was ready, ducking under the swipe with practiced grace, spinning about like a dancer and jamming the sparking end of her shock pike up in a vicious arc—right into the osvowraith's throat.

The beast's limbs splayed in all directions, sparks shooting out from under its chin in cascading showers. Its eyes wider than saucers, the osvowraith shuddered so violently, Ella feared the beast might explode into a million pieces. Finally, Jaellyn yanked the staff away and the beast sank to its knees without a sound. It was barely conscious, eyes dulled, swaying back and forth.

Jaellyn and Ella exchanged a look of disbelief. Then the Tarkathian picked up the pulse pistol from the ground. "Make an end," she stated flatly, tossing it to her human partner. The girl's fierce tone sounded more nasally and youthful when not on a comlink.

Ella caught her pulse pistol. Pointing it at the osvowraith's temple, she fired. *BZZAARK!* The osvowraith fell forward, kicking up clouds of red dust. Jaellyn drew back her hood, revealing a bald head with a scaly, grey-green complexion. Her triangular face sported several tiny, chalk-white bumps on each cheek. The Tarkathian's dark indigo eyes, with baby-blue star-shaped pupils, fixed on their prey in that grim fashion Ella had become used to.

"Too bad we need it alive," she said as casually as a being discussing a sports team's loss. Her button nose wrinkled at the stink of charred osvowraith flesh.

Ella stared down at the fallen beast, looking so frail and pathetic. She had lost count of how many times she'd dodged death since taking up the bounty hunter trade. Still, Ella couldn't stop trembling. Whatever weird psychic shit that creature did to her…she had never felt so utterly hopeless in her life. So naturally, Ella covered by lashing out. "Took your little ass long enough."

Jaellyn shrugged and kneeled next to the osvowraith. "Wouldn't have been an issue if you stuck to the plan." The Tarkathian pulled a glob of greyish goo out of her left boot pocket and slapped it over the osvowraith's mouth. Immediately, the grey goo wreathed around the beast's face and solidified into a smooth-surfaced muzzle.

"Well, I didn't," Ella spat petulantly, pulling a flat six-inch rod from her own boot.

"Clearly," Jaellyn shot back, unfazed. "We'll look at those ribs later." Ella made a rude noise and kneeled down to hold the rod over the beast's body. The rod took on a fiery glow, extending from the osvowraith's upper torso to its feet. Several beams of shimmering energy shot out of either end of the rod, wrapping around and binding the beast's body securely.

With the muzzle and EM restraints in place, Ella looked up at her partner. "Short-range teleporter?" Jaellyn nodded quickly. "Good." Ella rose to her feet and grimaced, needles of pain stabbing her midsection. "Let's go before our audience gets too nosy." Already, the beggars and alley vendors she had passed earlier were spilling into the passageway to see about all the commotion.

Jaellyn brought up her wrist and tapped a few buttons on what looked like a common chronometer. A half-sphere of gleaming blue surrounded them and their quarry. As the grimy Rimhara alleyway and its nosy crowd faded into a shimmering white nothingness, Ella realized how that could have been her grave.

Dying in an alley on Bimnorii. *God, how fucking sad.* Ella turned to Jaellyn to say "Thanks."

"You're welcome," the Tarkathian cut her off with tolerant expectation. Ella rolled her eyes and smiled. Rimhara was replaced by the familiar surroundings of their ship, the *Aurora,* parked just outside of Rimhara's borders.

The *Kyrior*-class stealth cruiser was small, but still large enough for Ella and Jaellyn's needs—mainly home and fast transportation. Most importantly, the *Aurora*—originally owned by a despicable and now-dead Tarkathian hunter—was where the pair first had begun their improbable partnership.

Now safely aboard, the bounty hunters carried their subdued prey to the ship's chaotic cargo hold—Jaellyn taking the osvowraith's shoulders while Ella struggled with the feet. Once inside the cargo hold, they reached the floating containment tube—over six feet long—and dropped the beast inside. Despite how startlingly light the osvowraith was, Ella's ribs shrieked with such protest she almost cried. The bounty hunters quickly secured the beast inside the tube with a series of passcodes and activated the sleep stasis function to keep it unconscious. Then, Jaellyn contacted Xubes to confirm the capture of the quarry.

"Superluminal!" the Xyobian exclaimed via 3D projection in the ship's helm, more surprised than delighted that they succeeded. He stood not much taller than Jaellyn. "You sure you got the correct species—Okay, I believe you!" he squealed after Jaellyn snarled at him. "I'll tell the client, and get back to you with a meet time and location."

Only then did Ella let Jaellyn evaluate her injuries: two ribs cracked, another three bruised, a mild concussion, and dark choke marks all around her neck. *Nothing that an injection of mendonanocytes and five shots of black dwarf couldn't cure...*

"Is this a good idea?" Ella slurred out, tipsy from pounding down liquor shots one after another. She currently lay on her stomach in bed, topless. Jaellyn, meanwhile, used a slim hypo-injector to infuse a payload of mendonanocytes into her partner's injured ribs. Ella winced. The uncomfortable tingling rippled through her body, signaling the start of the healing process.

"Is *what* a good idea?" the Tarkathian answered idly, packing up the medical supplies in a pouch.

"Delivering something so dangerous," she whispered, as if afraid that they weren't alone.

Jaellyn scoffed. "Silly human. It's just a job. What the client does with the bounty is their business."

Ella knew the Tarkathian was correct. "Right." Yet that didn't ease her conscience.

"And the pay is good," Jaellyn added gently as she stood up. "We will be set for near six months!"

"It'll be nice to pick and choose our next jobs," Ella admitted and smiled, stretching her arms out cat-like.

The Tarkathian stood at the exit, casting a long shadow against the light from outside. "Get sleep. We need to be ready for our client meet tomorrow."

Once the door closed, Ella pulled out a thin strip of lightspeed from her stash under the pillows. She pressed it to her nose and inhaled greedily. The hit shot up into her brain and through her body like a comet. Suddenly, a million sparkly dots of silver light danced before Ella's eyes, the good kind of sparkly dots. Then came a flood of tranquility that washed away all pain, leaving Ella delightfully numb as always. She sagged and fell face down onto her pillows. The twinkly dots blurred into infinite trails of light, shooting off into a distant direction, pulling Ella into a fathomless void....

The human came to several orvs later, sporting a mild hangover and slightly sore ribs. Jaellyn informed Ella that while she was sleeping, Xubes had gotten a time and a meet location— midday today at the furthest edge of the Sandstone Sea. The massive valley of high sand dunes and bizarrely-weathered rock formations was east of Orabesq, a remote settlement. After getting a look of the site on their 3D holomap, the Tarkathian thoroughly hated it. "Too easy for ambushes," she bristled.

Ella had felt her blood run cold as she scrutinized the location as well. It appeared far too similar to an earlier job months ago that had gone way south. That client had double-crossed and nearly killed both her and Jaellyn. She sucked in a calming breath, "We'll 'port in, keep our ship about a mile out and make sure the containment tube is rigged."

Jaellyn noticeably relaxed upon hearing this. Rigged meant syncing the tube to their heartbeats. If anything happened to either Jaellyn or Ella within a mile of their bounty, the tube self-destructed. This precaution was expected, given their profession's duplicitous nature.

Ella donned an ensemble similar to yesterday, the only variance was a white tank top, a reddish-brown armorweave vest, and letting her thick, black hair down. And unlike yesterday, she was beyond thankful to carry more weaponry on her person—her cherished RR-5 rifle which she hefted in her right hand, and an ArmoryTek DraCross 530 long pulse pistol slung on her hip. Jaellyn cast aside the hooded cloak, going with a navy blue, ribbed catsuit of oiled nanoclothe. She carried two long knives in her boots and two DraCross long pulse pistols.

After soaring for half an orv over a seemingly infinite stretch of rolling crimson dunes, the *Aurora* reached the coordinates Xubes specified for the meetup: a series of distorted, arching rock formations at the end of the rolling dunes, a precursor into a longer stretch of craggy, cracked desert.

"They're already here," Jaellyn stated grimly once they were a mile out, reading their ship's scans. "We should have gotten here first."

"But we didn't," Ella scoffed. "Let's just do this and get paid." With their captured quarry, Ella and Jaellyn transmatted in just under a far-jutting shelf of gnarled rock. It provided the perfect shade from the ball of bright cherry flame hanging in the clear sky. But the shelf provided no protection from the suffocating dry heat...or the half-dozen intimidating humans that surrounded the pair the moment they materialized onto the site. Jaellyn whirled around, always cagey as she took in their company.

Ella never flinched, even when seeing how exposed she and Jaellyn were in the middle of this rock structure. The Tarkathian gave her an *I told you so* glare to hammer home the obvious. Shafts of light pierced through holes in the rock shelf, giving a solid illumination of their grim-faced clients.

Ella recognized the Children of Earth at a glance.

The humans had sense enough to dress in dusty, tattered clothing, befitting of Bimnorii smugglers and prospectors. But the heavy-duty firearms they carried—ArmoryTek and Vega-Millum, to name a few—were definitely UComm military-grade. Their speakers introduced themselves: a lean, dark youth named Chidi, and Priyanka, a petite, dusky-skinned woman with a large hooked nose. Both stepped forward to authenticate the osvowraith in the containment tube.

Priyanka looked fascinated, waving a medical datapad across the tube's pane that displayed the beast's face and upper torso. Ella and Jaellyn backed away to give them space. Chidi, however, kept sneaking in nasty looks at the Tarkathian teenager, who returned them in kind.

Dios Mio, Ella swore, her nervousness contained beneath a blasé façade. The bounty hunter slipped into survival mode again, taking in her potential opponents with a quick glance. The Children of Earth had the edge in terms of cover behind the bulbous rocks, and superior firepower. Even if Ella and Jaellyn took out Chidi and Priyanka, they would never make it to the other side of this formation before getting cut down. Ella could at least console herself with the fact that if their client took them out, the quarry would self-destruct.

"Is there a problem?" she finally asked.

For a long, charged moment, Chidi locked eyes with Ella, his contempt obvious. The whole scene became loaded with an ugly, taut energy—Jaellyn looked ready to explode into action, her hands reaching for both pulse pistols. The other four gunmen behind Chidi seemed to coil with an alertness born from countless skirmishes. Ella let the hand at her side with the pulse pistol slip down gradually for a possible fast draw...

The moment passed, and Chidi shrugged with an easygoing smile. "Nope. Just admiring the pistols you two are carrying." Jaellyn remained rigid, keeping a wary eye on the Children of Earth operatives.

Priyanka brushed aside her blunt fringe of bangs, and whispered in Chidi's ear. He nodded. "Let's take care of payment." He pulled out a thin, black datapad and clacked away. Ella whipped out her 6" datapad to access their vault account, watching the exchange take place in less than a macrom. In fact, Ella gaped in shock at the sight of their second payment—twice the agreed-upon amount.

"The few bounty hunters that have actually captured an osvowraith seemed to think, 'capture alive' shouldn't include, 'in one piece,'" explained Priyanka, noting the bounty hunter's shock.

That won a laugh out of Ella, which died quickly under Jaellyn's disapproving frown. "You should now have the passcodes to open the tube," Ella stated soberly. "They'll be active in about an orv."

Chidi nodded gratefully. "Many thanks. We might call on you again." That both excited and turned Ella's stomach a little. The dark youth made a terse head gesture. Moments later the Children of Earth contingent transmatted away with the containment tube in a golden shimmer.

As soon as the last sparkle of their exit dissipated, Ella felt like she could breathe again. "Thank GAWD," she said in a gusty sigh. You okay?"

Jaellyn nodded, eyes still trained like lasers on the area their clients were just standing. "You?"

"Fuck yea," Ella blurted out with a gleeful clap, feeling very celebratory at their big payday. "All I want to do now is just drink myself stupid."

Jaellyn patted Ella on the head mockingly, "Didn't know drinking was needed."

Ella aimed a hard swat at the back of Jaellyn's head. But the Tarkathian easily ducked and dodged away with a playful smile. In those fleeting moments when Jaellyn actually acted her age, Ella thought her heart might burst. But she'd never reveal that to a Tarkathian, since sentimentality was something they usually distrusted. The two bounty hunters laughed while activating their teleporting device, which transported them back to the *Aurora* in a bluish shimmer.

Once more, the distorted rock structures at the edge of the Sandstone Sea lay barren under the blazing Noriida Major sun.

Aftershock

Usually, Pilot Pub's atmosphere of loud and stupid fun was infectious and unshakeable.

Tonight the mood inside the dingy, undersized dive bar was thick with tension.

News had spread across Union Space about an 'incident' on Alorum. The story UComm had spun for the news streams detailed a diseased betelydra escaping from Merrivel Nebula, and colliding with a UComm warship. Most beings in Pilot Pub believed otherwise, correctly assuming that the Korvenite terrorist Maelstrom was involved.

Samantha D'Urso couldn't fault the pilots' assumptions, nor would she confirm them. The truth about Alorum's surface had almost gotten her and Star Brigade killed.

On the outside, Sam was the epitome of relaxed, a crooked grin on her face and a half-empty drink in hand. Inside, her stomach roiled, anxieties bouncing back and forth like a swarm of angry bees.

She stayed focused on her teammate Liliana Cortés, sitting by her side on another floating bar stool.

Better that than eavesdrop on the noticeably loud speculations among Pilot Pub's mix of AeroFleet, private contractor, and freighter pilots.

Far better than paying heed to the ogling of a somewhat doughy earthborn space jockey at the far right end of the bar. He'd been trying to get Sam's attention with those 'fuck-me' eyes for a while now.

Not that she could blame him.

Unfortunately, he was audibly an obnoxious loudmouth amongst a bar full of obnoxious loudmouths. Even worse, by how much he was swaying in his seat, this one clearly couldn't hold his liquor. *Must be a UComm PLADECO pilot,* Sam mused, skin crawling.

She watched Liliana with concern. The young doctor, usually all long-limbed and lovely with perfect posture, was hunched over in dread. The poor thing shook so badly she could barely hold her tumbler glass of superluminal without the blue and white swirl of liquor spilling over. The black, long-sleeved tee and khaki slacks fit Liliana's tall, slender figure well. The shell-shocked expression didn't, in Sam's honest opinion.

Tonight she had made it her mission to wipe that expression off the doctor's face.

"Might want to drink some of that, while it's still in the cup," Sam insisted dryly.

Liliana hesitated briefly but did as instructed, taking the daintiest little sip in the history of the universe.

Sam snorted out a laugh.

Liliana glared at her. "What's so funny?"

"The way you drink," Sam answered between cackles. She tucked sleek locks of blonde hair behind both ears. "You act like you're carrying a live grenaser."

"So?"

"*So?* If I had just survived a mind-controlled betelydra, attached a Protectorate Base and discovered how secretly awful the Union can be, I'd be chugging down my drink. Like this." Sam snatched up her own glass of superluminal and guzzled down most of it in three big gulps.

That finally coaxed a faint smile out of Liliana. She straightened her posture and tossed her tumbler back again for a real gulp. Her face scrunched up as the superluminal ran hot down her throat. Now Sam openly guffawed.

"Please tell me that all our missions aren't always so," Liliana leaned in close, dropping her voice to a whisper like someone divulging government secrets, "so overwhelming."

"I could tell you that, but I'd be half-lying. Keep drinking," Sam encouraged.

Liliana did so without hesitation this time, and her gagging expressions lessened. The lighting cast a sickly purple glow over the tavern tonight, doing no favors for the low-grade HV screens showing football or the grimy lived-in texture of its walls.

Pilot Pub felt not quite like home, but safe enough to relax her guard just enough. Sam needed that tonight.

She took in Pilot Pub's scene with a smile, letting its familiar atmosphere fill her senses: the pungent, alien liquors permeating the air, the various rowdy debates ranging from what really went down on Alorum to if the Union should be in bed with the Kedri. Small groupings of patrons here and there, along with the solitary customers, were either lost in their own worlds or mindlessly watching whatever was on the HVs. Pilot Pub's clientele tonight included regular AeroFleet patrons stationed on Hollus, mixed with unfamiliar government-contracted freighter pilots just passing through or private military company on the starbase for training exercises—sentient beings from every corner of Union Space. It was an unofficial rule for Pilot Pub customers not in flight uniform to dress down. Sam always happily complied with that edict, hence her clingy grey tangtop and loose army green cargo pants with flip-flops.

Sam heard the familiar digitized sounds of a Cressonish voicebox, and glanced over her shoulder. The hulking Cressonish was a shaggy mass of silver-grey hair working the floor, greeting newcomers to Pilot Pub and catching up with frequent patrons. That would be Nan'oud, former AeroFleet and one of Pilot Pub's original founders. Sam caught his eye and they exchanged a friendly nod.

Working behind the bar was Solrao Ytod, a stork-like Ibrisian with a burnt orange complexion and not a single hair on her finely segmented skin. She was former AeroFleet, like Habraum and one of his oldest friends, as well as an occasional drinking buddy of Sam's.

Tonight the Ibrisian had been a mid-level irritant, constantly hovering near Sam and Liliana, trying to interject herself into their conversation during any lull in drink orders.

The only things I want from her tonight are drinks. Sam rolled her eyes and pushed away the aggravation, remembering that coming to Pilot Pub was as much for herself as it was for Liliana.

She had checked in on each SB-1 member after the Alorum incident— *even* Marguliese. Most of the team was coping just fine, except for Liliana and Honaa. The Rothorid had holed up in his quarters, refusing to see anyone. Sam would try again with him tomorrow.

Liliana was easier to engage. The doctor had been hiding in her Medcenter office barely holding it together, all the excuse Sam needed to suggest a few drinks to calm both their nerves.

It's the least I can do for the Brigadier who saved my life. "I never got to say thank you for what you did on Alorum," Sam admitted after Liliana had finished her superluminal. She wasn't the only grateful Brigadier, but V'Korram would never tell the doctor that. "We'd all be dead if not for you, lovey."

As expected, Liliana shooed away the praise. "I have Khrome, Marguliese and Captain Nwosu to thank for that," the doctor was now blushing. "But you more than anyone, Sam, for believing in me the whole time...and those extra training sessions these last few weeks."

That remark filled Sam with more gratitude than Liliana could ever know. Of course, her default response was a snide wisecrack—specifically at the expense of Habraum's pet Cybernarr—all to win a cheap laugh out of the doctor.

But Sam held her tongue. Liliana didn't need that now. She needed to recognize her incredible inner fortitude and embrace it. "Give yourself *some* credit, Lily," she reached out and gave the doctor a tender pat on the cheek. "We just provided the tools. You're the one who did the work to get this far."

"Well, I'm not there yet. I thought..." the doctor reclined back, folding both hands behind her head. Liliana's pixie cropped hair looked as black as her shirt under the dim lights and no longer spiked. Sam noted the slight but noticeable growth these last few weeks. She liked it better this length.

"I thought we were all going to die," the doctor admitted in a rush.

"Same here," Sam admitted easily. She leaned over the bar counter, finishing off her drink. "That was as close a call as it could get."

The doctor propped an elbow on the bar counter, scrutinizing her teammate through narrowed eyes. "Yet you're very *le zen* about the whole thing."

Despite Sam's devil-may-care attitude, the strange fear kept on buzzing inside her stomach. Masking her true feelings came as easy as breathing, given the countless times she'd stared death in the face and lived to laugh about it. But the Alorum incident...*that* had rattled Sam, as much as it clearly did Liliana.

Suddenly, all she wanted was to speak to the doctor like a true friend. Sam longed to admit how terrified almost losing another combat team had made her. Every cell in Sam's body burned to confess over the rush of emotions that had coursed through her when the Retributionaries were about to kill SB-1.

Then there was that devastating look of longing, or whatever that was, she and Habraum had shared when the end seemed certain.

And afterward in the Cerc's office, every moment between them so open and honest and raw…

Yeah, like Liliana wants to hear about my drama, she scolded, regaining some much-needed resolve and making those pesky feelings go dead as easily as if it were breathing.

"Two things help after a mission like that," Sam raised her glass, putting on her mischievously lopsided grin. "A few good drinks or a good fuck…usually both."

From the corner of her eye, Sam caught Solrao perking up and ignored the overeager Ibrisian.

Liliana turned her head from side to side, taking stock of Pilot Pub's occupancy. Her gaze landed on the tanked PLADECO pilot right as he tumbled out of his seat. She wrinkled her nose in disapproval. "Think I'll settle for another drink."

Sam gestured for Solrao's attention, pointing at her own and then Lily's cups. "Two more."

"Make mine a small one…" Liliana quickly pointed out, and then caught Sam's barefaced scorn. "A *large* one," the doctor amended with a laugh.

Solrao returned in no time with their drink orders. "You two look like you've been through it," she declared in her usual sleepy-sounding Ibrisi accent. "Hard mission?"

"That's an understatement," Liliana muttered after thanking the Ibrisian for her drink.

Much to Sam's displeasure, the ex-pilot didn't look ready to depart yet. "And yea, yea I know you can't officially confirm this," Solrao leaned in all conspiratorial-like. The blood-red limbic rings in her eyes rapidly narrowed and then widened, narrowed and then widened, the telltale sign of an Ibrisian's interest. "I'm guessing your mission had to do with whatever went down on Alorum? Am I warm?"

"We're good, Solrao. Thank you," Sam replied sharply, her taut smile saying, *Back the fuck off.*

Solrao took the hint and retreated to the other end of the bar, sulking. Sam watched her go, glowering. Indulging the needy Ibrisian a few weeks ago had been stupid. *I should cut her off for good.*

Solrao's hovering didn't go unnoticed. "Uh…which one of us does she wanna sleep with?" Liliana inquired, observing the Ibrisian with far too much curiosity.

"Why, you interested?" Sam joked. *God, please don't be.*

"Nooo," Lily shook her head, dead serious. "Something about her just screams too much baggage."

Sam nodded and continued nursing her drink. Smart girl.

As they continued talking, Liliana's silence on the Korvenite internment camps became glaringly obvious. Given how much the Alorum location had upset the doctor, Sam left that asteroid mine alone. So she broached another topic. "When you were flying the *Phaeton* by yourself, what did you feel…beside fear?"

Liliana frowned at her, confused. "Not sure what you mea—"

"Yeah, you do," Sam interjected briskly, searching the doctor's face. "And the answer scares the shit out of you, way more than Maelstrom's ambush did."

Even under the bad halolights, she saw Liliana turn bone white.

Christ, this girl had no poker face. Sam needed to work with her on that. At least her suspicions were dead on. "Now," she continued in low and huskier tones, "what *else* did you feel?"

"I…" Liliana looked like she'd rather be anywhere else. Then she seemed to calm, her eyes going vacant. "My blood was singing," she admitted, soft and trembling. Discovering this hidden aspect of herself was a clear jolt to her system. "The risks, the impossible odds… Even at one point, V'Korram got knocked out and I was alone, I've never felt so alive…so powerful."

A sister in arms. Sam tried not to smile, but pride had rendered her poker face as transparent as Lily's. At the Brigade all-hands where Habraum made his return, she had seen a glimpse of that steel within the doctor. But when

Liliana had stepped out of *Phaeton's* cockpit after rescuing them from Alorum, eyes ablaze with fear and fire and focus, Sam knew she was Star Brigade material through and through.

"On a mission like that when the odds seem insurmountable and death's coming at you from every turn?" Sam shook her head wistfully, jostling loose a few locks of hair. The familiar thrill she got from each and every field mission, nothing topped it. "Gets in your blood, like a drug."

Liliana shuddered. Clearly that kind of addiction didn't agree with her. "After all this time, can you imagine your life any other way?"

If Sam had been asked this question eight years ago, the answer would have been a resounding, 'yes.' Settle down somewhere on Terra Sollus, find a mind-numbingly boring civilian job, marry an adequate male, start a family— the expected things that normal sentient beings were supposed to do.

But that was eight years ago. Today, Sam sucked down more of her drink and shrugged. "Nah!"

The two humans burst out laughing, breaking the tension. They clinked their glasses with big smiles in a toast to surviving. Sam loved seeing Liliana not so uptight and timid. While she wasn't drunk, her growing ease in demeanor and posture became obvious.

And of course, just as she was becoming more fun and relaxed, Liliana called it a night. "Got some lab work to get through," she countered despite Sam's protests, rising from her bar stool. "More research on the overproduction of xenotrophin."

"Ah," Sam nodded, needing no further explanation. Knowing the personal obligation behind Lily's research, how could she keep the doctor away from that?

"But I can put it off till tomorrow," Lily added hesitantly, "if you need me to stick around."

Don't go. Stay a little longer, Sam wanted to say. For some reason the thought of being left to her own devices tonight chilled her from head to heel. "Please," she instead waved Liliana off lightheartedly. "Go be brilliant."

"Luminal!" The doctor's relief was palpable. "We'll *both* get sloshed up next time, mamita."

Sam leaned away in mock distaste. "So you think this is gonna become 'our thing' now, Ensign?"

Liliana froze. "I...no." Suddenly she was alarmed and stammering. "That's not...I wasn't—"

Sam let out a loud and bawdy laugh. "Christ on a *comet*, you're so easy it's not even a challenge! Of course there'll be a next time!"

The doctor slapped her hard on the arm. "*Pundeja*," she hissed, smiling again. "Thanks for the drinks...and the talk." The doctor leaned in, wrapping her slim arms around Sam. "Just what I needed."

"Anytime, sweets," Sam returned the embrace with an extra squeeze. "Love ya from the bottom of my bottom."

When Liliana pulled away, Sam found her no longer smiling. The doctor's face was lined with concern. "We have to find Maelstrom, Samantha," she stated in a quiet, urgent tone only Sam could hear. "We *have* to stop him."

Sam nodded, rubbing Liliana's back like a doting parent. "I know. And when we find him, we *kill* him." Liliana's features hardened, but Sam didn't care how coldblooded that sounded. Maelstrom signed his death warrant the moment he'd hurt her Star Brigade family.

"Good," the doctor decided, a flat and final response.

Sam watched her go with raised eyebrows, surprised and a little concerned by the glint of satisfaction in the doctor's eyes.

A few macroms after Liliana left, Sam motioned Solrao over again to order herself a nice big bottle filled with what looked like liquid gold. But to Sam, a bottle of hellburner trumped liquid gold.

More customers arrived, thankfully drawing Solrao away again. Sam turned around on her stool to face away from the bar counter, slumping back against it. She downed a lengthy swallow from her bottle. The thick liquor tasted bitter, salty, electric and honeyed all at once. She winced and immediately took another long pull. Nice.

Today had almost been another Beridaas, with Sam rendered just as powerless to save her teammates. SB-1 with all those young Brigadiers—even Habraum's pet Cybernarr—had all nearly been killed by Maelstrom.

Wiping her mouth with the back of her hand, the thoughts and fears and disappointments began to pile up like stones weighing on her chest.

Any hope Sam had of helping the Korvenites in the internment camps, exposing their deplorable living conditions—*definitely* killed by Maelstrom.

Hunting Maelstrom down while the trail was hot, ending him before he broke into another internment camp or killed more innocents—stupidly stalled by Union Command.

Sam bristled and tossed the bottle back again, draining more of it. All that tasted bitterer in her mouth than this hellburner. And the welcome haze of drunkenness wasn't kicking in fast enough. On days like this, when life clobbered over and over a being with gale force, Sam really hated having such a high fucking alcohol tolerance.

Her first instinct was going to Habraum, her rock…her *harbor*. After what happened on Alorum, just the thought of being around him again made her insides feel so fluttery, yet ache so deeply, the discomfort was near acute. A few orvs ago in Habraum's office when they spoke briefly, that same sensation had nearly overwhelmed her.

A grin tugged at Sam's lips. After all these years, those feelings just wouldn't die. A talk with her favorite Cerc would make Sam feel safe again and expel her worries.

Her smile widened, showing teeth. Habraum should be in his quarters now, maybe eating dinner…

…with Jeremy. Sam's smile curdled. The reminder was a hard punch to the gut.

No, I can't intrude tonight. It would be selfish, especially given the Cerc's struggles to balance Star Brigade with being a good dad to Jerm. She flinched away from the sharp disappointment and sighed, taking another pull of liquor.

She studied the bottle in her right hand, resting it on her right thigh. *Jesus, it's empty already?*

Then Sam noticed the liquor finally beginning to work its sweet magic, making her senses go tipsy and muddying up her thoughts. *Won't be enough,* she already knew.

Sam dared a glance at Solrao. The lanky Ibrisian stood all the way at the other end of the bar, leaning forward to chat up two swarthy and strapping crimsonborn. By their outfits the two looked like freighter pilots. *Out of the question,* Sam decided with a quick head shake, dismissing all three options. Both Cercs looked too much like Braum. *And Rae's gotten too clingy anyway.*

Solrao caught Sam's lingering gaze, and with a smirk the Ibrisian nodded her head toward someone in the increasingly crowded bar.

Sam turned away and surveyed the area that Solrao just indicated and Liliana had earlier so reductively dismissed.

The crowd was rather lacking in potential, until her gaze landed on a carroty-complexioned Nnaxan. He sat alone three tables to Sam's left, minding his own business, while nursing what looked like a BBT.

Sam gave him a quick, but thorough, onceover. Private military contractor pilot by the uniform. Tall and well-made in physique, a handsomely chiseled face for a Nnaxan, with a perfectly overarched brow, and a quartet of thick, fleshy craniowhisks spilling down his shoulders—each which Sam had a sudden desire to lick from root to tip.

And four hands, Sam gloated, her lips parting slightly. *Hope he knows what to do with them all.* She set her empty bottle on the bar counter with a *clunk,* and then lurched up from her stool with as much sensual grace as she could muster.

…an orv later they were on a beaten-up bed inside his small frigate ship, entwined under the dim red glow of halolights. Sam was on top and unclothed, a low and steadily rising moan in her throat, riding the Nnaxan ferociously.

His hands were touching all the right spots on Sam's body, fondling her senseless. This one had some dangerous fingers. She arched her back, curtains of disheveled blond hair tumbling down her shoulders.

If the Nnaxan had given out his name, Sam hadn't cared enough to remember it. Only her need mattered, feeling his coarse flesh against hers, the overwhelming desire to burn away that nagging ache and the memories of today—even if just for tonight. Exactly what she needed.

Samaritan

At first glance, the apartment was gorgeous. Two stories of aquamarine-walled luxury on the upper floors of a posh residential complex in Terra Sollus's Sheffield city-state.

That included unrestricted views showcasing Sheffield's dazzling forest of spacescrapers and the Avalon River below winding through the downtown corridor. The apartment's curved architecture surrounded a tube-shaped forcefield housing a massive saltwater tank. The circular pool on the second floor served as the tank's opening, reaching down to the first floor like an oversized middle pillar. The water tank oozed ripples of pale cerulean light throughout the unlit apartment.

However, the intruder sneaking through its corridors had little interest in those aesthetics.

The human/cybernetic hybrid known only as Darkstar crept past the brilliant glow of the water tank, exposing a broad-shouldered building of a humanoid at six-foot-seven. His cobalt-blue body armor, essentially a second skin of weaponized cyber organics, was etched with circular dull grey patterns. The sleeveless overcoat he wore was black as night, flowing just past his knees, ideal for hiding a variety of weapons and tools.

It had taken some doing, but Darkstar had finally found ways to circumvent the advanced Vigilance-Tech watching over city-states like Sheffield, allowing him to breach this complex unnoticed. He searched high and low over the apartment's furniture, focusing on anything that might look ordinary in a Galdorian's residence on a non-oceanic world. That might hold the proof he was looking for.

Hojkoddi Nolo, the apartment owner, was out this evening and would not return for another 4.5 orvs.

What better time to conduct a covert and uninterrupted search?

Darkstar scrutinized every coral sculpture with chalky colors and shapes fanning outward in contorted veins, examining them down to the minute cracks and chips. He ran his fingers along those aquamarine walls, scanning the technology behind them that powered this apartment's systems and protocols.

Nothing. Not in the walls, the sculptures, the angular tables and chairs, or the holoimages.

He shook his head in frustration, causing his long ponytail of thick copper braids to jostle from side to side. Had he arrived at the wrong address or wrong time?

No, my intel is sound, Darkstar reminded himself. A pricey yet trustworthy data broker had tied several disappearances to Hojkoddi Nolo through an intricate web of smuggling rings. Initially the connection to Hojkoddi Nolo made no sense at the surface level, and none of these disappearances were of anyone notable. More to the point, it had baffled Darkstar why a Galdorian restaurant owner would adopt this sudden fondness for abducting others?

Until he had discovered one unshakeable fact—each abductee had either dined or had a blood relative dine at one of the Galdorian's many restaurants over the last four months. And half of these abductees happened to be unregistered maximums.

Darkstar had seen this intricate pattern of abductions before: twelve members of a certain species captured, half might exhibit a recessive genetic trait, other times a third or a quarter or an eighth of the abductees would have a near vestigial genetic trait. Most likely, they would breed each group in a controlled and accelerated environment together to see which genetic trait thrived.

This reeked of Cybernarr behavior, meaning Hojkoddi Nolo was either a Cybernarr thrall…or an undercover Cybernarr himself.

Darkstar felt a chill just considering the latter theory.

But that was why he had arrived at this place, in this time.

Uncover and terminate the Technoarchy threat.

The tangible proof he needed had to exist somewhere in this residence. He moved toward the apartment's internal translifter to check upstairs.

Then he felt it, a shiver up his spine from something reacting to his presence.

Cybernarr technology definitely existed inside this apartment.

I knew it. But where? He turned slowly around, guided by that sensation, and found himself directly facing the water tank.

Darkstar inched closer at an unhurried pace. The gold faceplate shielding his nose and mouth took on an eerie green shimmer as he stepped fully into the aura of watery light. Only the forehead on his honey-brown face was visible, that and a beady pair of intense violet eyes widening in anticipation.

Standing up against the forcefield, he saw the delicate swirls of saltwater and a few steel-grey fish creatures native to Galdor. *A perfect cover*, he decided, fixating on some of the tinier bubbles, dull metal dots nearly microscopic in size.

The intruder cautiously pressed a hand against the forcefield, the warmth of the solid energy seeping through his protective gauntlet. In short order, a thousand little bubbles surged through the water and coalesced into a cloud of shiny foam around the spot where his hand rested.

Not even the most detailed observer would notice if a Galdorian plunged into the tank to swim through these innocent-looking bubbles, which were miniscule cybernetic organisms that interfaced with the Technoarchy Connectivity. Not unless the observer was a half-Cybernarr hybrid like Darkstar—or a Cybernarr sleeper like Hojkoddi Nolo. Probably either an Infiltrooper or Razor sub-class.

"Of course," Darkstar realized aloud, his voice bearing a deep, digitized cadence. No doubt the 'real' Hojkoddi Nolo, if he ever existed at all, had been dead for a while. The half-Cybernarr took no pleasure in his accuracy about this sleeper agent. Still, a giddy buzz flooded his insides. Stopping the Technoarchy's further expansion had been his sole mission in life for so long. And now, he'd found proof of their attempted foothold in Union Space.

Almost instantly those bubbles in the water lit up and flew apart in different directions.

Darkstar scowled and scanned about the apartment. Every translucent viewport fogged up and turned opaque. A security forcefield triggered by his presence. Now he couldn't transmat out. And Hojkoddi had been notified.

"He's coming," Darkstar stated. The hybrid backed away from the water tank and steeled himself in preparation, waiting.

Half an orv passed before Hojkoddi Nolo strolled through the front door.

The impostor was a head shorter than Darkstar, wearing a dark seaweed-thread suit of the finest quality, as if he'd just come from a Galdorian Aquopera performance. At first glance, he had all the typical Galdorian features—rubbery purplish-maroon skin, beak-like mouth, webbed hands and feet, two foot-and-a-half tall eye-stalks perched atop his head. But one look in those golden eyeballs told a different tale—cold, soulless intelligence, scrutinizing how best to dispose of him. And not once did his eyestalks ever bend or tremble to convey any form of emotion. The circuitry-like conduits beneath his Galdorian skin, though hidden to the casual observer, practically bulged out from Darkstar's perspective. Definitely not a real Galdorian.

"It appears that we have an uninvited guest," Hojkoddi announced in a perfectly croaky Galdorian cadence.

"I could say the same about your presence on Terra Sollus, 'Hojkoddi Nolo' or whatever your real name is," Darkstar flexed his left hand, a swell of pitch-black energy forming in it.

An ebon tanto blade at four-and-a-half feet took shape in Darkstar's clenched fingers. How could a full-fledged Cybernarr hide in plain sight on the Union homeworld? Some type of upgraded sub-class? He would find out before killing the beast. "I have a few questions, if you don't mind." He advanced toward his target with bold strides—until a female Galdorian slipped through the front door behind Hojkoddi.

Darkstar froze. He wasn't expecting her. His surveillance never indicated Hojkoddi having a companion. This complicated matters significantly. *Collateral damage*, he bristled.

The female Galdorian, slim in build and even shorter than Hojkoddi, flinched away from Darkstar in fright. "Is that...is he a...?" Fear seemed to have rendered her speechless.

"An unconnected halfling? Correct," Hojkoddi finished her question, those lifeless eyes of his never leaving Darkstar. "Now be a good poppet and eliminate him."

The female instantly launched herself across the room at Darkstar, webbed fingers curling with lethal intent. The about-face left the hybrid dumbstruck...for half an instant.

"A thrall," he hissed, catching the female Galdorian by the throat with his free hand. Tiny jagged veins of gold had appeared on various parts of her rubbery maroon skin. Her eyes bulged, turning milky white and losing any vibrancy.

She flailed her limbs violently, silvery claws bursting out of her hooked fingers to swipe and slash repeatedly at Darkstar's face. He lurched away from her swipes, knowing and seeing that her personality had been consumed by Hojkoddi's single-minded will.

Becoming a Cybernarr thrall was a fate worse than death, if not halted in time.

There was still time for this one. Under different conditions, Darkstar could save her.

He stared into the puppet's vacant eyes with a flash of remorse and whispered, "Sorry." The hybrid hauled the Galdorian off her feet. He then swung his black blade up in a swift, savage arc, slicing her open from crotch to cranium.

The Galdorian dropped to the floor with two wet clunks, inky blue blood splattering everywhere.

He returned his attention to Hojkoddi and saw he was gone—right as a knotted tendril of ribbed wires burst out of the wall to the left. Darkstar ducked low and slashed, cleaving it apart.

The false Galdorian had merged his physical form fully with this apartment's technology, wielding it as a weapon.

Two more thick corded tendrils shot forth from behind Darkstar. The Cybernarr hybrid somersaulted overhead, hacking the wriggling tendrils to pieces in quick, brutal swipes.

Half a dozen more snaked, one spearing Darkstar through the right calf. He grunted and almost buckled to a knee as a white-hot bolt of pain roiled up his leg. Another caught him flush in the upper back, then another through the left forearm and another through the gut. Each strike was searing agony, but the hybrid fought down the temptation to cry out. He would not give this Cybernarr the satisfaction.

Darkstar found himself skewered and strung up high in front of the saltwater tank, every movement an agony. His pulsating ebon blade slipped from trembling fingers.

Only then did a fountain of liquid metal spurt up from the apartment floor. The oozing jet swelled and took the shape of a Galdorian.

Suddenly Hojkoddi stood before him. Watery light bathed the Cybernarr's emotionless face as he marched forward, not sparing even a brief glance at the gutted corpse of his thrall.

Fear began slicing at Darkstar's resolve the closer Hojkoddi came. He thrashed and squirmed with every bit of strength he had, until the coils restraining him jolted his body with blistering fire. The hybrid gasped and drooped, held up only by the mesh of tendrils skewered through him.

Hojkoddi wasted no words or time to gloat. The fake Galdorian grabbed Darkstar by the chin, drew back his arm and shoved the hybrid's head back *through* the saltwater tank forcefield.

Suddenly Darkstar's world turned wet and azure and ice-cold. His face mask immediately sealed up and provided much-needed oxygen, but that was the least of his worries.

The tiny bubbles that reacted to his presence earlier now coalesced again into a silvery cloud, and then shot through the water at his exposed face on Hojkoddi's command. Darkstar could only guess that those 'bubbles' would infect his cybernetic systems with junk technorganic code, self-replicating until he drowned in toxic cybernetic goop. Or they would alter his systems and make his cybernetics mistakenly assume his human components were an infection.

Darkstar had seen others die one of these ways firsthand, and now he was next.

He tried to jerk his face loose from the Cybernarr's webbed hand.

But Hojkoddi's grip was unyielding. And Darkstar's demise was inevitable. Unless…

The hybrid closed his eyes, ignoring the sharp bite of his multiple injuries and the stifling pressure of the saltwater on his face and regained focus.

That focus ignited a burning in his chest that swelled and intensified, flooding his injured body with revitalizing power.

The spray of greyish bubbles were about to hit his face when Darkstar discharged a bright sweeping arc of concussive force from his body. Hojkoddi went flying back and for a brief moment, the darkened room was bright as daytime.

Promptly, the bubble cloud in the water tank dissipated, Hojkoddi's grip on his face was gone, and the tendrils impaling his limbs went slack. Free from the water tank, Darkstar lurched forward and faceplanted hard on the floor. His faceplate's filters opened up and he breathed in the freshly recycled oxygen of the apartment.

Too close, he told himself, sucking in laborious breaths. Straightaway, Darkstar yanked out the four tendrils still impaled through his body. Each removal hurt worse than the last, carroty-colored blood oozing out of every wound. He shook his braided head, spraying tiny droplets of water in every direction, and then struggled painfully up to his feet. Luckily, Darkstar had that concussive burst trick up his sleeve for whenever the odds weren't in his favor.

Across the common room, Hojkoddi began to stir. Darkstar whipped his head in that direction. The false Galdorian lay in a gruesomely twisted posture. Their eyes met.

Darkstar's attack had blasted away gaping chunks of rubbery purple skin, mainly from the Galdorian's face and upper torso, revealing bleeding cyberorganics of conduits and circuitry underneath.

For the first time, some semblance of emotions distorted the Cybernarr's ruined face—surprise and discomfort. That concussive burst had injured him more severely than he let on.

"A halfling…maximum? Interesting." Hojkoddi's vacant orange eyes flickered as his body began shuddering and losing cohesion, melding with the floor to escape.

Darkstar dove forward, determination chasing away the screaming pain of his injuries. He snatched up his weapon, and with snake-strike quickness stabbed Hojkoddi through the chest.

The ebon blade exploded out through the Cybernarr's shoulder blades in a gush of yellowish fluids.

Hojkoddi went rigid and arched his back, eyestalks standing straight up in agony. But the false Galdorian didn't scream. Darkstar frowned, sensing tendrils of wiring and conduits shoot from the walls behind him at Hojkoddi's command. He answered by channeling a pulse of bio-electric shock through his ebon blade into Hojkoddi, wracking the Cybernarr's sinewy frame with violent convulsions.

Immediately the tendrils dropped like limp rope. Darkstar ceased his attack, but connected with and slaved the false Galdorian's cybernetic systems to his own.

Instantly Hojkoddi drooped like a corpse. That disabled his control of technology, which kept the Cybernarr from escaping either physically or virtually from the apartment.

"Trapped," the hybrid tried to remove the relish from his voice, but it wasn't easy. "Now for my questions. How many of you are there in Union Space?"

Hojkoddi lifted his head and stared back with blank defiance.

Darkstar gave his blade a brutal twist, sending another bio-electric shock through it. "HOW MANY?" he roared.

Hojkoddi's face contorted in pain. Thick yellowish fluid oozed freely from his beaked maw. "This battle…against your own kind is…ultimately fruitless," he replied feebly. His eyes began to dull. "Destroy…me, and ten more will assume…my place. You cannot repel the Technoarchy."

"I'll take my chances," Darkstar grimaced. He unleashed a surge of concussive energy through his blade, bombarding Hojkoddi's injured body over and over until he was wracked with violent tremors.

At the same time, Darkstar linked with the Cybernarr's systems through their forced physical connection. He tunneled deep through blinking algorithms, barely dodging past cybernetic security protocols, soon pinpointing Hojkoddi's virtuessence—the cybernetic heart and soul of a Cybernarr.

Darkstar seized hold of Hojkoddi's virtuessence…and ripped it apart without a shred of mercy.

In the physical world, the false Galdorian's body jerked and flopped uncoordinatedly like a fish out of water. His scream bounced off the apartment's soundproof walls like the strident shredding apart of metal. A pleasant melody to Darkstar's ears.

Just as abruptly, the cold, golden light in Hojkoddi's eyes winked out. The Cybernarr was dead.

But Darkstar didn't revel in his very minor victory at all. Hojkoddi was just a soldier, and no doubt the Technoarchy would shift strategies because of Darkstar's interference.

"At least I now have proof," the hybrid allowed himself a small pat on the back. With a flick of his wrist, the ebon blade evaporated into nothingness. A wet circle of pungent yellow fluids pooled outward around Hojkoddi's corpse, which now showed signs of fissures forming at the outer extremities.

Darkstar rose up to his feet…and immediately wished he hadn't.

Every part of his body hurt, even his long, copper braids. Thankfully, Darkstar could feel his puncture wounds slowly begin to knit, his sheath-like armor supercharging the healing process. He'd be fully healed within an orv or three.

"Time now to make contact with UniPol," he lifted a gauntlet in front of his face and tapped a few buttons. In short order, a small holoscreen appeared above his wrist gauntlet with the broad and blocky face of a pinkish-skinned human male: Agent Puemri Tas of UniPol's Terra Sollus branch.

His buzz cut hairstyle notwithstanding, the bone-white locks with brick-red roots revealed his Pogollish heritage.

Puemri's fatigue morphed into shock and then disdain in half a heartbeat. "Darkstar," the stormborn human spat.

This individual was supposedly the one who would help Darkstar expose the Technoarchy's hidden scheme to penetrate and eventually corrupt Union Space. As his frosty greeting inferred, Puemri had been less than receptive to Darkstar's warnings. The half-Cybernarr warrior tried his best not to lose faith in this Agent Tas just yet.

"How did you get this frequency—" the UniPol agent began, and then reeled his fury in. Clearly he wasn't alone. "Never mind. I don't have time for another of your Technoarchy conspiracy theories—"

Darkstar cut him off succinctly. "There is something you must see."

The stormborn human gaped, as if the statement was blasphemous. "Do you know what tomorrow is?" he hissed.

Darkstar wasn't sure what he found more patronizing, the question or the tone. Of course he knew of tomorrow's significance—even a blind, deaf and mute sentient living inside a super black hole at the center of a galaxy knew about tomorrow's significance.

The Galactic Union and the Kedri Imperium were to engage in some ridiculous trade merger that would supposedly change the very face of this galaxy. No doubt every Union agency was on high alert, making sure nothing could derail this monumental moment.

If only they knew how ultimately pointless their efforts will turn out to be, Darkstar allowed himself an amused smirk beneath his faceplate.

But it wasn't his place to deride, and definitely not his place to divulge what he knew about that outcome. "What I have to show you is important," Darkstar insisted soberly.

On the holoscreen, Puemri folded his arms and scoffed, unmoved. "Ensuring this planet's safety from anything going wrong tomorrow is more important."

Darkstar glowered. Sometimes he wondered if what he'd heard about this man and his testicular fortitude had been massively inflated. "Very well. If you're not interested in thwarting a potentially hidden threat to the Galactic Union that you claim to serve unwaveringly—"

"Fine," Puemri ran nervous and impatient fingers through his hair. "Show me."

"You'll need to see this in the flesh."

For a long and heated moment, the stormborn ground his teeth so furiously, Darkstar thought they might crack. "What. Are. The coordinates?" he snarled out each word.

A smirk formed beneath Darkstar's faceplate. Maybe there was hope for this operative. "Come discreetly."

Puemri arrived over an orv later, transmatting directly into the dim apartment foyer in a bright flare of gold. He was a lean strip of manhood in his steel-grey denims, black Henley, and navy blue overcoat. The veneer of patience he had on, however, wasn't nearly as well-fitted.

Darkstar strode limping from the common room without as much as a handshake. "Are you alone?"

Puemri nodded, "I came 'discreetly' just like you asked." A lie, but at least the stormborn had the decency to enter the apartment alone. Darkstar had at least earned a modicum of trust during their short partnership, thanks to the leads he'd provided Puemri all eventually paying off.

The stormborn noted Darkstar's limping gait. "You're hurt."

"I'll endure," Darkstar turned back toward the common room. "Were you seen?"

"Of course not," Puemri snapped, his impatience evaporating. He stopped in his tracks, hands on his hips. "What are you showing me?"

Darkstar's probing yet dismissive onceover quelled the stormborn's insolence. "By the way, the wearable monitoring in your clothing won't provide any data to your backup stationed two blocks away."

Puemri's eyes grew the size of saucers. "How do you know?"

Darkstar turned away without answering, fighting back a grimace while he hobbled his way into the common room. Annoyingly, his wounds weren't quite healed yet.

"There's your proof," the hybrid pointed at the gruesome remains of the Cybernarr and his female Galdorian thrall littered on the floor.

Puemri grumbled something unflattering under his breath and marched up to Darkstar's side. For a long moment he just stared in stunned silence, clearly unable to mentally digest what lay before his eyes. Then dawning recognition drained the color from his face. "Holy tattshi! Those are…?"

"A Cybernarr agent and his thrall," Darkstar finished his sentence.

Puemri backed away slowly, breathing shallowly, body beginning to tremble. "Are they…?"

"Dead? Destroyed? Terminated? All of the above."

The stormborn ran both hands through his hair again and shook his head, as if refusing to believe any of this. The dim lighting of the apartment did little to hide Puemri's panic. "How many more sleepers are on Terra Sollus?" he asked in a small, shaky voice.

Darkstar folded both well-built arms behind his back and shrugged. "Uncertain."

Puemri gaped. "How many more are there in Union Space?"

"Uncertain, but undoubtedly more than just these two."

"Nonono!" Puemri's headshaking became more vehement, almost angry. "This cannot be happening. Not today!"

Darkstar got in the stormborn's face, seething. He towered over him by almost half a foot. "It *is* happening. Today." He itched to backhand some poise into this frantic human. But patience stayed his hand. Too much was at stake to lose his cool. "It has clearly been happening long before that. There are Cybernarr sleeper agents within Union Space. And your government needs to know before it is too late."

That reached Puemri. He paled, and the tension in his body slowly uncoiled. "How are you so calm?"

Darkstar's eyes narrowed into glowing violet slits. A ripple of watery light washed over his face. "Someone has to be. Now that I've given you proof of a possible Cybernarr incursion, I assume you and your agency have work to do." He'd done as tasked: expose a herald from the forthcoming Technoarchy threat to the Union. Hopefully the Union would now have a fighting chance. The cybernetic being turned on his heel to exit the common room.

"Wait," Puemri's request stayed his exit. "You're a Cybernarr. Why do you care what happens to the Galactic Union?"

Darkstar turned back around, his tattered coat fluttering about. "I'm *half*-Cybernarr..." he corrected evenly, "and I care as someone who knows how the Technoarchy deals with anyone or anything that they consider imperfect."

Puemri's frown suggested further confusion. "But of all the beings you could choose to tell, why me?"

Darkstar almost said nothing. Since he first contacted the UniPol agent over a month ago, Puemri had been too doubtful and arrogant to even buy the Cybernarr infiltrating the Union in plain sight.

But after he'd finally grasped how real this threat was, Darkstar threw caution to the wind and said, "Because you told me to...*six* years from now."

That revelation seemed to visibly break Puemri's brain a little. "*What?!*" he barked, eyes bulging in cartoonish shock.

Darkstar had revealed too much. "I'll be in touch," he said, transmatting from the apartment in a shimmer of light.

Passenger

Rouma came to, flat on his back, awoken by the lightning rods of agony shooting through his chest, back, and all the way to his fingertips. The golden Retributionary armor that once felt like a second skin now weighed down on him with immovable bulk.

He heard a distant roar of fury, closing in from all around. A charred stench of death and blood filled his nostrils.

Everything within his line of sight appeared staticky, meaning his helmet visor was damaged.

Even scarier to the Korvenite was the lack of sensation below his waist. But a more chilling realization than not being able to feel his own legs?

The Unlink, the babbling river of noise and verve that flowed through his mind, was silent.

Panicked, Rouma stretched out with Mindspeak. Other non-Korvenite minds were nearby, afraid from seeing Sollus attacked, grieving from losing friends or loved ones, pained from injury.

Rouma sighed with as much relief as his tortured chest would allow. *My psionics aren't gone*, he gathered, *just any communal link to my Korvenite brethren.*

Before Maelstrom freed him from slavery, Rouma had been deprived of the Unlink for years. But after growing accustomed to hearing other Korvenites' voices again, returning to that desolate silence was unmooring.

Rouma thought back to when he last sensed the Unilink. It had been when he'd crash-landed inside of some skyscraper with that human soldier he'd tried to kill—the one from *Star Brigade*.

He had snuck up from behind, taking perfect aim to finish off the earthborn whore...

...until some witless creature had warned her of the attack. Rouma had fired anyway, but regrettably the human had dodged and pointed her fingers at him like a gun. Rouma could never forget the immediate blast of concentrated sound that struck the Korvenite harder than any blow he'd ever felt—smashing through his chestplate and fracturing his ribcage.

The last thing Rouma remembered was blinding pain after he was thrown from the skyscraper, followed by a moment of weightlessness.

By Korvan's will…my armor…must have broken my fall and saved me…just barely, he winced, trying to sit up. Every cell in his body flared up, scorching away his already failing strength. He slumped back down, wracked by violent coughs.

Rouma didn't need his eyes to know that he was hurt badly. Several ribs were broken, spine perhaps shattered. His life's blood was oozing like a leaky pipe from the deep wound in his chest, wet and sticky within his ruined armor, a dark green ichor pooling around where he currently lay.

Even Rouma reaching for his helmet added to the anguish. But Rouma fought through as much of the pain as he could, frantic to know why he couldn't sense the Unilink.

Had Maelstrom been defeated? *Impossible.* This time the Anointed One's plan had been foolproof. Sollus was sheathed in its own defense shielding. Not even the Kedri would thwart Maelstrom this time.

Rouma fumbled at his helmet's delicate controls with fingers that had grown clumsy and weak until finally, the malleable helmet slid away from the Korvenite's face.

He breathed in the foul, unfiltered air and took in his surroundings. The Korvenite lay in a valley of twisted debris and ruin from the KIF's righteous assault.

The skyscraper he had fallen from was at least seventy or more stories high, resembling a jagged tooth jutting up into the dirty smoke soiling the blue skies—

Rouma gasped, and almost choked on another fit of coughs.

"[The skies are blue]?" he whispered fearfully in Korcei. The Korvenite could no longer see the golden forcefield that had bathed Sollus's heavens. Nor could he see the eclipsing shadow of the *Amalgam* hovering above him, or any Korvanes statues striding through the starscrapers. What Rouma did see were hordes of warships high above, both UComm and Imperium, swarming like angry bees around a gigantic smear of dirty black smoke and fiery embers.

Rouma's ravaged body went cold.

No. The Korvenite felt his eyes beginning to water as the truth dawned on him.

No! He could not believe it. He *refused* to believe it. Maelstrom had sworn to Korvan Almighty that the Korvenites would have their homeworld back.

Rouma stretched his mind out further than his injuries allowed, pain blurring his vision as he searched for any Korvenites still alive.

He found a number of his brethren either captured or dying or fleeing underground. Their thoughts all revealed the same horrible truth.

The Korvenite Independence Front, defeated and scattered.

The Amalgam, destroyed.

Lord Maelstrom, *killed.* The survivors had felt the deaths of him and every other Korvenite aboard the *Amalgam*, right before the Unilink went dead.

"[It's over…again]," Rouma heard himself say. And this time, he had no doubt the Korvenite race would be wiped off the face of the 'Verse.

Somehow he knew this would happen, his renewed faith in Maelstrom notwithstanding. No way would the Union just allow the Korvenites to reclaim their homeworld without consequences.

But that didn't dull the agony of those losses, or the heartbreak of failing to recapture their home.

Rouma's eyes grew blurry. Soon, tears were streaming down his cheeks, loosening the greenish blood caked on them.

Through the chaotic noises swirling around him, Rouma started to make out individual voices nearby. One sounded *human.* Possibly UComm soldiers?

They would never capture him alive, not after what the KIF had done. But the Korvenite would not let them be the ones to kill him.

With strenuous effort, Rouma turned his head to the right and saw a twisted spike of 112arasteel. Sharp enough to stab with, small enough to hold with both hands. A smile tugged at Rouma's torn lips.

He reached for it with a weak and shaky arm…

Rouma. The voice startled Rouma out of his single-minded struggle.

It took a moment of glancing around for Rouma to detect another presence inside his mind, a passenger. A few more moments passed before the Korvenite assigned an identity to this passenger.

"[You!]" He was beside himself with shock. His arm dropped, strength spent. "[I thought that…when the Amalgamation exploded. How—?]"

I jumped from my body into yours, right before…it was too late," the voice explained, sounding strong and hale for a dead Korvenite.

"[And the Chouncilor?]" Rouma asked, almost afraid of the answer, "[Did he die also on the *Amalgam*?]"

Escaped, his passenger admitted with clear shame, before changing the subject. *You're weakening, Rouma.*

"[Dying will do that.]" Rouma should have been angry at his psychic visitor for not fulfilling his promise to win back Sollus, should have been lost in despair over dying.

Instead, Rouma managed a smile. *Of course this one survived death.* That only proved beyond a shadow of a doubt that he was Korvan's Anointed.

High above, the swarms of warships began to disperse from the big black smear, which had almost exhausted its thunderstorm of blazing wreckage. While Rouma watched this, a world-shaking swell of sorrow not belonging to him overwhelmed his thoughts.

The two Korvenites mourned today's losses together in Rouma's body.

"Holy *tattsh*! Kiran, look what I found!" a nearby voice pulled Rouma from his grief. He sensed two sentients dangerously close. The Korvenite raised his neck as high as possible and eyed the slope of crooked debris and rocks ahead.

Humans. An older earthborn male stood in front, swarthy and balding, with a roll of pudge around the midsection. The other one who looked like a stormborn human male trailed behind him, young, lean and limber, a shock of white hair over beet-red roots atop his head.

The stormborn human's eyes widened. "Is that one of those armored Korvies that attacked Conuropolis?"

"Yup," the earthborn took a few nonchalant steps forward. "It looks fekt up!"

The older human stared at him with merciless eyes. Rouma could taste his loathing from afar. "Let's finish the job."

When this day began, these dungheaps cowered before the Korvenite. Now he couldn't even run and hide; his terror reached nightmarish levels from two normal, nobody humans with hostile intentions.

"Stay…back," Rouma wheezed in accented Standard. "I want no trouble."

"You telling us what to do?" the human advanced angrily. "After what you did to my homeworld?"

It's not your homeworld, Rouma almost screamed, but held his tongue. He was in no position to back such words up. And if they had any clue whom Rouma was housing inside his head… "Please, I'm already dying. Just…let me pass in peace."

"I don't think this is a good idea," the youth named Kiran warned, backing away. "We should leave, find shelter."

His partner was adamant. "Not until this blekdritt pays." He launched himself at Rouma and stomped his foot down hard on the Korvenite's chest. Rouma shrieked. Every pain receptor in his body ignited, even in the legs he could no longer move.

The earthborn was far from done. "You green-blooded, blekdritt piece of Grade-A *tattshi*!" the human roared, each word punctuated by a swift and vicious stomp. "You attack my fucking planet, kill thousands and think you can get away with it? Fuck! You!"

The attack was ugly and brutal, so much that the human almost fell over in his unending desire to stomp Rouma's chest in. The Korvenite couldn't even cover up. So his end would come at the hands of a human. As blow after blow crushed more bones in him, he just prayed to Korvan Almighty that the end would come quickly.

Don't fear, Maelstrom declared through the onslaught, *I'll handle this insect.*

Rouma's arm, the one he no longer had the strength to lift, snaked out on its own volition and grabbed the human by the leg.

"What the—WHOA!" The arm jerked back, yanking the pudgy human's leg forward and sending him face first to the ground. "Kiran, help!!"

Silence. The human's eyes went black as pitch and he began to convulse, limbs and head flopping about like a fish yanked out of water. Suddenly Rouma felt his passenger leave, and once more his mind was alone. The stormborn human who had hung back cried out inarticulately and dashed forward.

Meanwhile, his earthborn partner sat up and examined his body with disdainful hands. "This body will serve for now." His species and tenor were that of a human's. But the facial expression, the authoritative lilt of his voice and even his posture resembled the Korvenite that Rouma had revered and followed. Praise be to Korvan!

Kiran was almost upon Rouma, fear and hesitation giving away to fury and confusion. "What did you—"

The Korvenite-possessed human raised a calm hand. "Sleep." The telepathic command caused Kiran to slump forward in mid-sprint.

Turning away from the unconscious stormborn, the Korvenite-possessed human stood up on unsure legs. Rouma felt the possessed human link with him, projecting out thoughts via Mindspeak to Korvenites far and wide in—but using Rouma's voice. *It is over, my brethren. Maelstrom is truly dead. Flee now. Do not let them destroy you like dogs.*

Rouma stared up at the Korvenite-possessed human in disbelief. *Why did you lie?*

No one can know I am still alive, his comrade replied psychically. *Not until I correct my,* he gestured at his new body with unconcealed disgust...*my current situation.*

That consolation was the least of Rouma's concerns. The human's attack had hastened the inevitable, and he felt his life ebbing away more quickly.

The Korvenite-possessed human dropped to his knees and cradled Rouma up in his arms, holding his comrade as gently as possible.

"[Rouma, I am so sorry,]" the human said in spot-on Korcei, "[This was...Sollus was supposed to become home again for our species. I failed all of you, again.]"

"[You didn't fail me,]" Rouma chided, but his voice sounded so weak. The sensation had left his arms, and the world began to darken. "[Because of you, I have returned to our homeworld, and I am free.]" In the distance, Rouma heard vehicles soar overhead, closer than he cared for.

"[I won't stop…until our species is avenged]," Maelstrom continued, that familiar fiery passion engulfing his words. He glanced at the motionless stormborn nearby. "[I can save you…put you in that other body over there so we can—]"

Even as he lay dying, the thought of telepathically possessing another sentient—even worse, a *human*—sickened Rouma to his core. He shook his head with his remaining strength. "[My journey ends here…on our homeworld.]" Surprisingly, his leader wasn't upset by the refusal. Empathy radiated off the Korvenite-possessed human.

"[But I don't want to die like this…ebbing away…alone.]"

In his failing eyes, Rouma saw the human shake his head. "[I'll make it as painless as possible.]"

"[My…thanks… Anointed One,]" Rouma's words came out so soft he was afraid they went unheard.

Thankfully, they weren't. "[Enough with the titles and the aliases, Rouma. Call me…Isydryas. Until we meet again in Illyria.]" He rested a hand on Rouma's clammy forehead.

The surrounding charred debris, the dirty skies, and the chill numbing Rouma's body faded.

Now he saw rolling hills, sparkling lakes, and clear skies. The region now called Oklorada Basin, untouched by the earthborn defilers.

Sollus, as Rouma had remembered it almost thirty years ago.

In this illusion, Rouma was no longer armored or crippled. He could stand tall again, whole and healed. His companion and their two children, all killed years before the first Korvenite Rebellion, stood beside him.

In the real world, Maelstrom's arms wrapped around Rouma, one encircling his head while another snaked over his armored torso in the opposite direction. Both arms tightened, especially the one holding his torso steady.

Rouma barely felt that. *I'm finally home.* He gazed up at the sunny skies with a smile…

…right as Maelstrom gave his head a quick, hard twist.

A white-hot jolt shivered through Rouma's body. Then everything went black.

Together

"Now turn around."

Jeremy Nwosu did as told and turned to face the floating 8'x4' holomirror. This was the first time he'd been allowed to mostly dress himself. Too bad it wasn't for a more fun occasion.

Under bright and warm halolights, the boy saw himself very dressed up, in a black suit and collarless white shirt. His bushy, dark brown fro had been trimmed to a manageable length which he cared little for. Jeremy was in his small room cabin on the *Crimsonborn*, his father's personal freighter space yacht.

His light brown skin looked flushed, probably from how anxious he felt about today.

Behind Jeremy sat the human who'd helped dress him, his father Captain Habraum Nwosu.

In the holomirror, the large Cercidalean was taller sitting in a bed than Jeremy was standing up, bald and broad-shouldered with a trimmed goatee, and chocolate brown skin much darker than Jeremy's. Daddy had his full military uniform on, black and grey and high-collared, but with the colorful rank emblems and insignias he didn't usually wear. The crimsonborn silently studied his son's attire in the mirror, smoothing out or tugging at any rumples to straighten them out.

"Brilliant," his father exclaimed after several moments. His hands rested on Jeremy's shoulders, engulfing them in his massive grip. "You look grand, sprout."

Jeremy gave a little shrug and said nothing, watching his father intently through the mirror.

From Jeremy's experience, the older crimsonborn's hazel-gold eyes always reflected his moods: warm and liquid in happiness, cold and hard in anger, clouded and dim in sadness.

Though Daddy was smiling, Jeremy saw the sadness in his eyes. And he knew why.

Daddy's friend, Mr. Honaa, had died almost a week ago. Even worse, he had died exactly like Mommy had—in a ship explosion.

Now Daddy and his Star Brigade workfellows had come to Rothor IV for the funeral.

Jeremy had been only to one funeral before, his mother's. He had cried a lot, but didn't sob. "Cercidaleans are like the rocks of our homeworld, solid and durable," his father had said many times. "Cercs don't crumble when life tries to break us."

Jeremy was only half-Cerc, and hated funerals. But he promised himself not to cry like he had at Mommy's funeral, which would be easy. Jeremy didn't even know Mr. Honaa that well.

"Okay," Daddy rose slowly from the bed, very slowly. His strong-jawed face tensed up as if in pain. "We'll head over to the funeral in a few." He walked toward the room exit with a noticeable limp.

Jeremy made a face at the prospect of venturing out into the muggy outsides. But he said nothing, only nodding.

Before this week the boy had never visited the Rothorid homeworld. Within a day of arriving, he quickly decided he never wanted to visit again.

Everywhere he'd been in this region of Rothor IV was muggy, smelly, foggy and really, *really* hot. So hot, Jeremy thought at times he was sweating despite the TempReg tech in his clothes. He had wanted to go to Rothor IV and be with his father. Now he really wanted to go back home to Hollus Maddrone or to his grandparents' home on Terra Sollus like his father had suggested.

But Daddy was here with all his workfellows for Mr. Honaa's funeral. Daddy had been so sad all week. Suddenly Jeremy felt bad about wanting to leave Rothor IV.

And he knew exactly what his father would say if he complained about the planet. "Cercidaleans don't bellyache over nonsense like crap weather."

So Jeremy made an effort to say as little as possible and not to complain. That way he wouldn't upset Daddy. Especially since his father had been in the hospital a few days because of getting hurt at work.

"Been real quiet since we reached Rothor IV, sprout," his father said as he lingered near the door exit. "Everything ollrigh'?"

Don't make him upset. Jeremy nodded quickly and mutely.

That didn't convince his father one bit. "Use your voice. The Twins gave you one for a reason."

"I'm fine," Jeremy murmured, avoiding his father's unflinching gaze. He started fidgeting with his hands, but stopped.

"You don't sound fine," Daddy approached. With a look of great discomfort he lowered himself to one knee in front of the boy, tilting his chin up so their eyes met. "C'mon lad, what's this about?"

Jeremy let out a heavy sigh. He tried to keep quiet, but knew Daddy wouldn't take silence for an answer. "Because Mr. Honaa's dead. And you're sad. I don't want to make you more sad, like you were when Mummy died."

His father stared back at the boy in momentary disbelief. Then he chuckled and gave a slight shake of his head. "You sweet little boy." He placed a hand on Jeremy's left shoulder. "I'm going to be sad no matter what, lad. Honaa is…Honaa *was* a close friend. And your dad misses him very much." His father gave him a soft pat on the face, like he usually did. "You can ask any questions you have about this, yea?"

"Yes, Daddy," Jeremy nodded. Hearing that had lifted this weird heavy feeling off his chest. He had a lot of questions. Best to start asking, since it wouldn't upset his father more. "Is Mr. Honaa now in the same place as Mummy?"

The question made his father's mouth pull into a smile. His clean-shaven head gleamed under the room's halolights. "I'd like to think so."

Jeremy frowned. "But how?" he asked, confused. "They aren't even the same species. And Rothorids don't worship the Holy Gemini."

"Smart lad," his dad said with one of his long, serious looks that always made Jeremy feel so small. "What I do know is that they are both watching over us now…wherever they may be."

"Even if they're in different paradises?"

His father nodded and scratched at his trimmed goatee. "Absolutely, sprout. They're in…similar paradises."

Now Jeremy was more confused. "I don't get it. Why doesn't the Union just make every species worship the same religion?"

Daddy rose to his feet, wincing the whole way. "Would make it easier, yea?" he asked, trying to cover his pain with a chuckle.

Jeremy was serious. He put on his most serious face as he looked all the way up at his father. "But why don't they? Then we'd know Mr. Honaa and Mummy are in the same paradise."

Daddy shook his head then, still amused. He placed a hand on Jeremy's back and guided him toward the room exit. "The Union doesn't work that way, sprout. Now, we can get on about this later," his father said as the boy opened his mouth with another question. "I need you to be really good for Mr. Honaa's family and my coworkers at the service. Can you do that?"

"Yes, Daddy," Jeremy nodded his head vigorously. He promised himself today to be a rock, like a true Cercidalean. "Can I ask one more question?"

"Sure," his father said. Jeremy's room's door slid open before them.

"Why do our family and friends keep dying?"

His father froze in his tracks. He stared up at the ceiling, squeezing his eyes shut for a moment as if to steady his emotions, and Jeremy quickly regretted the question. *I made him sad*, the boy fretted.

He was about to apologize when his father spoke again. "Only the Twins know, Jeremy," the tall Cerc replied in a quiet voice. He began walking again, taking his son by the hand. "Come on, then."

The moment they stepped outside the *Crimsonborn*, the humid temperature smacked Jeremy in the face. The fact that he and his father didn't melt into puddles of goo was surprising. A Unionjack shuttle filled with Daddy's workfellows was waiting. All of them had on their formal UComm uniforms.

Jeremy saw Auntie Sammie, who looked pale and even sadder than Daddy. She did, however, have a smile and a hug for the boy. Everyone else was friendly and said 'hi'; the tall Terranborn Dr. Cortés; the burly metal-skinned Thulican, Khrome, and the lean ice crystal guy, Tyris. The tawny Kintarian that Daddy had referred to as 'Prydyri-Ravlek' said nothing, scowling at everything and everyone. Jeremy's father was really tall, but Prydyri-Ravlek towered over even him. His yellow eyes with their green flecks fell upon Jeremy.

The boy waved.

The Kintarian didn't smile back, but he did wink before looking away to scowl at the ceiling.

The only being not on the Unionjack was that scary cyborg lady friend of Daddy's. Jeremy didn't remember her even coming to Rothor IV.

"She couldn't make it," Daddy had said a day ago, without any further explanation. The tone of his father's voice had discouraged Jeremy from inquiring further.

Jeremy found it odd how Daddy and Auntie Sammie didn't say much to each other after everyone sat down. In fact, barely anyone spoke during the whole trip to the Temple of Greater Wuirothao, which took about ten macroms. Unfortunately, that meant they had to go outside again. Jeremy stifled a groan, remembering to be on his best behavior.

The Temple of Greater Wuirothao had been built on a vast bog, but visitors could enter by way of the hardlight bridges leading up to the entrance. Jeremy looked down at the murkiest, muddiest water he'd ever seen in his life. The thought of falling into that made him walk faster.

Even when they walked right up to the entrance, the massive spiral-shaped temple looked like just a dark brownish silhouette, thanks to all the muggy fog. Its three jagged pinnacles were shaped like teeth, rising up into a hazy greyish-brown gloom.

Once inside the foyer, Jeremy stayed at his father's side as he greeted what appeared to be a never-ending procession of Rothorids, some marooned-scaled like Mr. Honaa, others green-skinned. Quite a few had black scales or bluish scales. Jeremy had no clue which ones were Mr. Honaa's family, or if all of them were. Every Rothorid sounded alike with their hissing dialogue. Jeremy also noticed was how stick-straight their tails were when speaking with Daddy, which Auntie Sammie had said was a huge show of respect.

After the Rothorid parade ended, a number of other non-Rothorids came up to Daddy as they entered the temple's inner sanctum where the funeral would be held. All of them had on military outfits too.

The inner sanctum was shaped like a huge half-circle, with vaulted transparent ceilings and patterned walls, showcasing a smooth, shiny bronze color. The pitch-black benches were divided by two aisle ways into three sections, all in long rounded structures to fit with the half-circle design of the inner sanctum. Even inside a building, a faint humid mist hung in the air. A soft chorus of rattling combined with zig-zaggy-sounding hissing played in the background. This must have been the funeral music, but Jeremy couldn't find anything musical about those noises. He took in all the sights and sounds, until his eyes landed at the very front of the inner sanctum. The boy jolted back.

Floating to the right of the speaking podium was a 3D holographic bust of Mr. Honaa's head and shoulders, identical down to the triangle shape of the muzzle. Jeremy inched closer to his father, hoping they wouldn't have to sit close to that. But the seats all were beginning to fill up, so Jeremy tugged at his father's hand so they could grab some seats quickly.

"This way, lad," Daddy guided him forward. "We're up there with Mr. Honaa's family."

'Up there' meant the very front of the inner sanctum.

Jeremy cringed away. But his much bigger and stronger father kept moving, almost dragging the boy forward until he came willingly. *You promised to behave*, Jeremy scolded himself, and scurried to catch up with his father's long, limping strides.

While they walked, Auntie Sammie explained that since Mr. Honaa died defending the Union with Star Brigade at his side, the seating arrangement was a place of honor for Daddy, Auntie Sammie and their workfellows. Strangely, that made Jeremy feel less weird for having to stare at Mr. Honaa's head.

Jeremy sat between Daddy and Auntie Sammie in the front, while the rest of Daddy's Star Brigade workfellows sat in the bench behind them. Soon Honaa's family arrived: twin teenagers who looked almost exactly like Mr. Honaa, even down to his maroon skin. Then Jeremy saw three smaller Rothorids, clearly preteens like him. One youngling's scaly skin was bright green, another had a pale maroon coloring and a third was covered in cool ivory skin and blood-red eyes. All had super serious looks on their tightly clamped muzzles.

Behind the offspring stood a lean and petite Rothorid with darker green scales, muzzle clamped shut, eyes hard as diamonds. Though Rothorid males and females didn't bear too many differences in physiques, Jeremy knew immediately this Rothorid was a she-Rothorid and Mr. Honaa's partner. And that meant these five younglings were Mr. Honaa's offspring. Jeremy gulped. How bad was it for them when they found out about Mr. Honaa? Jeremy remembered when he was told about Mommy not coming back. At first the boy didn't believe it—*refused* to. Sometimes he had dreams that she was still alive.

Those thoughts made Jeremy's eyes get itchy and his stomach feel queasy, so he pushed the bad memories of Mommy away and focused on being as nice as possible to Mr. Honaa's family.

He smiled big like Daddy would when greeting Mr. Honaa's partner and her offspring. But they were all very terse in their hellos, not friendly at all. Jeremy frowned, wondering what he had done wrong.

"Rothorids almost *always* look serious," Daddy whispered after seeing his son's reaction, "even when they are happy about something."

Once everyone was seated, the rattling music stopped and the ceremony began with some rail-thin Rothorid priest speaking first. He spoke in Wuiroth tongue, all hisses and rasps that grated at Jeremy's ears. A few other Rothorids came up with their hissing and rasping. After the fifth speaker Jeremy had tuned them all out, not even bothering to look at the translator screens.

How long is this going to go on? he wondered impatiently. The boy hated funerals, and looking at the holo bust of Mr. Honaa's face was *beyond* creepy.

Finally, it was Daddy's turn to speak. Auntie Sammie gave Daddy an encouraging rub on the back as he stood up. But the dread on his father's face made Jeremy feel cold all over, despite the humidity.

Daddy took his place behind the podium, standing there alone. He stared down at the floor as if to gather his wits. After a long moment, he looked up at the crowd, still quiet, drawing in a deep breath.

Right then Jeremy remembered his father standing behind a similar podium, a year ago on Cercidale—the day of Mommy and baby Nwosu's funeral. Daddy had spoken about how much Mommy meant to him and everyone in her life, how the heavens had gained two more stars. Jeremy didn't like thinking about that day ever, but it just popped into his head. Then the boy recalled how tears had been running down his father's face the whole time he had spoken about Mommy.

At one point his father, his strong-as-a-rock Daddy, had gotten so emotional during his eulogy that he almost couldn't continue…

Jeremy jumped to his feet and ran.

He heard the chorus of surprised hissing from all the Rothorids and the gasps from the non-Rothorids. Auntie Sammie called out his name as loud as she dared, but the boy didn't stop.

His father's jaw dropped in disbelief as Jeremy dashed up to his side.

The boy grabbed hold of his father's massive hand. "Y'ollrigh'?" he asked, looking up at Daddy, searching for his sad eyes.

Daddy looked so staggered that Jeremy might have laughed if they weren't at a funeral. His father's hazel-gold eyes brightened for the first time in days. The crimsonborn straightened up and sighed. "I think I am, sprout." He gave his son's hand a gentle squeeze.

Jeremy felt good hearing that, and seeing Daddy genuinely happy. "Okay."

Daddy smiled broadly at his son. "Let's do this."

Jeremy grinned back in agreement, and then looked out into the crowd. Many of the Rothorids looked befuddled by this change in events. Khrome and Dr. Cortés were beaming at him. Aunt Sammie had a hand over her heart and mouthed, "Love you, Jerm." Her eyes were all wet like she was about to cry. Jeremy mouthed back "Love you, too."

"Seems my speech translator finally arrived," Daddy told the crowd, pointing to his son. "Better later than never, yea?" The whole crowd laughed, mostly Rothorid sissing, with a distinct jumble of human laughter and other alien sounds of mirth. And Jeremy couldn't miss Auntie Sammie's big, loud laugh.

"Who was Honaa Ishiliba to me?" Daddy continued, bold and brave as ever. "Well, before I answer that question, I'll start with how we first met…" Then Daddy began his speech.

It was kind of long, but Jeremy still liked every moment of it.

Birthright

When the skies of Terra Sollus turned blue again, the whole town of Big Victory erupted in joy.

The young and old hugged each other and danced together, jumping around in the makeshift dirt streets that weaved through the dilapidated spaceships serving as Big Victory's business establishments or homes.

It mattered not if they were earthborn humans, stormborns with their bone-white hair and colorful roots, scaly Rothorids, ivory-skinned Korvenites with their purple hair or whatever the species.

Terra Sollus had been saved. Maelstrom and his ministry of brainwashed extremists had been stopped. The town in the most isolated part of Terra Sollus's Oklorada Basin had united in a deafening celebration that went well into the early evening. It would have surprised no one if Brightwater, the closest town at about twenty-eight miles east, could hear them clearly.

No one, however, was happier or more ashamed than Antur.

The sharp winds were needling the Korvenite's whitish skin through his casual dark slacks and shapeless blood-red tunic. Antur, while not very tall at five-foot-nine, kept his physique lean and hard for someone north of fifty years. He had his waves of violet hair with a thick streak of gold pulled back in a shoulder-length ponytail.

Currently, the Korvenite stood silhouetted against the sinking sun. A faint smile brightened his sharp features as he observed the whirlwind of joyous activity around him. He couldn't help but psychically feed off the town's impromptu celebration, letting the exuberance flood through him. By the time night had fallen, Antur lost count of how many hugs or exclamations of relief he had exchanged with his many longtime neighbors.

But then he looked at the other Korvenites in their gold and ebony eyes, everyone filled with tension and dread. That was when the shame and the memories seeped in to darken his joy.

This morning all his nearly forgotten fears had returned with nightmarish force after Terra Sollus's planetary shields painted the skies gold, followed by that psychopath Maelstrom spewing out his xenocidal endgame for every news streams to broadcast.

On that terrorist's order, those shields were set to unleash radiation that would wipe out every sentient being on Terra Sollus, except the Korvenites of course.

Antur had been certain he would be witnessing another Earth Holocaust. The longer the planetary shields remained active, the more his brain conjured up the worst-case scenarios of watching Maelstrom's hijacked battle station burn all his non-Korvenite friends and neighbors to death.

None of the 406 Korvenites in Big Victory were in danger had the Korvenite Independence Front's 'purge' succeeded. But that mattered little and less.

Since its founding in the year 2370 from a cluster of rundown spaceships, Big Victory had known no racial barriers. Every sentient in Big Victory was family.

Today, despite the town's modest yet slowly expanding sprawl, that tenet of family still held true.

Antur and the other Korvenites had lived here in secret for over twenty-five years, building new lives in a time when their species was being enslaved or hunted like game. So as a member of this town and its council, The Korvenite had buried his own worries in favor of offering reassuring words and calming embraces when needed. Any of his Korvenite brethren able look past their own fears followed his lead, keeping Big Victory tranquil.

Losing a homeworld, triggering so much chaos, Antur had considered, *all due to the stupidity of a dozen*. What a well-deserved dose of cosmic karma for his past crimes.

And even if the Union and Imperium warships breached Terra Sollus's compromised defenses, what would stop the Kedri from declaring war on the Union? Maelstrom's attack had not only ruined the Union-Imperium Trade Merger but had embarrassed both hyperpowers involved on an intergalactic scale.

...All due to the stupidity of a dozen...

Thank Korvan that the heavens had turned blue again, and the Kedri departed from Terra Sollus without a single shot fired at UComm forces.

Only then did the weight of the galaxy leave Antur's shoulders. Only then had that sweet sigh of relief left his lips.

Four days after what the news streams had called 'the Battle of Terra Sollus,' fear still hung heavy amongst many of Big Victory's 6,800-plus citizens. Not just for their safety, but for that of their Korvenite neighbors.

Everyone knew what Maelstrom's attacks meant for any Korvenites discovered on Terra Sollus's surface. The afterglow of celebration and relief had long faded, replaced by palpable dread of UComm warships casting eclipsing shadows over Big Victory to seize friends and neighbors.

That was why, under a moonlit sky, Mayor Sunshine 'Sunny' Nakamura addressed her town tonight. Well-placed streetlamps cast pale yet ample lighting over a town square teeming with hundreds of Big Victory's residents. Ringing the massive town square's borders were nine metallic tall, angular and twisty sculptures lacquered in silver, all constructed from the innards of nonfunctioning ships.

In front of a rusted military command cruiser now serving as the town hall, the earthborn woman stood on an elevated podium shaped like an enlarged half-tablet. Even dressed in a casual chunky ash grey turtleneck and dark blue denims along with a brown Kurthahide jacket, she carried an unmistakable presence. Sunny cast a sweeping gaze over her constituents and shrugged. "Wish I could say I was up here tonight just because I'm a sucker for your applause."

The nine sculptures around the town square sonor-amped her quip across the settlement, and a collective chuckle rippled through the audience. Antur allowed himself a brief laugh. He was just one of many in the crowd watching Sunny's speech. A quick, psychic scan of the gathering revealed the taut worry and at times animosity over the events in Conuropolis. Most blamed Maelstrom and his brainwashed cronies, while small pockets of some humans blamed *all* Korvenites. For Antur, those reactions weren't unexpected or worrisome…yet.

"Unfortunately," Sunny's voice sobered and she straightened up in posture, "we all saw what happened four days ago. Let's pray for those living in Conuropolis, Sheffield, and every city-state that suffered from Maelstrom's attacks, those who lost their homes and loved ones. We may be worlds away from them big megapolises, but we're all of the same planet and the same Union."

Steady applause followed Sunny's declaration. Age had etched fine lines around her almond-shaped eyes and pouty lips. Yet for a fifty-one-year-old, Antur still found her handsome by any humanoid's criteria. Her thick, flowing hair was a bright shade of powder blue, which she had perma-dyed several years ago when the white hairs began outnumbering the black. Tonight she draped her customary long braid loosely over the right shoulder, her blunt and heavy bangs skimming just over the eyebrows. "However, as much as we support our fellow Unionists in other parts of Terra Sollus, we must look to our own community.

"There will be a lot of blame and hatred being lobbed at the Korvenite species over the next few weeks or months or years. The Korvenites in this town will need us more than ever."

"What if UComm comesss?" someone shouted out in the crowd, the hissing cadence indicative of a Rothorid. "What are we ssssupposed to do?"

"Well, Rojuic," Sunny cast a melodramatic eye toward the speaker, addressing her by name, "here's hoping we never have to answer that question. But if we do, the answer is plain and simple." Her dark, almond eyes filled with fire as she continued. "Just like over a quarter of a century ago, we protect all Korvenites in this town, hide them in the underground bunkers where the UComm's scans and probes can't reach. If that doesn't work, then we will make a case of it with the courts, and let everyone see how much the Korvenites in this town mean to the community. Big Victory protects its own, no matter what."

Antur's pride threatened to burst from his chest. The human had a gift for this, owning the crowd yet making each and every citizen feel like she addressed them directly. His pride notwithstanding, that declaration received a more mixed reaction. The Korvenite exchanged glances with some of the many Korvenites scattered throughout the crowd, unmistakable by their ivory skin, purple-colored hair and their physical similitude to humans. The forty-plus Korvenites in the crowd were connected with each other through a telepathic Unilink, and all shared varying degrees of unease.

Crowd's a bit agitated in my area, a Korvenite named Isydryas commented, *especially the Kent and Gutiérrez clans.*

A female named Kumett chimed in. *Got a few Rothorids not buying what Sunny's selling, dead-set on ratting us out if UComm comes around.*

Relive their tension a little, Antur replied to the Unilink. *Remind them to feel safe around us.*

Isydryas and other Korvenites stretched themselves with their Mindspeak gifts. Almost instantly Antur sensed the doubts and resentment of several in the crowd simmer down. Soon, only flickers of unease and doubt lingered amongst the citizens tonight, but nothing warranting any further concern.

Antur sighed, forgiving himself as always for the manipulation, and returned his gaze to Sunny.

"I understand everyone is scared. So am I," the earthborn woman admitted in high and ringing tones. "But we cannot let our fears and worries drive us apart. The Korvenites in this town had nothing to do with the tragedy that took place in Conuropolis. They are family. And in Big Victory, we protect our family," she then gestured down to a Korvenite standing in the front of the crowd, "even Tharace."

The crowd howled with laughter over that, and Antur sensed the Korvenite she spoke of seethe with embarrassment.

"For now, go home, spend time with your loved ones and your friends. Let us enjoy the very things we've labored for and fought hardest to protect—our family." The crowd burst in applause, then the cheering from days ago returning in full force. Sunny nodded and voiced her thanks to the crowd. She then angled a look in Antur's direction with a subtle askance that only he saw.

Antur nodded his approval. *You did great, Sunshine,* he telepathically reassured her, *as usual.*

And then Sunny let her shoulders sag in relief. A big smile played across her lips as she waved and soaked in the appreciation from Big Victory's citizens.

Antur watched her in amusement. Yes, she really was a sucker for all the applause.

A few orvs later, Antur and Sunny had returned back to the warmth of their home, a modified mini-luxury space yacht. The walls were blood-red and gold, stylish enough but maintaining a rustic quality. Antur's longtime partner sat before a holomirror, her face pinched and serious. The silky, lavender robe she had on was untied and hanging loosely on her slender frame. Sunny's powder blue hair was unbraided and spilling down to the waist, with Antur combing out any tangles with an oval-shaped brush. Several holo-motion portraits of the couple adorned their walls, displaying them throughout the years. The soothing sound bath of a celestial symphonic melody filled every room in their home.

"What's the temperature out there tonight?" she asked quietly. Even this late in the day, her work as mayor was never done.

"Concerned and scared," Antur answered. "Some of our more remote citizens were ready to give us up if UComm ever visited."

Sunny gave him her look through the mirror, collected but pointed. "I assume the weather's cooled?"

Antur set the comb down atop a drawer next to the holomirror. "Do you even have to ask?" To keep the peace in Big Victory, Sunny had tasked Antur and the other Korvenites over the years with training the townsfolk in 'psychic defensive.' But in truth this allowed the Korvenite familiarity and access to occasionally sway public opinion to benefit their standing in Big Victory, like ensuring that Sunny's two-decade rule as mayor remained unopposed.

"Smooth winds for now," he placed both hands on Sunny's slim shoulders to start rubbing away the knots. Antur was one of Sunny's chief advisors on Big Victory's town council, and her partner in everything else.

He sensed Sunny's lack of regret for any actions taken to protect this town, as well as her already ebbing relief. "Let me know if anything else comes up."

The Korvenite couldn't help but smile. "You worry too much."

Sunny closed her eyes and let her head loll forward, surrendering to the massage. "You never worry enough," she sighed.

I worry more than you could ever know, Antur said to himself, feeling a sharp pang deep in his chest. "You carry enough worry for us both."

Sunny opened her beady eyes and shrugged. "Have to. I'm the mayor."

"Not in this house," the Korvenite declared in his sexiest voice and continued kneading away his partner's worries. They had made a rule to try and not let town politics affect their personal relationship. For the most part, the rule had worked for them.

"Maybe..." Sunny cooed once the Korvenite pulled his hands away. She rose to her feet, standing about three inches shorter than him. "...maybe I need a reminder." The impish grin on her face made Sunny look twenty years younger.

Lust jolted like lightning through Antur. A soft caress on the cheek from her, a lingering kiss on the mouth from him and soon they were tearing each other's clothes off. He took Sunny's hand, pulling her eagerly toward their bed.

As her bare pink flesh pressed up against his alabaster white skin, Antur was reaching out telepathically to weave their minds together. By the time the two lovers were deep in the throes, Antur and Sunny's thoughts were merged completely. Every memory of his were laid bare for her to experience, all except that one cataclysmic day from almost three decades past.

...the sheer horror of watching Earth's atmosphere burn, the allegedly righteous pact with eleven other Korvenites that had set Earth's ruin in motion...

Sunny would never know that side of Antur. Years of practice had allowed him to bury those memories from his paramour whenever their minds merged, without her ever realizing.

The sound of Sunny's contented moan drew Antur back to the pleasures before him. *If tonight is my last night as a free Korvenite,* he mused, *then I will actively enjoy every last moment.* The Korvenite clasped Sunny's hands, pinning her to their bed, and sank on into the warmth between her thighs.

After they finished, a telepathic call roused him from his slumber.

Antur. The Korvenite sat up in the dark, recognizing the firm cadence of longtime friend Vycho.

Something wrong? In the background Antur also sensed quiet mental chatter like a babbling brook, several Korvenites he didn't recognize. That icy fear returned, but he couldn't figure out why.

You're needed in the Underground Hub, Vycho continued. *Tharace found something.*

Tharace was also a longtime acquaintance and sometimes friend. She was also the best tracker amongst Big Victory's Korvenites. If she required

Antur's presence, then Tharace must have found a potential threat to this town. His breathing grew labored with anxiety.

He glanced to the left. Sunny continue to doze peacefully beside him, swaddled in only sheets and shadows. The human was dreaming of sparkling Galdorian seas she once visited as a child.

No need to wake her. *I'll be there in ten macroms.* Antur swung his legs off the side of the bed.

After throwing on some clothes, Antur ventured out into the chilly night toward the edge of town. The more rural and scattered residential areas of Big Victory were evident by the increased dilapidation of the ships-turned-homes. Antur ventured to one of the mobile homes, an ancient mini-starliner so rusted over that Antur couldn't recall its original color. After entering through the vessel's helm, the Korvenite soon found himself in the luxury section of the ship.

The halolights came to life as soon as he entered that gutted section, revealing eight circular transmat platforms of crimson coloring, lined up in two rows of four. The walls of this former luxury section, however, were as timeworn as the outside of the ship.

These transmatters had been smuggled in sometime before the Earth Holocaust, allowing quicker transportation to and from the massive tunnels beneath Big Victory. The underground Hub was the refitted military bunker where the Korvenites in this town had been hidden, keeping them safe from global gene scans until UComm assumed they'd captured every Korvenite on Terra Sollus. When needed, the Hub also served as a meeting place for the town's Korvenites.

"Computer," Antur spoke. Immediately, a rainbow of blinking consoles lit up in the room. Antur stood on the circle closest to him. "One to transport. The Hub." The insides of the transmat center vanished in a shimmer of white, replaced by the gloom of the subterranean tunnels beneath Big Victory. The transmat platforms were identical to those in the starliner, even down to their metallic sheen.

Upon stepping off the transmat platform, he was greeted by two senior members of Big Victory's Korvenites. Vycho, stocky in build and sporting a mop of dark curly hair, offered Antur an anxious smile. At his side stood Tharace, petite and pudgy. But her pudginess was the only thing soft about the female Korvenite. Tharace's crewcut lilac tresses were as severe as her flinty expression. Antur had known these two since before he'd made Big Victory his home, so he expected such greetings.

The babbling of thoughts he'd sensed from earlier was stronger and more pronounced. Several new Korvenites, most confused, some relieved, quite a few angry—all of them Retributionaries.

A chill swept over Antur. "[What's going on?]" he asked in Korcei, approaching the duo.

Vycho led the way into a larger, more open room. "[See for yourself.]"

Antur stepped out of a short corridor and into a bowl-shaped meeting room built to fit hundreds. It had been his home for almost a year after the Earth Holocaust. This room was just one section in a vast underground complex capable of housing the whole town if needed.

Antur spotted over two dozen Korvenites who worked town security, all armed with pulse rifles. He exchanged greetings with them as well. Antur was far less welcoming to the new group of Korvenites, nameless faces under the dim lighting of the Hub.

Their complexions were white as snow, like his own; their hair, varying shades of purple similar to his; their eyes, black on gold exactly like Antur's. Korvenites, birthed from the same world. *But they chose to murder willingly,* Antur fumed. *They are nothing like me.* He lost count of how many were present but noted that all appeared robust and well fed. Yet many sported wounds that ranged in severity; from minor cuts and bruises to poorly bandaged wounds and serious burn injuries. The majority wore next to nothing, and shivered from the brisk drafts underground. Clearly these Retributionaries escaped the ruins of Conuropolis after Maelstrom had been thwarted and killed.

And now, they have found Big Victory. That icy fear from earlier had seeped into every cell of Antur's body. Regardless of his private fears, the Korvenite approached the gaggle of his own kind with as much confidence as he could muster, speaking with them telepathically.

We want no trouble, a Korvenite female named Cymae assured him. *Only sanctuary. There's nowhere else for us to go.* Cymae's plea mirrored all of these Korvenites'. They needed shelter and safety. There was nowhere else for them to go. The ice filling Antur's insides thawed then, but not the fears.

Some were older and had known freedom before the Earth Holocaust. Most of these Korvenites were either younger or children, whose only homes had been the internment camps. The bitterness and anger ruling many of these younglings' thoughts tasted of poison, but not nearly as much as the unanimously staunch hatred all of these Korvenites harbored for anything human.

Antur knew without question that Big Victory did not need this infusion of rogue Korvenites. But *they're still my brethren*. If he turned them away, their chances of survival dropped to nil. "[How did they find us?]" Antur asked after putting some distance between himself and the new Korvenites.

"[I sensed their presence a day ago and led the group to this location,]" Tharace declared, as if he'd asked a stupid question. "[They've been walking through Terra Sollus's subterranean tunnels for days.]"

Antur rubbed at the bridge of his nose, sensing the onset of anger, arguments, and a massive headache. "[Are you sure they weren't followed?]"

"[Yes,]" replied Joreis. The young and brawny security guard kept shooting uneasy glances at this new group of Korvenites.

Antur's heart thundered hard against his chest as he considered what to do next. "[Check again with the military scanners,]" he ordered Joreis, "[We can't be wrong about this.]" After Joreis departed, Antur gave both Vycho and Tharace pointed looks before stalking even further from the gathering.

His mind was a mess. The other non-Korvenite citizens were on edge as it was after the Battle of Terra Sollus. The arrival of Korvenite extremists that had tried to wipe them off the face of this world could ruin everything. A quick read on his fellow companions told Antur most of what he already knew. Vycho wore a heavy disquiet on his face and his thoughts. Tharace, while concerned about the town's reaction, had no conflict in helping these arrivals. The trio walked away until they were out of earshot.

Once the Korvenites had all properly shielded their minds from any psychic eavesdroppers, Antur immediately asked. "[How many?]"

Tharace's irises gleamed bright gold in the tunnel's gloom as she said, "[Seventy-four.]"

Antur's eyes nearly popped out of his head. "[Sweet Korvan, you two!]" He turned and began pacing, hands on his hips. How could he let these butchers into Big Victory's mostly non-Korvenite population, yet how could he turn them away to be captured and slaughtered by the UComm? The conflict was a whirlwind inside of him. And by Vycho's contorted features, Antur wasn't alone in his ambivalence.

"[You expect us to allow that many Retributionaries into our town?]" he asked the female.

"[Maelstrom is dead,]" Tharace stated flatly, "[These Korvenites have no further ties to him.]"

Antur stopped pacing and pivoted toward his two longtime friends. "[No further ties except for their crimes and their hard hatred for humans. How are we supposed to spin this with our neighbors?]"

Tharace appeared offended by such a question. "[We can spin them in any direction we want.]"

Vycho gaped at his partner. "[Keeping the town in line for events like Maelstrom's attack is one thing. Manipulating them to accept a group of Korvenites that nearly eradicated them all?]"

The female Korvenite shrugged. "[We've persuaded them on other matters.]"

Antur frowned. Even after so many years, he was continuously galled by how Tharace's passion to protect their species outweighed her need for scruples. "[You've grown far too comfortable bending others to your will.]"

She folded her arms and made a rude noise. "[Like you have with your Earther puppet?]"

Antur bristled. "Watch. Your. Mouth," he warned in Standard.

The venom in his voice wiped the sneer right off Tharace's features. She pointed at the cluster of Korvenites standing far from their debate. "[If it wasn't for us, these Korvenites over there…our brethren…would still have a homeworld.]"

Antur recoiled as if she'd slapped him, except the slap might have stung less. These three Korvenites leaders shared more than just a long friendship. If anyone knew the dark secret that had brought them to Big Victory, Antur knew that no place in the galaxy would be safe for them.

"[She's right,]" Vycho blurted out. He looked Antur in the eyes, standing half a head taller. "[We ruined Earth. And the entire Korvenite species still pays for our sins. Maelstrom wouldn't exist if not for us.]" Vycho shook his curly-haired head with such sorrow. He carried his guilt over the Earth Holocaust like weights around his neck. It had pained him only a little more than when Antur and Tharace had convinced him to sneak back onto Terra Sollus instead of leaving Union Space, like the rest of their group had originally agreed. "[Some of these Korvenites have never stepped foot on their rightful homeworld.]"

"[And after what Maelstrom and his brainwashed sycophants have done,]" Tharace pressed on, "[do you think the Union will let the remaining Korvenites live?]" Despite Antur's distaste for her methods, he could not help but be mesmerized by her zeal. "[As stupid as they were to follow that fanatic, this group could be all that is left of our brethren in this universe.]"

Antur absorbed her words and quickly saw no other choice. Neither did her partner, Vycho. "[Very well. Let me discuss this with Sunny first.]" Antur owed his human lover that and more after everything she had done to support the Korvenites in Big Victory.

Tharace looked appalled. "[You need your human's *permission*? On Korvenite natters?]" she spat. "[Do you also need her consent to wipe your own ass too?]"

"[Show some respect, you piece of flotsam,]" Antur got right in the female's face. His irises vanished, eyes turning pitch-black in anger. "[She is this town's mayor.]"

"[And she will *remain* Big Victory's mayor,]" Tharace snarled, not backing down, "[unless we say otherwise.]" Her eyes had also turned blacker than night.

A green flush crept up Antur's neck at her words. He itched to slap the insolence off Tharace's smug face. Thankfully Vycho stepped between the two Korvenites before wish turned to action. "[This isn't just about Sunny. Bringing in these Korvenites affects the whole town.]" The import of his words reminded Antur of the larger picture. He was still too angry to forget Tharace's disrespect, but currently he had to deal with the issue of these refugees.

"[They stay underground and out of sight, for now. We tell the others to persuade the non-Korvenites first.]" Tharace stated in cooler tones. She refused to look at Antur directly. Whether out of disgust or remorse, he had no interest in probing her mind to find out.

Nonetheless, Antur nodded in agreement with her solution. "[Keep an eye on them while I talk to Sunny.]" He turned around and headed back toward the transmatter that had brought him here. "I see no reason why she wouldn't grant them asylum," Antur decided, confident in Sunny's answer.

After waking up his lover and explaining the situation, the Korvenite had assumed wrong.

"Absolutely not!" Sunny Nakamura threw back as soon as he finished.

"Sunny!" Antur yelped in surprise. Her refusal was a knife thrust to the heart.

She stood in the middle of the hollowed-out ship helm serving as their warmly lit common room, hastily dressed in her silky lavender robe. Sunny shook her head, causing her thick mane of powder blue hair to spill down her shoulders. "I *won't* allow those murderous xenophobes anywhere near Big Victory."

Antur had expected some hesitation as was Sunny's way, but never such blatant refusal. He tried a different approach—begging. "These Korvenites are lost, leaderless and afraid. Most have no idea how to function in the outside world. They have nowhere else to go."

"And whose fault is that?" the human sniffed.

Mine, and your species as well. "Maelstrom's fault, I know," Antur detailed instead, nodding.

"Then they chose wrong," Sunny concluded with an insolent toss of her hair.

Antur leaned away. How could she be so heartless? He thought that she understood his brethren's plight. "We've provided shelter for several Korvenites in the past. Most of Big Victory's Korvenite population came to this city seeking refuge...*including* myself, Vycho and Tharace."

Sunny shook her head defiantly. "Totally different. You never tried wiping out every Earth human!"

Antur winced at the falsehood. He prayed that Sunny read that as his reaction to her resistance. "These poor creatures were thrown into internment camps, treated terribly for most of their lives and someone offers them a way out. What choice would you have made in their place?"

That finally reached Sunny. Her vehemence bled away and suddenly she looked very exhausted. "Antur…" the human began with a sigh.

Antur overrode her before she could reply. "All the Korvenites in town will take full responsibility for these newcomers," he took her gently by the shoulders and looked his lover right in the eyes. "We'll help them acclimate into the town. It will work out."

"And what about when UComm comes, huh?" she shrugged off his grasp and began pacing around him. "What if these Korvenites lead UComm back to you and every Korvenite in Big Victory?"

Antur bit down his annoyance at her inability to stay still and trailed her pacing. "Then we'll go underground, just like after the Earth Holocaust." The Korvenites living in Big Victory when the Earth Holocaust happened had hid underground to avoid deportation. UComm never found them. "Even with our larger numbers, this could work again. Everything will be fine."

But Sunny kept pacing, still unconvinced. "You don't know that." Her worry and her anger were tangible things, billowing out around her body.

The Korvenite weaved around and blocked Sunny's path. "You're right. I don't know," he admitted. "But Sunny, these could be all that are left of my species. We have to help them."

Sunny's mouth became thin and petulant. Antur could sense the resistance building up inside her. "No, you don't. I chose you, Tharace, Vycho, Joreis and all the other Korvenites living in Big Victory. After what these Korvenite Independence Front crazies just tried to do, I do not choose those murderers." Her last words harbored a spiteful contempt. "I won't."

You did choose a murderer. Three, in fact, Antur winced, *you just don't remember.*

"Even if I wanted to grant these Korvenites asylum, do you think I'll be alone in my opinion from the other non-Korvenite council members? Or the non-Korvenite citizens?"

Antur could find no plausible comeback for those inquiries, which was all the answer Sunny needed.

"I am sorry, my love," she looked pained and sad, but resolute. "My answer would be the same regardless of their species. I'm doing what's best for Big Victory." She reached for his hands. "Please tell me you understand."

Antur squeezed his eyes shut, fighting back tears. "I understand perfectly." With cat-quick speed he took both sides of Sunny's head in his hands. The Korvenite pushed past the self-loathing, and with his Mindspeak talents plunged into the human's psyche.

Sunny gave a surprised grunt, and her face emptied of all expression. The human woman's eyes glazed over as Antur forced his telepathic will onto her. "This land was ours before it was yours." When Antur opened his eyes, they were blacker than pitch. "No *human* will deny us of it."

Antur pressed in deeper, and Sunny's vacant eyes also turned black. "You will welcome these Korvenites into Big Victory with an open heart and mind. You will refuse them no courtesy. And if anyone protests in this settlement, you will defend these new arrivals wholeheartedly. Big Victory is their home now." Antur breathed in deeply, and his golden irises reappeared.

The Korvenite let both hands fall to his sides and stepped back, hating every aspect of himself for what he had just done.

Today wasn't the first time he'd influenced Sunny. Over the years, Antur could count on one and a half hands the times she'd needed a 'nudge.'

But those 'nudges' were only to ensure that certain mayoral decisions favored the interests of Big Victory's Korvenites. He loved Sunny as she was, not as some brainwashed puppet. Fifteen years ago was the only other time Antur had forcibly changed her mind.

They had just married, with Antur believing Sunny's love to be unconditional. So he had stupidly confessed his role in the Earth Holocaust.

Sunny had replied with disbelief, then horror, followed by an eruption of screams and curses. Antur never forgot the hatred in Sunny's eyes. Nor could he bear sensing as her love for him rapidly evaporated.

So before she told anyone else, Antur had wiped her mind clean of his foolish admission. And suddenly he had won Sunny back—that smile, those adoring eyes, her love.

Antur was drawn back to the present by the sight of Sunny's beady eyes returning to their white sclera and brown iris color. She blinked twice and shook her head, as if waking from a deep slumber.

"You're…right, Ant," the human uttered, her words thick with fatigue. She massaged the bridge of her nose. "These Korvenites deserve a chance."

Antur's stomach twisted and soured. But there was no other choice. "Thank you so much," he whispered, and drew the human into an embrace so she wouldn't see his eyes watering up.

"Anything for you," Sunny kissed Antur's neck. "Don't cry. It's okay. Your brethren are safe now." She gave him an extra squeeze around the waist. A salty flavor filled Antur's mouth. It was all he could do to not vomit.

"I have some work to do still," Antur said once they'd pulled away from each other. "Go back to bed. I'll handle everything else." Those words were spoken with a gentle telepathic nudge.

Immediately, Sunny yawned. "Yeah, I am tired." She leaned in and gave Antur a peck on the lips. "Don't stay up too late."

Antur watched as she walked back into their bedroom, refusing to forgive himself this time. So he would live with his choice, bottle it away and let it sear at his very soul as punishment. But for now, his focus had to remain on protecting the remnant of his species. He reached out to Vycho, still down in the Hub, *Tell Tharace to get the townsfolk ready.*

Did Sunny agree willingly or did you have to convince her? Vycho thought back.

Antur bristled. Tharace would be laughing her head off when she found out. *Does it matter?*

Vycho's remorse tinted his thoughts. *I'm sorry, Antur.*

Antur was in no mood for anyone's pity. *Get those Korvenites in the underground barracks,* the Korvenite snapped. *I don't want them anywhere near the town until we know they're not a threat. I'll come back to the Hub shortly.*

Understood, Vycho replied dutifully. His thoughts receded, leaving Antur alone in his common room.

The elder Korvenite sank into the common room couch, placing his head in his hands. The Korvenite opened himself up to the guilt and the anguish of all that he had done, and the millions who had died thanks to the actions of him and his eleven companions. It didn't take long before his body began shuddering with silent sobs.

When the tears finally stopped, Antur stood up and dried his eyes, whispering a prayer to Korvan, a god whom he stopped believing in years ago. Old habit. The Korvenite then headed back to the Hub.

He had worked to do, for both Big Victory *and* the Korvenite race.

Memoria

For the past week and a half, since the battle for Terra Sollus, a certainty had taken root inside Habraum Nwosu's mind. The Star Brigade Senior Executive Officer hadn't spoken it aloud during the convalescence from his extensive injuries in a Hollus Medcenter bed, or when he had delivered the news to Honaa Ishliba's widow. Even at the funeral ceremony on Rothor IV almost a week ago, Habraum had kept that illumination to himself.

He should have died instead of Honaa Ishliba.

Sleep had been an elusive target the past several nights since Honaa's death. A quick workout made sense to clear his head and take an edge of the grief. Being cleared for light exercises this afternoon had been a blessing from the Twins themselves. As Habraum wore the black body training suit, short-sleeved and fitting a bit loosely due to his recent convalescence, he was hoping to shake off this frightening nihilistic outlook with some target practice.

Hit the target at least fifty times, and get right in the head.

Habraum stood alone across the floating coppery sphere target within the neon blue walls of HLHG Suite 4. Instead of working on his aim, the crimsonborn's thoughts revolved around the borrowed time he continued living on.

He should've been the one to die. Instead, Honaa used his power of intangibility to toss Habraum out of the exploding space station.

Habraum closed his eyes, easily calling to mind every aspect of their first meeting eight years ago. Honaa had been the Star Brigadier who recruited the former AeroFleet pilot with no purpose after the Ferronos Sector War.

"Ssstrategic Assssault & Reconnaisssssance Brigade, Habraum," Honaa had explained to him eight years ago, his smile displaying teeth that resembled daggers, his Ss punctuated with a hiss like all Rothorids. "Star Brigade. We protect the Galactic Union against extraordinary threatsss that most citizensss never know about. And we would love to dissscuss you working with usss."

That memory twisted into Honaa's stoic expression before *Amalgam*'s exploding inferno consumed him whole. Remembering the Rothorid's end sent a cold shiver through him.

Honaa deserved to live out the rest of his days surrounded by the family he loved so much, on the swampy homeworld to which he longed to return. After giving so much to Star Brigade, staying when the going got tough while Habraum fled, Honaa deserved to bow out on his own terms. Instead, the brave Rothorid died saving Habraum's life.

It should have been me, Habraum realized again, tasting bitterness with each word.

At least Honaa's children still had a parent, another voice entreated. If he had died instead, his sweet Jeremy would be an orphan. Honaa knew that, making the guilt of Habraum's survival that much more world-crushing.

On countless Brigade missions, ever since the Ferronos Sector War, he had been cheating death. This brought no relief. Not while other, better sentients kept dying around him.

Habraum raised his fist up and fired off a thick crimson blast—missing the moving target completely. He irately fired with his other arm, still tender from a recent dislocation. The target dodged again.

"FEKT!" His fury soaring, the Cerc unleashed a sweeping backhand arc of concussive force, finally smacking the spherical target to the ground. It bounced away. Habraum stalked it, going no faster than a hurried limp. The sphere attempted to float off the ground.

Habraum angrily pounded it back down with a glowing fist of pure kinetic force. He cried out to the Twins, to the whole universe, caving the sphere in with repeated, savage blows. "WHY?!"

His glowing fists rose and fell, hammering the ruined target into flattened sparking scrap.

He raised his fist again, and something grabbed him by the wrist. Lost in his fury, Habraum twisted free and whirled about with his blazing red fist cocked.

Seeing his 'attacker' then, fury instantly gave way to surprise…and shame.

Marguliese stood before him, golden and statuesque as always, studying him with those emotionless cerulean eyes. The Cybernarr said nothing, nor did she have to.

What the hazik is wrong with me? Pull yourself together! Habraum straightened up with as much dignity as he could muster and shook his arm, sore from the sudden exertion.

"No one saw you," the Cybernarr said flatly, answering the question he had dreaded to ask. Habraum dared a glance up at the walls behind him, the indistinct location of the holovid cameras that broadcast HLHG sessions to the HLHG ObDeck nearby.

Thank the Twins. How could Habraum's subordinates respect him again if they had seen that unripe outburst?

He took fleeting comfort in her unemotional demeanor…and remembered that she would be leaving as well. After how effective Marguliese had been, Habraum didn't want that. However, the Cerc had promised Khrome that she would be gone once this Maelstrom business was finished. Plus, her presence placed the entire Star Brigade at risk should she be exposed.

"I should…get some sleep," Habraum decided. Marguliese made no move to follow him, but he could feel her eyes on his back even after the HLHG Suite doors closed behind him.

Enough of this pity party rubbish. Habraum shook his head to clear it out. Jeremy needed his father, not some bloke bludgeoning himself over what can't be changed. *With Honaa gone and Marguliese departing soon, Star Brigade needs me more than ever.*

So did Sam, his second-in-command…his best friend.

Habraum voiced his frustration with a loud groan and limped into an open translifter booth, hands on his head. What he wouldn't do right now to see Sam's irresistible smile. But that smile had been as absent from Habraum's life as she had been.

On the surface, Sam D'Urso's resolve appeared ironclad. She had helped with Jeremy and keeping Star Brigade steady while Habraum had been convalescing. Sam had even been spending time on Terra Sollus with that Korvenite lass who helped stop Maelstrom. She *seemed* fine…on the surface.

Habraum saw through the visage, recognizing the emptiness in her eyes. But Sam had no interest in his comfort. Since Honaa's demise, Sam had been keeping herself buried in work, shutting everyone out.

According to Solrao, a few nights since Star Brigade had returned from Honaa's funeral, Sam had been leaving Pilot Pub tanked-up. And usually not alone.

If that's how she was coping, then Habraum wouldn't judge. All he wanted was to be there for his friend when the grief became too much. *And it will…*

Just this morning, they had started having breakfast briefings in his office to go over Star Brigade's status. She and Honaa had been doing this for the past year, so Habraum figured it would do well to continue the tradition. He had worn his black and grey Brigade captain's uniform while Sam went casual in a baby blue variant of the kurthon hooded tracksuits she favored. That was as far as Commander D'Urso took her casual air. She barely touched her peach oatmeal, and outside of one question about Jeremy's wellbeing, made no effort to engage him beyond the meeting agenda—very unlike her.

At the meeting's end she rose to leave, her farewell cold, curt and perfunctory.

"Sammie…" Habraum had called out, more from desperation than anything.

Sam gave him an uncomprehending look. "What?" she had snapped after the silence between them stretched on too long.

Thankfully, Habraum had found his voice quickly. "I'm telling you again. I'm not going anywhere." Sam's expression had frosted over into a bloodless mask, giving away nothing. "Whether that's today, tomorrow, next week," he continued, "I'm here when you're ready to talk."

When Habraum finished, a thin, disdainful half-smirk pulled at Sam's lips. She gave a slow shake of the head as if the entreaty amused her before turning and leaving without a word.

Habraum would've been more frustrated if he hadn't been surprised. Sam dealt with personal loss by not dealing with it…until she had no choice. And despite their differences, she did care deeply for Honaa. However, experience had taught Habraum that pushing Sam too much would backfire.

She'll come to me when she's ready, he told himself again as he arrived at his quarters.

The Cerc stepped into his foyer. His plan for the night was to tackle some intelligence report reading and then sleep, until he tasted it. The gloom of his quarters carried a faint fragrance. Vanilla firespice.

Habraum smiled his first genuine smile since seeing Jeremy after the Battle of Terra Sollus. A quick glance confirmed she wasn't in the living room. *Upstairs.* He climbed the stairs, feeling close to a hundred years old when moving as fast as his aching body would allow. The closer he got to his bedroom, the more anxiety poured acid over his excitement. What was she going to say? Would she be angry or sad or just more of what he got this morning? Too many questions. *Best to barrel head-on and not go skittery over it*, he told himself.

Walking slowly down the darkened upstairs hallway, the Cerc stopped instinctively in front of Jeremy's room. He then quickly reminded himself that the boy had been at his grandparents' on Terra Sollus since Habraum returned from Rothor IV. Given how close he had been to the KIF danger, Jennica's parents had wanted to see Jeremy to confirm that he was truly alright (since Habraum's word was clearly not good enough).

He had actually been glad Jeremy spent the past four days with his grandparents. It gave the Cerc time to get his head sorted before resuming his fatherly duties.

He found her on his bed with legs crossed, hands limply on her lap. The dim lighting left her half-shrouded in gloom, but Habraum could make out her black short-shorts and green t-shirt with the university name 'Wellington' inscribed in white lettering across her chest. Her blond mane was pulled back in a high ponytail. She sat perfectly still, gazing blankly at the wall across from the bed.

She didn't react to his arrival or his easing into a seat next to her on the bed. Habraum waited patiently for a response, waiting so long that when she finally spoke, her voice startled him.

"Haven't slept well since Honaa…you know." Sam sounded tired, her voice throatier than normal, lacking any vitality. "Then, tonight I had this dream that I didn't catch you in time when you fell from the *Amalgam*." She shook her head slowly, as if disbelieving the words she uttered. "Felt so real, and you had this calm look on your face...like when you were actually falling...as if you were all too ready to die."

Shame crawled like cold fingers up Habraum's spine. He had willfully forgotten that dishonorable moment, but now it barreled into the forefront of his thoughts.

"So I came over," Sam continued in that low, dead rasp. "But...you were gone, and for a moment...for a moment I thought the dream actually had happened."

The Cerc couldn't forget how she'd rescued him yet again or that fleeting displeasure afterward, knowing he wouldn't be reunited with Jennica. That wish, so selfish in hindsight, had been the only thing keeping the terror at bay when death seemed imminent.

Had Habraum died, Sam would have been the only veteran Brigadier left. Instead, it was just her and him from Star Brigade's previous incarnation. "We're the last of the old guard," he offered quietly.

"I know," she nodded. By the strain on that lovely face, the notion didn't agree with Sam. Habraum's past combat team came to mind unbidden. He cringed away from those thoughts. Maelstrom's manipulation of his guilt over their murders and his wife's demise still hurt too much to think about.

Sam looked up and turned to regard his face. Her russet eyes looked dead, blacker than pitch in the low-lit room. Sam reached out, stroked the side of his face with delicate fingers as if to confirm that he really sat beside her. Her touch sent warm tingles through Habraum from head to heel.

She slapped him.

"Oww. Okay," the Cerc groused, more surprised than stung. So she was angry. *Anger, I can sort.* He turned his head back to her.

She slapped him.

Stars danced before Habraum's eyes, one side of his face burning. Sam moved fast, rolling over and straddling him in one fluid motion. She pinned him down with her hands on his chest and a stare that could've soured fresh water. "If you *ever* give up like that again...I will skin you alive."

"I'll...right, then," the Cerc blurted out, knowing his second-in-command was in no joking mood.

Sam moved to roll off, to flee from him and her anguish.

Habraum grabbed her forearms, holding her in place. Sam fought and writhed and yanked to break free, but Habraum refused to let go. Sam had always been deceptively strong. Had this been right after he'd left the Medcenter a week ago, she might've succeeded. *If I let go, she'll hide behind her walls again.*

"*Stop*," Habraum's voice dominated the room. Sam ceased her struggle, squeezing her eyes shut.

A single tear rolled down her left cheek. She looked barely able to hold the agony at bay. Seeing Sam in pain stabbed through the Cerc's heart. Only alone with Habraum would Sam ever display her wounds. He reached out on instinct, thumbing away her tears gently.

Sam swayed at his touch, and slowly inclined her head toward his. For a searing instant Habraum thought she might kiss him. His body tensed. *Should I stop this or not?*

Instead, she rested her forehead against his and lingered there.

Habraum sighed in quiet relief. They remained like this a long while, eyes closed. He heard the raggedness in her breaths settling now. Sam's nearness, the unnatural warmth of her body soothed away his sorrows. Habraum's heart pounded, his hands slipped unbidden along her sumptuous waist and hips. The blissful scent of her vanilla firespice fragrance flooded his nostrils in disquieting ways. It would be so easy to pull her in and—

No, Habraum turned his head, cursing his own weakness. *Not when we're so raw.* The thought of Jennica and the ugly mockery Maelstrom made of her memory intensified his guilt even more.

Sam didn't seem to notice. She melted atop him and slid both arms around his waist, nuzzling her face against his neck. Habraum gathered Sam up in his arms, and she gave a little moan.

"You disappeared on me last week," he whispered.

"I know. Sorry."

"I'm sorry too," Habraum whispered again.

"I know." Sam brushed her lips by his ear, sending another jolt through him. "You feel like home," her murmur was thick with longing. She kissed his throat softly and the strength seemed to go out of her. Soon Habraum heard gentle snoring.

Habraum let his cheek rest against hers, feeling the world fade away…and woke up abruptly.

He didn't know whether it was Sam's balmy warmth on top of him or her increasingly loud snores. They'd both been out for a few orvs, just enough to restore his clarity.

And now that she was here, Habraum recalled what they both needed to do still. For Honaa.

"Sammie," he murmured in her ear, squeezing her arm for extra emphasis.

Sam stirred at the sound of his voice. "Mmmmm…" Then she went still.

Habraum shook her again by the shoulders. "Samantha," he said right in her ear.

"Whaaat?" She jerked her head up, leveling a drowsy-eyed glare at him.

"We need to go pay our respects."

That woke Sam up. "I'm not ready." Her abrupt tone permitted no further discussion.

"Nor am I," sighed Habraum, expecting this reaction. "We have to."

Sam jerked back into a straddled position. "Habraum—" she warned.

"Samantha," Habraum overrode her tantrum, barely raising his voice. "We still have to."

Five macroms and a brief squabble later, Habraum and Sam stood side by side inside a translifter briskly weaving its way down and right and diagonally toward their destination.

Neither said a word during the entire ride. The Cerc's stomach was in a tight, uncomfortable knot, just like the last time he'd come down to give tribute to the other teammates and friends he had lost over a year ago. Habraum sure as *hazik* didn't want to go there, but it had to be done. This was the tradition for any Star Brigadier killed in combat.

He stole a glance at Sam. She glared straight ahead, lost in her own separate pain.

Before Habraum knew it, the translifter stopped, its doors hissing open. They had arrived.

He clutched for Sam's hand tightly, not so much to keep her from bolting but to fortify his own resolve. Ripping open a still fresh wound was not on Habraum's list of enjoyables. Sam gave his hand a squeeze. Suddenly Habraum felt a rush of courage that forced his legs forward.

The Memorial Hall loomed imperiously before them. Habraum wasted no time standing in front of it, hesitating and contemplating. He steeled himself against the expected waves of pain and led Sam forward. The doors slid open, and halolights switched on.

They were all there: close to a hundred or more Star Brigadiers dating back to Leonardo Osawa of the first Star Brigade combat team twenty-seven years ago. More recent additions, the eleven murdered last year on Beridaas stood in the forefront. The tenures of every Star Brigadier was recorded in Star Brigade archives. Only those active Brigadiers killed in combat were immortalized via 3D holograms in the Memorial Hall, as well as the Remembrance Wall outside Star Brigade's Command Center.

The knots in Habraum's stomach tightened to the point of nausea. Visiting the Memorial Hall before to honor the teammates he'd lost over a year ago, that had been a slow-roasting hell. Having to do the same with Honaa Ishliba felt worse.

A single silvery empty platform was situated in a clearing amidst these life-sized holos.

Habraum released Sam's hand and limped forward through the holos, fiddling for the datacard in his pocket. He focused on that platform. Something in Habraum would break if he stopped to behold Jovian or Ariel or Dr. Pel or any of his old team.

All the holograms of dead Brigadiers were silent specters as he slid a small, razor-thin datacard into a slot at the base of the circular platform.

"Activate," the Cerc whispered and backpedaled to Sam's side, wincing at his own haste to distance himself from these ghosts.

An instant later, Honaa Ishliba's life-sized holo blossomed into being. The height, the sinewy build and maroon scales, the tail length and thickness, even the cutting amber eyes were immaculate.

Habraum's breath caught, convinced in a moment of deluded grief it was actually the Rothorid.

He knew better. On command, the holo could speak or produce a data scroll of Honaa's career with Star Brigade, his whole life in fact, as well as how he died.

But it would never be Honaa.

"Let's do this," the Cerc muttered. Together with Sam, he began the words recited for any Brigadier entered into Memorial Hall: "Captain Honaa Ishliba, you fought with courage. You fought with merit. You gave your all in the name of Star Brigade and the Galactic Union. Your sacrifice will never be forgotten, Star Brigadier." *The epitaph I should've given my old teammates.*

They finished and the room answered with tomb-like silence. The knots inside loosened just enough, and Habraum could breathe again. He watched Honaa's holo, foolishly hoping against hope it could speak Honaa's words, give Honaa's guidance.

Nothing. All Habraum had now besides this life-sized holo were his own memories and years of the Rothorid's holorecords. *Not enough*, he thought bitterly. That would never be enough.

A sharp intake of breath pulled Habraum from his inner perdition. He turned to see Sam squeezing her eyes shut, quivering like a leaf, fighting with all her strength to hold it together.

Habraum's heart ached for her. He placed a hand on the small of her back, stroking up and down. "It's alright, Sammie," he said softly. "It's alright. Let it out."

After a long moment she finally did, turning and collapsing into Habraum's waiting arms. In the privacy of the Memorial Hall, Sam D'Urso began sobbing. She buried her face in Habraum's chest, streams of tears saturating his shirt. The desperate way she'd held onto his waist felt as if Sam was terrified to let Habraum go. He tenderly kissed the crown of her head to reassure her otherwise.

Habraum recalled Honaa's last words, as if the hologram was speaking to him. "Lead them well."

I will, Honaa. Fresh tears began to blur Habraum's vision. Another sob shuddered through Sam's body. The Cerc held her closer. *I promise.*

Gifted

Kasiaph had never stayed in a Medcenter recovery room before.

Then again, he'd never purposely plunged a spreader knife through his lower left arm before either.

By now, the nine-year old Nnaxan and his family should have arrived at Hyperion Interplanetary Spaceport on Terra Sollus.

Instead Kasiaph was still on Terra Gima, in East Poston city-state to be exact. The Nnaxan sat glumly on the bed of a recovery room in a fourth-rate medcenter, the closest his family could find. His lemony complexion was pale from blood loss, his still-growing craniowhisks limp. The sight of where he'd stabbed his lower right forearm was now just a dark, fading bruise. Three small square holoscreens floated like disembodied ghosts around his bed: one monitoring cardiac rhythm and blood pressure, another observing respiratory function, the third neurological function.

Kasiaph bristled at the latter holoscreen. He was *not* crazy. At least…he didn't think so.

Rhyne's morning light, partially shrouded by clouds, streaked through the viewport and gave the room a lukewarm glow. "I'm in big trouble such," the Nnaxan boy muttered under his breath.

The boy knew this by how his paternal's long and thick craniowhisks had gone rigid with anger. The way his maternal just glared at him from across the room, eyes full of such disappointment. Her own craniowhisks hung limp with sorrow, all four arms wrapped fretfully around her slender, cobalt blue-skinned frame.

Kasiaph stared out the window at the crisscrosses of hovercar traffic passing near downtown East Poston's anemic skyline. He thought of his older sisters Kaccia and Kecienne. They would have murdered him damn near if his paternals hadn't kept them at home. Kasiaph couldn't fault them for that. As it was, the air in the recovery room was thick with fury and resentment.

But the Nnaxan youngster had thought long about what he had done, and the havoc his actions had wreaked on his family.

The pain had exploded straight up Kasiaph's arm, through his craniowhisks, and needled into his brain, making his knees give out. He stayed conscious, barely. Blood squirted everywhere, painting the family living room floor with splatters of rusty orange.

Still, Kasiaph believed he had done the right thing.

I have no choice, was the single-minded thought that had driven his gory actions.

"Matee, Patee," Kasiaph implored his paternals. "I'm sorry." Actually, the boy lied. He felt no sorrow for making his family miss the event, just for the dismay this caused them.

Kasiaph's father leveled a hateful glare at him, seeing through the lie. "No you're not," he snarled.

Matee gaped, her braided craniowhisks unraveling in surprise. "Louruus!" she chided her husband.

But Kasiaph's paternal would not contain his fury. "A once-in-a-lifetime opportunity!" Patee's dark grey complexion was actually turning a shade darker in anger. "I paid a small fortune for those tickets! And you *ruined* it for your family! Why?! Just to get attention *more!*"

As expected, his maternal shrank before Patee's towering anger. But for the first time, Kasiaph did not. Rage blossomed inside him like wildfire. He never asked for these visions. The least the Nnaxan could do with them was save his family. "But if we went to Terra Sollus we would die!"

"*No one would have died!*" Patee roared so loudly, Kasiaph felt the vibrations through his craniowhisks. "Spare me your false predictions!" His paternal spun around, craniowhisks rigid so much they barely even moved as he stormed out of the room—leaving Kasiaph and his maternal to stare uncomfortably at each other.

The boy turned again to the viewport, his lip quivering. Somehow he kept himself from crying. No way would Kasiaph let anyone see him cry, not when he was half grown. But his eyes stung, blurring East Poston and its traffic. Kasiaph knew how much his paternal had spent on those family pack tickets to Terra Sollus for the Union-Imperium trade merger celebration.

But Kasiaph could not have cared less about who was merging. As much as his paternal's anger stung, the Nnaxan boy was grateful just to have his family all alive and safe still.

If his family had travelled to Terra Sollus as planned, they all would have died.

The reminder shook Kasiaph to his core, and suddenly the memories burst through his mind.

For a month Kasiaph started seeing his family in these dreams—no, *nightmares*—that had been plaguing him.

....He and his family on Terra Sollus, watching the Kedri Sovereign and the Union Chouncilor finalize their historic trade deal... heat from Terra Sollus's sun Rhyne beating down on him....

...then, a massive station blotted out the sun, spitting jets of heavenly fire down onto the crowds...

... screams of terror in far too many dialects to count, the nauseating smells of living flesh burning...

...before he too was consumed by the flames, Kasiaph watched his family burning and screaming as white-hot fire reduced them to ash...

At first, Kasiaph thought these were just bad dreams. But every night, dreaming the same dream, seeing the same horror, dying the same way...it never once deviated.

The only aspect that kept changing for Kasiaph was remembering more details each time he woke up—like the region of Conuropolis' Diktat District, between downtown and Earthtown, where heavenly fire had incinerated his family. That location was displayed big and boldly on the event tickets his paternal had bought. The fancy clothing his maternal had bought for the Trade Merger event not two weeks ago? The very clothes they and his siblings wore in the dream.

The final detail that pushed him over the edge was when a first look at the joint Galactic Union/Kedri Imperium space station was unveiled on a holoview military channel a week ago—matching the silhouette of the very same station in Kasiaph's dreams that would slaughter millions.

Waves of fear threatened to drown the boy since then. Kasiaph never believed really in the silly creed of his paternities, the Church of the Holy Gemini, but maybe he should now.

Kasiaph had warned his family everything about these bad dreams every day for a week.

No one believed him.

His paternities wrote it off as his imagination running wild, while Kaccia and Kecienne ridiculed of him relentlessly.

Telling anyone at school was out of the question. Most kids at school actually envied Kasiaph for being able to go. Plus, his family had moved to Terra Gima from the Nnaxan homeworld Hommodus less than three months ago. Kasiaph had just started making friends. No need to be called 'crazy boy.'

"The Kedri Sovereign will be there with a small contingent of his army and advisors," his paternal had said last night after Kasiaph pleaded for them not to go. But his patience was waning visibly. "Same with the Chouncilor. He'll have his Honor Guard plus the might of the UComm Armada. Conuropolis will be the safest place in the known galaxy. Now stop this nonsense before I get angry."

That should have made Kasiaph feel better much. But last night's dreams were so real—the death cries from the crowd as the fire from heaven took them, smelling the flesh burn off his paternities and sisters, the blinding flash of light from above before his own end was upon him—Kasiaph had woken up shrieking at the top of his lungs.

So this morning, as Kasiaph and his family had prepared to leave…and meet their end…the scared boy had taken action—and jammed a butter knife through his lower right forearm.

Thank the Gemini their dwelling sat near a short-range transmatter hub or…let's just say Kasiaph might not have made it to the Medcenter.

The Nnaxan child was drawn back into the present by the sound of his maternal's irritated bleating. She defended Patee, of course. She took his side *always*, no matter how wrong he was. "You do this to everyone, how? You know your Patee and siblings were looking forward to this, much!"

His maternal kept blathering on. Kasiaph ignored her, but not out of spite. A hush had fallen over the bustle outside his recovery room, the only sound being news streamcaster voices in various dialects blaring on top of one another in a smearing roar.

Matee was still yapping her mouth off when Kasiaph's paternal reentered the room, his face painting a picture of horror. His craniowhisks trembled in fearful little ripples, all four arms hanging at his sides like dead things.

Kasiaph knew something was off. He had never seen his paternal this scared, even after the spreader knife incident this morning.

"Patee?" the boy asked. His paternal turned to his young son and stared.

The mix of disbelief and fear and regret in his almond-shaped orange eyes told Kasiaph everything.

"Matee, can you please turn on the HV?" the Nnaxan boy asked, a chill flooding every part of him.

"Why?" Matee asked, swiveling back and forth between the two males, her limp craniowhisks whipping about. "What's—"

"Iobe, do it just!" Kasiaph's paternal barked.

Somehow Kasiaph already knew what the holoview would show him. His maternal griped to an audience consisting of herself before uttering a few commands for a holoview screen.

A large 67-inch holoscreen appeared out of thin air in front of the boy—presenting a collage of horrific destruction.

The massive station thought to be a symbol of unity between the Galactic Union and the Kedri Imperium blotted out the sky, raining down white-hot fire onto Conuropolis, the capital city-state's most majestic buildings that scraped the stars imploding before the barrage. Massive Korvenite statues that once stood as silent, majestic guardians at the borders of Conuropolis now animated and stomping through the streets of their patron city-state with nihilistic abandon; the abnormal, seemingly impenetrable golden forcefield covering Conuropolis. Clearly the Kedri weren't behind the attack, as the news stream footage effusively showed their warships viciously firing on the forcefield alongside UComm vessels. One stretch of footage highlighted the far-flung civilian section where Kasiaph and his family would have sat to watch the event on massive skyview screens.

The section, meant to hold at least 300,000 occupants, had been scorched black by torrents of energy from the renegade space station. Not even skeletons remained of the corpses on the scalded earth.

Sobs and gasps erupted then outside of Kasiaph's room. Doctors and nurses along with patients and their loved ones were all watching floating holoscreens in Medcenter recovery rooms and hallways that showcased the devastation on Terra Sollus. Everyone was digesting the horror of the terrorist attack on the Union capital world in varying degrees.

Tears trickled down Matee's face as her whole body shook with sobs. Kasiaph could not take any of it, squeezing his eyes shut and covering his earholes. *I was right.* But the validation left Kasiaph so drained and sad. "I should have said something. I could have prevented—"

"NO," Patee cut him off. All of a sudden, the firm pressure of four burly arms had wreathed around Kasiaph's little frame, causing his eyes to snap open in surprise.

"My sorrows, child! My sorrows!" his paternal pleaded, enveloping his son with a firm hug.

Kasiaph rarely saw such emotion from his paternal, which made his apology hit that much harder. He gripped his father desperately and soon his maternal as she joined in on the hug.

"What do we do now?" the boy asked, a tremor of fear making his voice crack.

Kasiaph's paternities said nothing, answering only by embracing their son tighter.

Over the next several days, the only thing on the news streams and the holoview entertainment channels was nonstop coverage of the attack on Conuropolis.

More and more information emerged. A group of Korvenite fundamentalists were behind the attack, many of them captured or killed. But the damage had been done, both literally and politically.

Most of downtown Conuropolis, the Diktat District in particular, was destroyed. The death toll had climbed into the millions. Both Union and Imperium governments had been humiliated by this breach in security. But the news that hit like a megaton explosion had to be the Kedri had withdrawn from the Trade Merger and was closing their borders to the Union for the foreseeable future.

What did this mean to nine-year-old Kasiaph, who had seen this devastation all coming?

First off, his family totally forgave him. The news streams hammered home their potential fate with graphic footage of the smoldering hulks of wreckage that was the Galactic Union's greatest city-state. All that death and destruction left Kasiaph's maternal a bawling mess. His sisters weren't much better.

Secondly, the dreams of a ruined Conuropolis had finally stopped. Kasiaph's slumber was dreamless for the first time in over a month.

Thirdly, Kasiaph's paternities took him to get tested. Blood tests, psychological tests, physical tests, any test that could determine the cause of his prophetic dreams.

His paternities insisted on heading back to the Medcenter for a battery of tests the day after the Conuropolis attack. Kasiaph fought with all his heart to stay numb throughout this whole period. Too overwhelmed to shout or cry or scream angrily, he went along with everything asked of him. Any action that required more mental energy and the young boy felt like his head might explode.

After the third day of tests, Kasiaph's doctor found something in his blood—which had never been identified because they weren't looking for it. This newly-discovered chemical had been causing his dreams, a neurotransmitter found in a small but growing percentage of Union citizens with abilities beyond those of normal sentient beings. The neurotransmitter offered understandable variances depending on the species, but the common name is 'xenotrophin.'

"Our son is a…*maximum?*" Patee asked their doctor in mild horror.

"Don't worry," the elder doctor reassured them. His craniowhisks and gestures were calm and loose with poise, unlike the rigid twitching of Kasiaph and his paternities. "Whatever your son can do is not a danger to himself or you, as far as we've seen."

"What can we do to find out more about…what he can do?" Matee asked, her words dipped in dread.

"Well," the doctor answered calmly. "It's good that we have spotted this when his abilities manifested just. But, I would recommend a visit to the Section M office in Poston."

All he got in return were blank stares. "Er…what is a Section M?" a befuddled Kasiaph inquired.

Section M, according to his doctor, was the Galactic Union's government agency that handled maximum affairs. Giving the growing number of beings with maximal abilities, there was now at least one Section

M branch on every single Union memberworld. "Registering known maximums, helping them cope with their abilities, providing training for maximums with issues controlling their abilities. They are the experts on all things maximum-related," their doctor hashed out. He smiled affably at Kasiaph. "I think you might benefit from this, youngling."

At first, Kasiaph's paternities were hesitant about this Section M. The boy had no objection to meeting with this agency, if they could help about his dreams. "I might not be a maximum even, Matee," Kasiaph tried to reassure her on the ride back home, which had the opposite effect.

Their doctor took care of the appointment for the next day and sent all types of information into Patee's data spectacles about this Section M agency.

Bright and early the next morning, Kasiaph left with his paternities on a twenty-macrom shuttle ride to East Poston's grander, prettier, sister city-state. The Section M office in downtown Poston was not a large building, but Kasiaph thought its hexagon structure was nice-looking from the air.

After a five-macrom wait in the building's angular and pointy lobby, a rather stern Galdorian with his eyestalks bobbing up and down approached and led the Nnaxan family to a translifter. Kasiaph forgot the Galdorian's name right after he announced it. Big surprise, since the moniker was overly Galdorian—in short, hard to pronounce—and began with 'H.'

"You have nothing to worry about when it comes to your son," the Galdorian assured them in flawless Standard dialect. The translifter zoomed up a few floors and then zipped sideways to the left. "Helping maximums adjust to society at large is our specialty."

Patee and Matee looked less than satisfied, their craniowhisks twitching nervously. Kasiaph couldn't help but mirror their actions and feelings. "I read somewhere that Section M had some corruption problems a year prior," his paternal offered in fluent but rigid Standard. "What happened?"

The Galdorian frosted over. "Management restructuring," he offered cryptically.

As soon as they got off the translifter, Patee and Matee were ushered into a fancy, hi-tech looking office. Meanwhile, Kasiaph waited outside on a bench in an obsidian-glossy corridor. For a number of macroms, he just sat steeped in worries and fears that had been planted on the shuttle ride to Poston.

What if they take me away from my family?

What if they dissect me to see how my powers work?

What if I'm not a maximum?

When will the next 'dream' happen?

"Hi-hi! You must be Kasiaph," called a chipper, girly human voice from his right, interrupting his paranoid musings. The Nnaxan turned to see a short human female heading his way. She had a surprisingly fleet-footed gait for someone so plump and compact. Kasiaph could tell she was most likely earthborn human. There were no garish pastel colors in the roots of her evenly bob-cut brownish hair, and her beady, almond-shaped black eyes didn't glitter like minerals. Plus, her skin had a peaches-and-cream color to it.

"Yea?" Kasiaph replied in Standard dialect.

This human, practically bouncing on her flat heels with excessive glee, primly adjusted her formfitting grey dress suit as she sat down next to Kasiaph. "My name's Cameron Song," she continued, a megawatt smile in her already chipper voice. "How *are* you?"

The Nnaxan shrugged, taken aback by the human's cheeriness. "Fine, I guess." Close up, Cameron's elfin features looked like a mix of human subspecies, typical of earthborn and Martianborn humans. Kasiaph could tell by the subtle creases around her eyes and forehead that she was older than she looked, but his paternities told him it was rude to ask a female's age. "Are you a maximum?" he asked instead.

Cameron shook her head. "Nope. Just a regular baseline human."

"Do you work for Section M?"

"Yep, I do," Cameron nodded so eagerly her double chin jiggled like that human dessert gelatin. "By the way, I just met your parent—sorry, Nnaxans say 'paternities,' yes?"

Kasiaph nodded indifferently. *Does that matter?* "Yea."

"Okay. Anyway, just met your *paternities*," Cameron looked so pleased, her eyes sparkled with barely contained delight. "They're great. Very worried, but really great."

Kasiaph pictured his doubting paternal's fury as clear as a holoimage on a wall. And the maternal who wouldn't side against her partner, puncturing her son's heart again. Kasiaph shrugged. "I guess so."

"I got an idea," Cameron exclaimed, as if it were the best idea any being had ever conceived. She fingered her choker of thick pearls. "Let's you and I go for a walk."

They both rose from the bench, and Kasiaph was struck anew by how *not* tall this human woman was, standing barely half a foot taller than him.

Outside was overcast, but with golden shafts of sunlight piercing through the grey gloom sporadically. They strolled through the labyrinthine gardens in the complex's northern wing, a crimson-leaved sprawl. Cameron, seeing the boy's bewildered interest, stated that most of the garden's plant life came straight from the isles of the oceanic colony world Mekaal. During their walk, the human woman did most of the talking; being born and raised on Terra Sollus by a father from San Andreas in Western Vesspuccia and a mother from the Asian nation of Sino-Formosa; using her mother's maiden name instead of her father's due to him being well known in government circles; revealing her experiences working with maximum children.

Cameron seemed overly nice, to the point of phoniness. Regardless, Kasiaph offered her as much information about himself as he felt comfortable with when she asked him questions; talking about his family, the tough transition of moving from the volcanic Hommodus to the rather flat agribiz world Terra Gima. It shocked him how Cameron avoided any mention about his incident, so the boy didn't bring it up. *She thinks my doctor was wrong, maybe.* Hopefully. Kasiaph really wanted to return to Terra Gima. The boy was also surprised to see so many beings of all ages and species roaming through the gardens; an elderly human male, clearly a stormborn human by his shock of white hair with rusty orange roots, jogged by. A young Kheldoroshii crawled by on all its limbs like a caterpillar with its Galdorian chaperone.

"This Section M Center also serves as a living facility to those maximums who might consider themselves a danger to society until they get their abilities under control," Cameron explained to Kasiaph.

Seeing so many facility residents, all with chaperones of differing species, sat in the Nnaxan's stomach like spoiled food. *Could this happen to me?*

Kasiaph then noticed another pattern. Every chaperone they passed always acknowledged Cameron Song with distinct reverence...sometimes a touch of fear even. And she always greeted each sentient by name with her huge smile. The Nnaxan boy regarded her with renewed caution. This Cameron Song female was a big deal unmistakably around Section M.

About twenty macroms into the walk, Kasiaph found that he had run out of things to say. So he stopped talking. Cameron quickly filled the silence. "So when I spoke with your paternities…they told me about your 'dreams.'"

The way Cameron said 'dreams' with that happy-bubbly voice sounded mocking. The boy felt his craniowhisks stiffening. "Yeah?" he answered defensively, stopping in his tracks.

"What do *you* think they were?" the human asked curiously.

"I care not if you think I'm making my dreams up—" The Nnaxan's fatigue and frustration burst to the surface in an ugly eruption.

"No, no! I believe you, Kasiaph," Cameron held up both hands beseechingly, her voice still irritatingly cheerful. "Your dreams are actually called *precognition*, the ability to see the future."

Hearing this, Kasiaph unwound a bit. His craniowhisks drooped, but remained a bit tense. "Can all maximums do that?" he asked.

Cameron shook her head, causing a few stray locks of hair to fall past her round cheeks. "Not everyone. The abilities depend on the sentient…even the species."

"Well, precognition sucks!" Kasiaph spat, kicking out a foot in anger. His craniowhisks went so stiff with anger they throbbed. "I *want* not to see the future! I want to scare my family no more!" The boy folded his upper and lower arms angrily over his chest and stomach respectively.

Cameron stood stock-still, absorbing his tantrum without flinching. Only after he huffed out most of his fury did the human female speak again. "Kasiaph, your family is alive," she soothed, taking his lower set of hands into her own single pair. Cameron's voice sobered, but hadn't lost its soothing silkiness. "You saved them. *You*, because of your abilities. Being a maximum doesn't make you a freak. It means that you're gifted." She squeezed his hands.

Without thinking, Kasiaph squeezed back. "I know these abilities are hard to handle," she continued. "But with Section M's help…and my help…you can control them and maybe save more people. Do you want that?"

The Nnaxan nodded, wanting more than anything in the universe to feel normal again.

Cameron smiled broadly. "Me, too. I think you and I are going to become good friends."

Kasiaph looked up to her. Something about her made him feel so safe. Rhyne finally burned away most of the murky overcast, casting its warm rays across the garden. "I'd like that, Cameron." For the first time in weeks, Kasiaph smiled.

"Let's go back and discuss your future with your paternities." Cameron grasped the boy's upper left hand with her one right hand and led him back toward the building, leaving all of Kasiaph's worries and fears behind in that garden.

Reunion

"Apparently *everybody's* got a space rocket in their pants for Star Brigade now."

From the sourness in Sam D'Urso's words, Habraum Nwosu could picture his second-in-command's appalled expression over their audio-only transmission.

He would've shrugged at her colorful word choice, if not currently doing a handstand in the middle of his common room, both legs pointed straight up. Each of the Cerc's hands gripped an antigrav balance ball, small and gunmetal colored, both floating three feet off the ground. Rivulets of sweat beaded down his shirtless torso and black trunks.

"And our new fanfare bothers you because?" Habraum grunted, slowly dipping his strapping six-foot-five-inch frame down until his face and clenched hands were level. Every muscle in the Cerc's body trembled from the exertion. It felt wonderful, as did being back in sync with Sam on a friendship level and professional level.

"Not three months ago, almost all these agencies *and* UComm were ready to write us off," Sam scoffed as if the answer was obvious.

"That was three months ago. From what Hollienurax told us, we are UComm's most valuable asset for the moment. Let's forge quality alliances instead of nursing old grudges." Habraum's recently healed shoulder ached, plus his lower back and right leg throbbed in protest. He ignored the pains, holding his handstand another three nanoclics. The handstand pushups were an improvement from last week, but the Cerc hadn't completely recovered from Maelstrom's handiwork on him—physically or emotionally.

"Yeah, yeah," Sam agreed with less tartness. "Who do you wanna partner with first, flyboy?"

The Cerc already had an answer as he pressed upward for the twentieth rep in his fifth set of handstand pushups. "Whichever agency's running an active op against the Children of Earth." He harbored a special loathing for the human supremacist group after their brazen Corowood Zoo attack, which put both Jeremy and Sam in peril. If not for the Korvenite Independence Front threat, Habraum would have focused Star Brigade on that vile group months ago.

"My thoughts exactly," Sam agreed with a bite of anger. "I want to find every one of those xenophobes so I can personally roast their goddamn skins off."

Habraum made a face, unsure if he was more enthused or scared by Sam's ruthless vow. "Probably shouldn't phrase our request like that," the Cerc quipped, and lowered his now trembling frame down for another rep. Until a severe ache flared up through his lower back and right leg, making his vertical posture wobble dangerously. Habraum accepted his current physical limits with a growling curse and drew himself into a crunch position.

"You alright, chief?" Sam asked. "Sounds like a starship died over there."

The Cerc winced as he gingerly landed on his feet again. "I'm taking advantage of Cortés clearing me for advanced PT and light hand-to-hand training."

"FINALLY," Sam exclaimed.

Habraum snorted. "You and me both." Spending extra time with Jeremy these past few weeks had been a blessing, but the sooner Habraum could return to field-active shape, the better. His need to get back in the field was a thirst that couldn't be substituted by just working on his target practice.

"In that case," Sam purred, "swing by my place before dinner tonight for a few warm-up drills…if you're up for it."

The challenge in her low, husky tones sent a jolt through Habraum. He shook it off with a chuckle. "I'll keep that in mind."

"Alright, back to adventures in parenting." She would have been present for their daily morning briefing, but was still settling into a routine with Tharydane.

Samantha D'Urso, a mother. *Knew you had it in you.* Habraum kept the boast to himself with a smirk, knowing how much she 'loved' him proving her wrong.

"Bye, goldilocks." Habraum ended the transmission, toweling the sweat off his face and bald head.

Within moments, another transmission chirped on Habraum's personal line from Pilot Pub.

Habraum scratched at his trimmed goatee, feeling a familiar disquiet. There was but one reason the pilot-themed bar was ringing him—again.

"This is Nwosu," he answered stiffly, bracing himself for a new tale of another Solrao drinking bender.

"Braum!" Solrao's drowsy drawl filled the common room, completely sober.

The Star Brigadier cracked a smile. "Solrao! Howzabeen?"

"Every day's a gift," was the Ibrisian's blithe reply.

That amused Habraum. "How very illuminated of you."

"Free for lunch today at Pilot Pub?"

Having no set meetings during that time, Habraum planned to work through lunch. But he always had time for one of his old fighter pilot mates. "Sure. Midday works best."

"Luminal! See you then." The transmission ended, leaving Habraum pondering the lunch's purpose. Maybe Solrao wanted to discuss getting back on as a copilot for Brigade field missions. *Here's to hoping*, the Cerc mused as he stretched his sore shoulders.

After a quick breakfast and hydrobathe, the Cerc's day moved with insane briskness. Habraum oversaw the SB-1 training session in HLHG Suite 2, but didn't participate. That was followed by a UIB holoconference discussion over tracking down the Korvenite warship *The Libremancer*, still at large after the Battle of Terra Sollus. Next up came a target practice session back in HLHG 2 with Tyris, Sam and the Voton rookie Surje.

Before Habraum knew it, lunchtime had arrived. He made his way down to the small pilot-themed bar named Pilot Pub on the lower levels of Hollus Maddrone starbase. Pilot Pub was every bit the dank and dimly lit watering hole its name implied. Currently, the Pilot Pub's array of tables and booths were mostly empty, though the sight of patrons already tossing back drinks this early didn't shock Habraum. The Nnaxan barkeep behind the serving table gave him a welcoming head nod.

"Heya!" The Cerc turned at the sound of Solrao's voice. The rangy Ibrisian loped up, grinning broadly. Her segmented, ocher skin was pronounced in the dim lighting, as did the many blood-red concentric rings in her colorless eyes.

"Hi Sollie." The two friends embraced, and Habraum's nose wrinkled. Midday and already Solrao reeked like a distillery. "What's this about?"

When they pulled apart, the Ibrisian deliberately avoided his critical glare. "Follow me." Her hand, with its three fingers and two opposable thumbs, grabbed Habraum's and led him to the back of the bar.

They reached a private room, with far better lighting than the rest of the bar, and stepped inside.

The black-hued room had a wall stocked with various alien liquors and a small round table with four seats. Two seats were already taken.

One occupant, a human about as tall as Habraum, rose from his seat. By his violet eyes and smooth dark-honey skin, he was clearly crimsonborn, with square-jawed features and wavy chocolate brown hair. The other being, a Kheldoroshii, sported an exoskeleton and rear carapace with muddy green coloring. When Habraum entered the room, his two enormous cherry-red eyes lit up.

Habraum's heart leaped into his throat. "Rukk! Fll'gwl!"

"Glad that you're upright, Braum," Rukk Rigeff marched up and pulled his childhood friend into a fierce bear hug.

After that, Habraum turned to embrace Xo Fll'gwl as the Kheldoroshii got up on his eight hind legs. "We wanted to check in," Fll'gwl's shrill chirruping voice needed an attentive ear when speaking Standard, like with most Kheldoroshii, "so Sollie set it all up."

"This is a proper surprise," the Star Brigadier eyed Solrao, more thankful than he could express. By the smile tugging at the Ibrisian's white lips and how the limbal rings in her irises grew wider, she definitely understood.

Solrao rounded the table and snatched up a nice slim bottle of shireport. "Hope you're not too busy for a long lunch today." She shook the bottle like one would a bag of jewels.

"I'm the boss, so I'll make the time," Habraum quipped, drawing laughs from his former AeroFleet mates. He'd purposely kept today's post-lunch schedule clear. Unless some major crisis arose, the Cerc intended to spend the rest of the day with Jeremy when the boy's school transport returned late afternoon.

The door into the private room closed and Habraum eased himself into a seat as his three other friends did the same. Food came courtesy of Pilot Pub's floating server mech: frosted tulips and pollen- coated pine bark were served for Fll'gwl while Habraum, Rukk and Solrao devoured healthy servings of yosk steaks with Galdorian sponge dough bread.

The wine started flowing, which got the four friends reminiscing. As if by some unwritten rule, no discussion of the Union's failed Trade Merger with the Kedri or the Chouncilor resigning ever came up. The quartet's conversations were dominated by war stories and pranks from their shared youth as SACOS fighter pilots. Rukk was the life of the gathering, as always. Solrao, when not detailing her many pranks pulled on their superiors, was giggling so hard, shireport came snorting out of her nose. Fll'gwl, though not as extroverted, made sure to correct his friends if some random fact was erroneous.

Eight years since they'd served together in AeroFleet melted away, with Habraum's laughter coming more freely and more frequent over the course of their two-orv lunch. By the end, he couldn't remember the last time he had eaten so well or enjoyed himself so much. It was exactly what he had needed.

Once he'd thanked Solrao, the Cerc saw Fll'gwl and Rukk off at one of Hollus's hangar bays. The walk back to his office came with a less noticeable limp. He even found enjoyment in manipulating a fifty-inch holoscreen displaying training footage of the Brigadiers.

A chime briefly interrupted the mundane task. "Enter."

His visitor was Khrome. The burly and squat Thulican lieutenant with silvery metallic skin shuffled into the room.

"What's new, Khromulus?" he glanced at his SB-1 tech, surprised at the unusual seriousness ruling the Thulican's deep blue face—the type of serious that promised unpleasant news.

"I found something," the Thulican announced, his digitized tone cryptic, "updating the Star Brigade dossier like you asked, in the strike file of Addison Raichoudry."

"Raichoudry?" Habraum recognized the name, but kept his gaze on the holoscreen before him and pulled up training footage for a Voton Brigadier. "The rookie who went batty and washed out, yea?"

Sorrow filled the Thulican's rounded yellow eyes, so expressive despite lacking pupils or irises, making Habraum regret his rash assessment.

"Right," the Thulican folded his burly arms. "I found an encryption in Addison's file that can only be opened by a Brigadier of captain rank or higher. It was created three days before the meltdown that led to her resignation."

Habraum cocked an eyebrow, curiosity piqued. "Which officer added the encryption?"

"Captain Jovian Ivers."

The name made the Cerc flinch, like hot coals pressed against his chest. Flashes of slain Brigadiers filled his vision, their maimed bodies strewn in every direction across Beridaas's charred plains. In a heartbeat, the memory obliterated Habraum's happiness from moments ago. He turned around slowly to meet Khrome's gaze, remembering.

Addison Raichoudry, a human maximum teleporter and topnotch shriker from Gavron Colony, the last of Ivers's young female protégés. Back then her resignation over beating some Galdorian analyst bloody had been a small blip on Habraum's radar. Still, the Cerc recalled how surprised he and others had been by Ivers's indifference to his apprentice's ousting.

A few months before Beridaas, Habraum realized. The odd timing grabbed his undivided attention. "Continue," he urged Khrome after a long moment of silence.

"I wouldn't have even detected the encryption, which I'm guessing was the point. But I noticed a minor error in Addison's file and tried to fix it. And a captain-level encryption came up. Now, I could just bust it wide open." Khrome's cocksureness came flooding back with that admission. "Because, you know, I'm *me* and all."

"Until you realized it'd be wiser to tell your superior officer, yea?" Habraum inquired, fixing on the Thulican with a warning look.

An innocent stare replaced Khrome's cocksure smirk. "Of course, oh fearless leader."

"Glad we understand each other," Habraum gestured to the holoscreen before him. "Bring the file up."

The Thulican strolled up to Habraum's right and did as ordered. A life-sized holo of Raichoudry appeared before them, adjacent to a brief scroll of stats and bio information.

Addison Priyanka Raichoudry was listed in her profile as Bengalistani Indian, a fact bolstered by her coppery complexion and smooth black hair. She stood just under five-foot-four, petite, compact and limber in physique. Her thin and sharp features conveyed a hardness not aided by her wide nose and humorless line of a mouth. Raichoudry's close-set eyes conveyed less-than-subtle disdain, as though she'd rather be doing anything other than taking this profile shot. That might've made Habraum laugh under different circumstances.

Khrome laughed anyway. "That's actually her resting 'happy' face."

The Thulican's booming mechanical guffaw shook more memories loose as Habraum studied the profile.

He'd definitely seen Raichoudry's face around Hollus Maddrone before his sabbatical, that unblinking self-seriousness belying her twenty-four years of age. She had come with that exceptional batch of recruits two years ago which included Khrome, Liliana and Tyris. Habraum had never exchanged so much as a word with the girl, but before her disgrace the Cerc had heard of Raichoudry's undeniable potential as a field operator.

Khrome finally calmed and turned to leave Habraum's office. "Uh-uh, lad," the Cerc's raised hand gave him pause. "You found Raichoudry's file. You're in it now. We solve this together."

Habraum located the encryption his subordinate spoke of at the bottom of Raichoudry's scrolling profile, tapped on it and chose the optical scan option. In moments, a new section appeared just below Raichoudry's existing profile—paragraphs of concealed data.

At first both Habraum and Khrome read through the decrypted sections with their mouths ajar, like two beings who missed the punch line of a joke.

The pieces began gelling in Habraum's mind, and hit like a punch to his gut.

Khrome's exclamation described the Cerc's feelings perfectly. "Shut. Me. Down!"

According to this addendum by Jovian Ivers, Addison's meltdown and resignation was a ruse.

Ivers had been training her a month before her resignation to infiltrate one of the most notorious Children of Earth cells on Seredonia in a covert joint op with UniPol.

Also stated, no one in Star Brigade except Ivers knew about this assignment or had contact with Raichoudry except himself.

Khrome furrowed his hairless brow, still befuddled. "Why would he keep this a secret from Brigade Intelligence or any Brigade higher-ups?"

"Maybe UniPol instructed him to," Habraum assumed, "probably out of fear that the Children of Earth had informants and spies within Star Brigade's personnel."

"Her assignment was supposed to last no more than four or five months." That left Khrome stricken and his round yellow eyes brimming with sorrow.

Ivers died on Beridaas over a year ago. Habraum sucked on his teeth and shook his bald head with such sorrow. "Uh-uh. Rogguts, that poor thing…"

"Are we going to pull her out?" The Thulican asked.

Good question. Habraum steeled away his sentiments about this situation and looked again at what data Raichoudry's profile had provided them. As helpful as this had been, Habraum realized how much they still didn't know about this dilemma. *Best start there*, he told himself, and looked at Khrome. "Only after we get all the facts. Movements right before and right after leaving Hollus Maddrone a year ago. Her whereabouts and activities on Seredonia, if she's even still on Seredonia. What CoE cell is she in deep cover with?"

Habraum limp-walked over to his desk and brought up the Star Brigade dossier module on the surface console. After his handprint and optical scan had been captured, he said, "Captain Level access, Khromulus Threedwok. Forty-eight orvs." The Cerc turned back on Khrome. "You now have unrestricted access to the dossier files. It's temporary," he warned at Khrome's widening Cheshire grin. "If any more encryptions come up, just knock them down. Go through all of Ivers's old files to get more information on this mission and how Raichoudry had been contacting him. I want to know whoever Ivers's UniPol contact was. And for now, keep this between us until we know more."

"Affirmative," Khrome paused at the door. "Captain?"

Habraum paused to look over his shoulder at the Thulican. "Yea?"

"Do you think…?" Khrome appeared hesitant to finish his thoughts, a rarity. "After all this time with no contact from Ivers, do you think that Addison might have turned?"

That hadn't occurred to Habraum. "We'll find out after we track Raichoudry down and extract her," the Cerc replied in his most composed tone. He'd rather not consider such a dark notion…yet.

Once alone, Habraum leaned heavily on his desk. He voiced a command that activated his companiomech to pick up Jeremy and watch him for the afternoon. *Sorry, sprout,* he apologized and forgave himself. Studying Raichoudry's profile and sullen features, Habraum began assembling the details for a possible rescue op.

The team had to be small, no more than four operators, strictly Star Brigade. Working with another agency might take too long for approvals or get back to the wrong beings that could unintentionally blow Raichoudry's cover.

The Cerc then considered which operators he'd lead into the field—

You're not field ready yet. Meaning he couldn't lead his team into combat himself. The truth slapped him hard across the face. Swearing under his breath, Habraum slammed a fist onto his desk. The Cerc's frustration went beyond the need to get back onto the field. The Twins only knew what Raichoudry had endured and was still enduring to protect her cover. Or, what if Khrome was right, and she had joined the Children of Earth after months of no contact from Ivers?

Or worse, what if she's been made…and then murdered? A cold dread filled Habraum then, surmounting the sting in his knuckles. But he pulled his mind away from the black and focused on one obstacle at a time.

Not being cleared for field missions created a huge issue with who would lead an extraction team. Habraum's first thought went with Sam. She had the experience and would drop everything to lead an extraction for a fellow Brigadier. Especially one connected to Ivers.

The Cerc completely dismissed the idea for that reason. *She needs to focus on Tharydane, getting her settled. At least for this week.* If half the requests from other agencies panned out, then Habraum knew there would be countless chances for Sam to lead her own team soon.

"I'll take point remotely," he decided. Next up, the team needed a member focused solely on getting them in and out of Seredonia or wherever Addison might be.

Marguliese was a viable option, but Habraum wanted her focused on training the Star Brigadiers not on a combat team.

He waved away Raichoudry's profile and pulled up Star Brigade's very short list of field-ready copilots. All three were solid and talented, but with no experience on covert ops missions.

Not like myself or— The epiphany came suddenly. Habraum straightened up and smiled. He had a pilot in mind.

Less than fifteen macroms later, the Cerc arrived down at Pilot Pub yet again. The air was filled with raucous shouts and laughter. A late lunch crowd filled the small saloon to its brim. He spied Solrao across the pub working the bar. By the sureness in her movements while dishing out drinks and jokes, she'd clearly sobered up since their meal.

Habraum caught the Ibrisian's eye and gestured her toward the Pilot's Pub's entrance. After a couple macroms, she succinctly ordered a servermech to take over and weaved through the crowd toward Habraum.

"Need your help," Habraum announced quietly without preamble once they stood far down the corridor outside of Pilot Pub. He gave Solrao sparse details about a Brigadier needing an extraction, leaving out whom and why.

When Habraum finished, the Ibrisian looked confused. "Why me? You have at least two other field op copilots to choose from."

"The Brigadiers I'm sending out there are still green. With me not cleared for combat, I need the second best pilot I know watching over them."

Solrao laughed, but it felt half-hearted. That didn't fill Habraum with much confidence.

"I can't, Braum," the Ibrisian stared at the ground with that demoralized look he'd seen one too many times since the Ferronos Sector War. "I just...don't have it in me to fly like that anymore, and I don't want to disappoint you again."

In the past, Habraum would have placated her inexhaustible remorse with kind words and accepted his friend's self-flagellation with a forgiving smile. Aside from when they were amongst their old flight group telling war stories, this round and round of apologizing and forgiving had defined their relationship post-Ferronos Sector War. But a pile of murdered teammates on Beridaas filled Habraum's thoughts, joined by Honaa hissing his last request before the firestorm consumed him. *Lead them well.*

He had no patience for placating today. "Rogguts, why can't you move the fekt on, eh?" Habraum snapped, his anger barely contained.

Solrao recoiled as if stung. Her eyes narrowed in surprise. "Excuse me?"

"You want to stop letting me down? *Stop living in the past.*" The Cerc got right in Solrao's face, his piercing hazel-gold eyes pinning her to the wall. "What angers me," he seethed, lowering his voice, "is you wasting your life away by hiding in a bottle."

Solrao stared back at the Cerc like she would some terrifying stranger. It took the Ibrisian a few moments to find her voice. "I...I told you before I'm not doing that—"

Habraum barreled over her meager defense. "Who do you think made sure you were tucked in after those benders these last few weeks?"

Solrao had no response, and seemed to deflate under that hard truth. Ignoring the curious stares from patrons entering or exiting Pilot Pub, the Cerc took his friend by the shoulders gently but firmly. The distance between the concentric rings in Solrao's eyes widened, a sign of Ibrisian fear.

Something tugged at the Cerc's chest at this reaction, for causing it. But he was tired of Solrao's supplication, tired of watching a once bright soul figuratively and literally killing herself over a mistake he had forgiven her for ages ago. "There's an undercover Brigadier out there who probably thinks she's been abandoned, and the combat team I'm sending to extract her needs an extraordinary pilot to get them in and out of a hostile situation. I wouldn't ask you, Solrao, if I didn't need you. Just this once." His words had adopted an imploring tenor, but Habraum was past ego or pride to care.

Solrao stared up at Habraum, eyes and pupils wide with dread. And she stared. And she stared. After what felt like an eternity, the Ibrisian nodded, almost imperceptibly but decisively. "Okay, Braum."

It was Habraum's turn to exhale, this time out of relief. "I'll contact you when mission prep starts." He turned and swept away from the Pilot Pub without further discussion. Habraum had his pilot. Now he needed a team to rescue a fellow Star Brigadier.

T-2

(Deleted Chapter from Star Brigade: Resurgent)

Habraum Nwosu could remember the last two times he'd stared at himself in the mirror with reflective detail. The first time? Almost four years ago in the year 2390, right before his graduation from the Union Command AeroFleet Academy.

Then he had been, barely 20 years of age, finally becoming a fighter pilot for the AeroFleet—his dream since his childhood, growing up on the rocky red world of Cercidale. His reflection that day had been lean but muscular for his size, filling out his fitted AeroFleet uniform excellently. His smooth, dark-brown face was beaming with so much pride, he thought it might burst. His kinky black hair cropped low and glossy, hazel-gold eyes alight at the endless possibilities that lay before him. At that moment in his life, Habraum indulged in his youthful sense of invincibility, reveled in the excitement of getting to traverse across the star-spanning Galactic Union of Planetary Republics and see its many member worlds.

Then came the reality of AeroFleet fighter pilot with all its combat drills, that only fed his obsession to be the best, the joy of meeting his current girlfriend Jennica—a loving respite from the rigors of military life—the wonder of seeing a Thulican for the first time.

Habraum never forgot that day when a dozen of the stout mechanoid-like race arrived at the Galactic Union's capital world Terra Sollus, asking for help against their enslavers, the Cybernarr. Until that point, the Galactic Union had an uneasy armistice with the more humanoid-like Cybernarr—stay out of the Ferronos Sector and we'll stay out of Union Space. This, despite reports of the Cybernarr's cruel half-a-century internment of the Thulican race. And like most Union citizens, Habraum expected that to stick. But when reports came that the Thulicans not only offered their technology, but their twin homeworlds Ferros Arietis and Ferros Khanosis for membership to the Galactic Union, Habraum's fears became a reality. Thus began the

Ferronos Sector War between the Galactic Union and the Cybernarr Technoarchy.

It was almost two years later when Habraum gave himself that second, contemplative stare—right after the bloody Battle of Cassiopeia's Cross. One of many space clashes the Union Command had lost. There Habraum stood in his weathered flight suit in his tiny quarters aboard a UComm Command Cruiser, mourning yet another group of fallen AeroFleet comrades. At this point, he'd let his hair grow into a thick shock of big, kinky curls. Prickly stubble covered his lower jaw from neglect. Dark circles surrounded his eyes from lack of sleep. He was much leaner, having lost the baby fat and innocence of youth much more quickly than most. But those changes weren't the ones that startled him. It was the eyes staring back at him. Since Habraum's fighter pilot squadron the SunRiders had been on the frontline of the war, his eyes had seen much those past two years. They had seen the true horrors of the Cybernarr's occupation of the Thulican Twin Planets, witnessing the mighty military power of the Galactic Union's UComm failing to remove the Technoarchy from the Twin Planets, even with the Thulicans' technological upgrades, having lost so many fellow pilots whom he had graduated with. Habraum had never seen such ruthless butchery before.

But while he had lost that feeling of invincibility and childish cockiness of being a fighter pilot, Habraum knew more than ever that the Union had made the right choice in choosing to engage the Cybernarr. With what the Technoarchy had done to the Thulicans, it would only be a matter of time before they moved against the Union. But despite the fire ignited in his hazel-gold eyes, Habraum privately could not help but ask himself, "How are we going to win this damn war?"

That was before the Galactic Union began winning more and more battles, finding better strategies. And well before the Union got more aid in the form of the Kedri Imperium. There was no love lost between the Union and the war-like, honor-obsessed Kedri. But the Kedri hated the Cybernarr, so naturally they helped taking them down. Once that alliance formed, the tide truly began to turn, driving the Cybernarr out of the Ferronos Sector altogether. The Galactic Union was winning, finally. And now, a year later, Habraum Nwosu gawked at the strange reflection staring back at him.

"*Rogguts*, will anyone recognize me?" he whispered, his heavy lilt from Cercidale's northern Vanderoyce Province. Habraum ran a finger across the beard covering his strong jaw. He was getting a good look at himself after the Union's string of wins against the Technoarchy put it on the brink of victory. After he was captured at the Battle of the Kyrn Rift.

He would never forget that day, his SunRider squadron and a group of Kedri fighter pilots attacking a Cybernarr slipstream hub meant to assault Union Space. The slipstream had been destroyed, but at a huge loss of lives. The SunRiders and Kedri had been ordered to retreat. Almost everyone followed this order. All except for a Kedri pilot named Dagra Kel, fighting on like a savage with something to prove. And just as expected, Dagra was about to be overwhelmed by the Cybernarr's deathstrike ships, slashing through his fighter jet's shields like night-colored daggers. So Habraum flew back against his better judgment. Hurtling in with a blaze of photonic blasts and neutrino missiles, he saved that idiotic Kedri's life and covered the escape of his entire squadron. But with all the damage his own ship had sustained, it had been too late for Habraum to escape. A Cybernarr cruiser's gravity well made sure of that.

But once his fighter jet was taken into the dank, dark interior of that Cybernarr cruiser, Habraum had not made it easy for them. He leapt from his spacecraft as the shapeless cybernetic horrors slinked out of the dark to claim him, and he fought back. Yet Habraum attacked his captors not just with his fists and feet, but with abilities far beyond those of a normal being—abilities that were his birthright as a maximum. Ever since those powers manifested after his 17th birthday, Habraum hated the term 'maximum' as much as he did his abilities, feeling both to be hindrances that could prevent him from joining AeroFleet. So the Cercidalean had learned just enough about his powers so he wouldn't be a danger to those around him.

But when those bright crimson blasts of concussive force had issued from Habraum's hands, chasing away the shadows, punching holes straight through anything that tried to grab at him, the pilot finally thanked the Maker for this gift. By no means did he believe that he would make it out of this alive. The Cerc had accepted that the moment his ship was captured. But he would fight with any weapon in his arsenal. Yet Habraum wasn't quick enough, not trained enough in the use of his powers to target every threat. Something...or someone struck from behind, plunging him into unconsciousness.

And now, still a prisoner of the Cybernarr for the past five months, Habraum Nwosu was staring at the results of his capture on the liquid metal walls inside of a Cybernarr space vessel.

He had lost so much weight—muscles looking somewhat withered, ribcage plainly visible on his lanky, six-foot-five-inch frame. He absently rubbed the circular Union AeroFleet tattoo that he had branded on his right shoulder two years ago, just to make sure it was still there. His only attire was the techno-organic mesh supplied for him, a shimmering grey material that fit like a sleeveless robe.

His dark brown skin was noticeably lighter, but in a sickly way. Probably due to lack of sunlight, with some discolored scars on his arms and chest. The soft curls of black hair that he used to pride himself on were gone, cleanly shaven off during his incarceration. But he didn't mind it. All traces of body fat had vanished, burned away from the five alleged months of his imprisonment. He traced his hands over a face that was now gaunter than he remembered and covered by a short, curly beard.

Even his own gold-hazel eyes frightened him. No longer carefree, they were incisive, restless and telltale of someone who had experienced far too many horrors at such a young age.

This stranger staring back at Habraum was the result of the Cybernarr's particular brand of torture. Habraum had thought he knew what pain was, only to realize that his definition was an outright lie. The thought of what they had done to him, the depth of how much they abused him—Habraum squeezed his eyes shut as if to stop the recollection. But his thoughts were already there, yielding painfully to a bursting dam of memories reliving every bit of agony in vivid detail.

Soon after he had woken up, stripped of clothing and light, the torture began. The pain had been soul crushing, devouring his every waking moment for longer than he could fathom. Habraum's voice had gone hoarse and raw quite quickly from all his screaming. But he couldn't stop if he tried.

In those brief respites between torture sessions, Habraum had only known the stifling darkness of his cell. Sleep came in spurts whenever the pain had subsided. And then, all too quickly, it began again.

One technique, he couldn't remember or see how they'd executed it, felt like a thousand white-hot knives had been stabbed into his spine. That had sent a scalding agony shooting through his veins, scorching his insides like flames. Habraum had to endure that one for two days straight.

And not once had the Cybernarr ever asked him any questions. They only administered enough vital fluids to keep him alive and then kept up round after sadistic round of torment. After some time, he had learned to zone out, go to a place filled with memories of Cercidale with its endless rock formations, his strict but loving parents, his rowdy brothers and whipsmart sister, his AeroFleet family. Jennica…

…The memory of his lover floated up into Habraum's thoughts as the torture became more severe. Jennica Hoang was a petite little thing, which belied her firecracker personality. Every detail about her enveloped him with an urgency he never remembered before: the long raven-black hair that shimmered under sunlight, a pale creamy skin that smelled of warmth and luna blossoms, brown almond-shaped eyes that sparkled like stars whenever she spoke of the children she educated at her teaching job. Her quick smile that always disarmed him, and then there was her melodious laughter…

But after a while, the Cybernarr adapted the torture to bleed through that safe haven.

And then Habraum, a proud Cercidalean who never begged, wanted to beg for death just to stop the pain. Habraum sagged against his reflection, gasping for breath as if he had been running for days without rest. He hastily shoved away any thought of his treatment. Thinking of it again would be the end of his sanity.

The Cercidalean righted himself and tore his eyes away from the reflection, then paced back and forth in the hallways of the Cybernarr vessel. The walls around him were draped with smooth and continuous cybernetics that went on for kilometrids, gold and crimson in color. The floors were flat, not at all sinewy like the walls. The whole ship was alive, one mechanical, beautiful marvel.

While Habraum bottled away his past suffering, the memories of how his torture had ended flowed freely through his mind. On the day he had wanted it all to end, what appeared to be a female Cybernarr entered his prisoner cell. The sudden light that heralded her arrival after so long in darkness caused Habraum to squint in pain at first. This was his first time seeing a live Cybernarr up close.

This one stood before him, exceedingly tall and slender in figure. Its skin bore a golden metal sheen, like a humanoid mechanoid but far more advanced. Below its shoulders was a tapestry of dark, sinuous cybernetics that flowed into and out of its skin with perfect harmony. It had no hair on its face or head, the several short crimson nodules jutting out of its gleaming skull.

What drew all of his attention were the pupil-less cerulean eyes staring at him, so inorganic, so detached from emotion that they seemed to stab through his soul like icy blades. A part of him could not help but marvel at the terrible beauty of this Cybernarr, this perfect union of organic and cybernetic.

But after all Habraum had endured, the seething hate keeping him upright overrode any fatigue. The lives lost to this…*thing* and its race of butchers demanded that he stayed defiant to the end. He didn't have the energy to use his powers, so hatred was Habraum's remaining weapon to wield.

And that's when it—or rather 'she'—asked him a question in a mechanical feminine tone as cold and sharp as her knife-like gaze, "**Why do humanoids give each other nicknames?**"

For a long moment, Habraum had sat there staring at the cyborg in stupefied disbelief. He hadn't been sure if this was a bad joke or a test. His silence lingered so long that she had repeated the question.

A baffled Habraum remembered speaking with a voice damn near gone from constant screaming. His answer was something about how nicknames can either be a name given for affection or mocking.

She absorbed the response, then presented him with a plate of real food and a water glass like something out of a dream, and left. Habraum shoveled down the meal with his bare hands like someone from the most primitive parts of the galaxy. His father would have chastised him for such barbaric eating.

Orvs later, she returned with two more questions, both trivial and meaningless to Habraum. He answered. She left him another actual meal, which he ate with the provided utensils this time. The Cybernarr also supplied him with the techno-organic mesh that he now wore. She departed once more.

This continued at least a dozen more times, each visit came with more questions inquiring of the nature of life in the Union. What was the purpose of taking a holiday which served no work function? Why did the five races that started the Union – Earth humans, the Voton, the Kudoban, the

Rhomerans and the Galdorian – allow other races who joined equal say in the government? Questions of that nature.

None of them pertained to anything of relevance to the UComm defense protocols or secret codes. However, none of these questions were accompanied with any type of torture. So Habraum played along, fearing that this new situation wouldn't stick if he refused the Cybernarr.

After she had provided yet another meal to reward his answers, this Cybernarr then stated, "**It has been almost six of your customary weeks.**" And then she left. *That was it?* Habraum remembered thinking in relief. But he still had no expectation of freedom…or seeing his loved ones again.

Soon these interrogations became debates about how Cybernarr and non-Cybernarr live as they do. Habraum then felt bold enough to ask his own questions. Where is Cybernarr Space? How many worlds are in the Technoarchy? Why had they enslaved the Thulicans? And the Cybernarr answered openly. This went on for weeks, always proceeding her bringing him a meal, a minor but vital courtesy.

Soon Habraum actually looked forward to these. It gave him something to do and to focus on. Plus, the food was good. And though her mannerisms never showed it, Habraum had gathered that this cyborg might just be curious…or even lonely. Why else would she come back so routinely?

She no doubt had been following orders in regards to his torture, just like Habraum had in the AeroFleet when he blew several Cybernarr ships to kingdom come. This softened his once blanket stance on all Cybernarr being soulless automaton butchers. Well—at least in reference to her.

This Cybernarr female had revealed her name once, a long series of digital noises Habraum would never have any hope of enunciating. So he had given her a nickname, that of a character with intense blue eyes from one of his favorite holonovels, *Skydancer Swift*.

"Marguliese. My nickname for you," Habraum declared as the Cybernarr, emotionless as ever, eyed him with the barest hint of distaste. But she indulged him and answered to the name when he used it.

The need to know about the war or anything that took place outside this cell gnawed at Habraum's gut like a physical thing. Had the Technoarchy invaded Union Space completely? Had the Kedri Imperium sent more resources to aid the Galactic Union's war effort? But Habraum kept his concerns contained, barely, never once bringing it up. And neither did the Cybernarr. Until two days ago.

"The war is over." Marguliese stated suddenly during one such debate. **"The Technoarchy will leave the Ferronos Sector and return to our realm in the Dracius Cluster shortly."**

And Habraum nearly spat out his water. "Wait…you lost?!" Marguliese said nothing, but Habraum could have sworn a flicker of anger flashed across her gaze. Shuddering, he had quickly shifted the discussion on his situation. "What does that mean for me?"

"I was ordered to eliminate you," she replied flatly as if it were on a daily to-do list. **"And since your government declared you dead four months ago, it is the logical action."**

Habraum's throat had gone dry. And suddenly, the fear he should have felt in this cyborg's presence seized his bones. The hate that had been replaced by a sense of almost camaraderie twisted in his gut sourly. He remembered feeling so stupid, to not think that his capture would not end this way.

"But…" the Cybernarr arched a non-existent eyebrow as she continued. **"I see that as unwise. From how you speak of your family and related constituents, they clearly gain emotional sustenance from you and vice versa. So I am returning you to your homeworld."**

Home. Habraum had given up on even wishing for it. The thought of this launched him into orbit.

"I…I'm going home." Speaking this aloud made it so unbearably real. Habraum crumpled to his knees and burst into tears. He had thought he'd known joy before—relief. But before this moment, before believing that he may never see his loved ones again, everything before had been empty. Habraum had looked up through tear-blurred vision. "Thank you, Marguliese!" he said, his words just a whisper. The Cybernarr stood like a metal statue in the face of his euphoria. But he couldn't have cared less.

Remembering that joy still made Habraum smile, which went so unused during his internment that the facial movement felt unnatural. They had been traveling for two days now, back to Union Space from wherever they had been. During this time, Marguliese had allowed him to roam freely all over her vessel. And Habraum explored almost every section, gawking at it all like a kid at an amusement park-town.

The pilot in Habraum would have loved to watch the ship's journey, especially because they were traveling in slipstream—a flight technology no race but the Cybernarr had mastered. But his mind was in a million different places: his family, his girlfriend, the sensation of being free again. What was he going to tell everyone about how he survived? The young Cerc glanced up at one of the smoother regions of the Cybernarr ship's walls. Many of them also reflected him perfectly. But his gaze didn't linger long now before moving on to another section of this cyberorganic wonder.

"**Habraum.**" Habraum nearly had a heart attack. Marguliese, speaking through the ship's comms, sounded as if she stood at his side. That was so unnerving. "Yeah?" he replied after taking a breath.

"**I apologize for alarming you, but we have arrived outside of Cercidale's orbit.**"

Habraum's anxiety fell off him like a cloak. Resembling a kid on Christmas morning, the Cercidalean bolted toward the ship's bridge. Once he got to the entrance, he found it closed off by a smooth metal door not unlike the mirror-like walls all over the ship. But once he stepped closer, the door melted away like liquid metal, revealing a wide cavity leading right into the bridge.

Sitting before Habraum was a spherical chamber, soaked in deep crimson lighting, at least 20 metrids across and 7 metrids high. Just like outside, the walls were lined entirely with pulsating cybernetics, their beginnings and endings never clear. The only differences were the many circular viewscreens embedded in various regions of the wall. On the smallest viewscreen was an outline diagram of the ship and all of its readings, constantly refreshing with new data so quickly that Habraum got a headache looking at it too long. Other screens were also awash with rapidly changing data, but in a peculiar numerical code. A massive viewscreen just right of the main viewport held a holographic map covering all of GUPR space, divided by sector using different colors. The chart stretched nearly a quarter of the wall, but lacked the input consoles or navcomputer that a Union Command starship would have. But because this was a Cybernarr biomechanoid vessel, it only needed a Cybernarr hooked up to it for proper navigation.

In the room's center, Habraum caught a circular dais seven metrids across and rising a half metrid off the ground. The golden metal that covered it pulsed and throbbed with energy. There were six of these built on top of each other like a pyramid, each circular base smaller than the one below it.

Standing tall on the highest and smallest dais was Marguliese, her back to Habraum. The dark, sinewy cybernetics had different patterns on the Cybernarr's toned back. Writhing cords from the vessel's ceiling were directly connected with the nodules on the Cybernarr's head, giving her control over every aspect of the ship.

But all that barely held Habraum's attention for even a moment. Once he entered the bridge, the young pilot gaped at the large ovular viewport in front of the Cybernarr. On it was the inky black of space, dimly lit by countless twinkling stars. But what took up his attention—and a majority of the screen—was a rocky planet, reddish-brown in color, gigantic in size and majesty. They were facing its daytime side, which boasted a mountainous surface somewhat hidden under swirls of feathery white and pockmarked by scattered lakes of blue. Cercidale.

"By the Maker, that's a sight for sore eyes!" Habraum exclaimed, his voice heavy with longing. He dashed up the dais to stand next to the Cybernarr. There was his homeworld in all its red, rocky glory.

"We are just outside the orbital defenses," the Cybernarr said in her flat, mechanical cadence. She fixated on Habraum with glowing, cerulean eyes. That sharp, angular golden face was like a work of art, but came off so robotic and emotionally sparse. To Habraum she looked like a figure from Earth's old Greek mythology with those cables sticking out of her head, minus the petrifying ugliness. **"I will require the location on Cercidale you desire to be transported."**

"Oh—uh, right." Habraum reluctantly looked away from Cercidale and faced the Cybernarr. It had taken him two months to meet her penetrating stare directly without getting goosebumps. "Nobleton Province, Medillius, Orodon Apartment Complex." The bustling city of Medillius was his home during the rare times he had shore leave. Jennica had moved in with him less than a month before his capture.

Jennica. He was going to see her again. Habraum's whole body shivered with so much happiness.

"The coordinates have been logged." Marguliese's eyes shimmered against the bridge's crimson luminosity, snapping Habraum out of his trance. **"I will transport you at your discretion."**

"Well, Marguliese, this is it," Habraum tried to put his hands in his pant pockets, until he realized that the techno-organic mesh he wore had none. An uncomfortable silence followed. Feeling a bit awkward, Habraum directed his gaze at his homeworld. "It's been a ride for you and me, hasn't it?"

Oddly, the young Cercidalean held no grudge or bitterness toward the Cybernarr female. Just her, of course. In fact, there was a small stitch of regret in his heart for leaving Marguliese.

"This would appear to be the conclusion of our association," said Marguliese, her voice as emotionless as her face. Habraum frowned as he then noticed a sinewy growth forming on the Cybernarr's left shoulder, followed by two smaller juts that looked like welding tools.

The tools on the Cybernarr's shoulder worked furiously at creating an item that the Cerc couldn't identify. Habraum gaped at the result: a flattened grey disk, not much bigger than the cavity in a human ear. The juts in the Cybernarr's arm reverted to their former state and popped the disk into her awaiting palm. **"However, I desire to keep in contact. You can do so through this device."**

Is she serious? Habraum thought in shock. He struggled to keep his expression neutral as he cautiously plucked the disk from her hand. **"Situate the device in your earlobe, focus on it, and you connect to me directly."** Something in her eyes flickered. **"There is much that I have learned from you, Habraum Nwosu, about the emotions and temperament of other sentients, and I wish to sustain those conversations."**

"We will, Marguliese," said Habraum, truly meaning it. "I can't say that this has been the greatest romp for me, but it showed me what really mattered in my life. And for that, I thank y—"

"UComm vessels have detected me," the Cybernarr stated abruptly. **"Farewell, Habraum."**

"Goodbye Mar—" The air sizzled with dazzling white and his whole body stretched beyond normal limits for a quarter of a nanoclic. "—guliese? What the hazik?!" Habraum spun around in utter confusion. It was as if someone had flashed a blinding floodlight in his face and then shut off all the lights at once. When his eyes readjusted to the gloom, Marguliese, the bridge, and the view of Cercidale were gone.

Replacing them was a smooth cylindrical tower overlooking a clump of thick trees, probably less than 5 metrids in front of him. By the room lights visible on each of its thirteen floors, this was obviously an apartment complex, not unlike the one he resided at in the Cercidalean city of Medillius.

The rest of the wide and glassy boulevard behind him was lined with countless other complexes, some were squat and short, others were the same height as the building before him. Aside from the blaring headlights and the zipping hum of an occasional hovercar, the street looked deserted. Halolight posts cast a pale glow on the boulevard; they were 3 metrids apart on both sides of the street, lined up as far as the eye could see.

Cool night winds carried the aroma of quillgrass mints to Habraum's nose, making him notice that he stood in a large patch of downy green quillgrass stalks reaching up to his waist. Stepping back so as to not tread on too many, Habraum winced as his shin banged against the automated grey walkway of the tower next to him. Predictably an equally exquisite quillgrass patch resided on the other side of the walkway.

"I know this place," Habraum muttered. He tried recalling it while looking up at the night sky.

What he saw were five moons cascading a spectacular radiance on him. Something about their positioning instantly caught Habraum's attention. The largest moon was almost purple in hue, its craters visible even from its distance in space. Above the purple moon were two smaller ones and below it two even smaller moons also. It looked like a straight line with a disproportioned center.

Habraum froze. "That moon formation!" he cried at the heavens. The Cercidalean moon chain, which happened once every 400 days of a Cercidalean year. That explained why this street was deserted, as most would be at the many canyons or mountainsides on Cercidale to celebrate the Moon Chain.

"I'm home! By the Maker, I'M HOME!" He jumped high above the quillgrass, not caring if he was seen. He was about to clap his hands in delight when his eye caught actual cloth on his wrist. In a stunned silence, Habraum held up his wrist and then looked at his body.

No longer was he wearing the odd techno-organic mesh. The formal suit he now wore had a white color with navy blue bands around his neck and wrist collars, topped off by obsidian shoulder pads and intricate gold buttoning. Completing the suit were the long white slacks and navy shoes precisely of an AeroFleet Lieutenant Commander uniform—fitted for his current, scrawny build.

"Thanks, Marguliese," Habraum murmured at the night sky, thoroughly moved. He then looked at the complex before him, noticing the small holosign above the entrance in a royal-looking Cercidalean font.

ORODON APARTMENT COMPLEX #12

Habraum was beside himself with joy. "This is too good to be true." Both his pant pockets jostled as he sprang onto the walkway. Upon closer inspection, he discovered that his right pocket held the small communication disk that Marguliese created for him. He had completely forgotten the latter item wasn't in his hands. The abrupt halt of the automated walkway caught him off guard, nearly tumbling him forward. He gazed at the Complex #12 foyer. His "home" would have looked foreign to him even if he hadn't been a captive for five months. This war had kept him away from Cercidale for far too long.

He stood under the small archway that extended well past the foyer. The double-door entrance was platinum-white like the rest of the building and constructed of sturdy ferroment. Next to it was a black comm console that allowed a guest to tell a resident of their arrival. Buzzing the console to see if Jennica was home had crossed his mind, but after five months, Habraum doubted that she would even be here.

"ID scan complete. Welcome home, Habraum Nwosu."

The automated voice startled Habraum from his thoughts. He had completely forgotten how the security systems would briefly bioscan a resident and let them in upon verification. He strode inside, still not over the shock of being free. The ornately designed lobby was empty. It boasted smooth, flat walls with mini-viewscreens running constant visuals of the numerous Cercidalean landscapes.

Habraum paused to take in the scenery. "*Rogguts*, I've missed this," he whispered. The viewscreen showing the ice-covered Corde Vedriis Mountains held his attention longer than the others. That was near his parents' ranch. Then a chronometer reading at the bottom of the screen caught his eye.

"It's almost one in the morning?" Habraum gaped. "Fekt, will anyone still be awake?" He moved toward the three translifters straight ahead and strode briskly to the middle one.

"Floor six," Habraum said while entering the spherical translifter. Responding to his command, it shot up to his floor in less than ten nanoclics. But in Habraum's impatient mind it felt far longer.

Habraum stepped off the translifter to Apartment 6B, second door to the right in the well-lit hallway. He placed a hand on the handprint ID panel next to his apartment's entrance, and it slid open with a soft hiss.

As he entered, the hallway's halolights cast a long, golden lozenge straight through the living room. The entrance hissed shut behind him, and an open square viewport was now the room's only light source.

The Cercidalean moon chain's multicolor glow filtered into the viewport, jogging Habraum's memory of the surroundings. The common room was more spacious than he remembered, light blue walls, with a plush kurokoos-hide couch against the wall opposite him. Just in front of that was a translucent plasteel table littered with holozine charts and unopened ANCOR packages. The table faced a wide holoview viewscreen at least two metrids wide, the "gogglebox" as he called it. A few metrids to the left was a kitchenette. Beyond that, a short corridor, pitch-black, led to his bedroom.

In the past he relished the chances to come here and wind down for a few days of leave. That would last all of a day before the craving to soar across the stars seized him again.

Habraum knew it was probably better that Jennica wasn't here anyway. As much as he wanted to see her and his family, the euphoria had worn off, and Habraum realized how sapped he was. Just standing upright was a chore. He would contact them first thing tomorrow after a good night's sleep. He started to call for the room's lighting, but the words died in his throat.

Someone was in his bedroom, evident from a faint voice down the hall. Sucking in a nervous breath, Habraum focused as the biokinetic energy that was his maximum power surged through him and his fists began to crackle bright red. After what he'd gone through, one could never be too cautious.

He stalked down the corridor without a sound, getting closer, his powers casting an eerie red glow along the walls. Presently he tried recalling any combat training learned in AeroFleet while struggling to stay calm, which only made his head ache. But he had to. The door was half-open, splashing dim blue light onto the corridor walls. Habraum stopped just in front of the opening and the voice from the room became a bit clearer. The remaining hair on the back of his neck stood on end.

The voice from the room was him, sounding happy and carefree, so full of himself. He peered in the room to see a bluish, full-sized holo of himself in his pilot suit, bragging and joking around, facing the left side of the room. There was the unruly shock of curly black hair. It must have been at least a year old.

Habraum relaxed. He powered down the red energy immersing his hands, which faded to nothing. He chuckled as the holo went on and on about flight accomplishments. "*Rogguts*, that hair," he muttered.

A wretched sob broke Habraum from his reverie. He peered past the half-open door and saw who the holo was facing. Sitting on the bed and bathed in the holo's bluish light was his girlfriend, Jennica Hoang.

At the sight of her, Habraum felt a jolt run through his body, like the rush of a sudden free-fall. Five months were too long to have been denied such beauty. But she was crying, her body shaking. Habraum didn't have to guess why. She thought he was dead, as did everyone else in the whole Union.

The petite human female was dressed in a loose grey sweatshirt, staring at the holo. She quivered with such raw grief, it hurt to watch. The holo's light sparkled off the tears streaming down her face.

"H...Habraum. I miss you," she just kept on weeping, running a shaky hand through her long hair.

Seeing Jennica so broken and saddened cut through Habraum's heart like razors. He shut his eyes tightly and turned away. But he could still hear Jennica's sobs. And she was not done.

"It's been hard without you, so hard. The little things around Cercidale...all remind me of you..."

Habraum felt violently sick, his knees nearly buckling. How could he think about himself when his loved ones were suffering because of his alleged death?

"I've finally accepted that you're gone," Jennica said quietly. "But I...I will never stop loving you."

This was just too much. "Computer, end holo and illuminate room," Habraum ordered, bursting in. Instantly, the holo fizzled out of existence just as the room's lights came back on. Sporting bare white walls, the room's only furnishings were an unmade bed, a large viewport and a rectangular closet door on the right-hand wall. Everything he owned had been cleared out, obviously due to his alleged demise.

None of that mattered now. Jennica's almond-shaped eyes widened with fright at Habraum's sudden appearance in the bedroom. A lump in his throat constricted his speech. Rogguts, he had waited for this moment for five months and now he couldn't think of a thing to say!

"Wh—who?" Jennica, already deathly pale from grief, turned even whiter at the sight of Habraum. She slid off the side of the bed, keeping her disbelieving stare on him.

"Jennica," Habraum forced the name out of his mouth. "Jennica, it's me, Habraum."

For a long macrom Jennica stood there and stared at him. "No, no," she whispered, starting to quiver again. No, not quivering. Shaking her head in denial, and it became more and more furious by the nanoclic. "No, No, NO!" she shouted, as if yelling the word would make it so.

"No, Jennica," Habraum just about choked on his own grief. "It is me. I'm back!" He started toward her. All he wanted to do was hold her tightly, kiss away her suffering.

"GET BACK!" The terror in her voice froze Habraum in his tracks. "You're dead!" she stabbed an accusing finger at him. "You died five months ago. And I'm seeing things...I've finally lost my mind!"

"No, Jennica! I'm real...and I'll prove it! Computer, confirm the two occupants in this apartment."

"The two current occupants of Apartment 6B are Jennica Hoang and Habraum Nwosu."

"You see, Jennica," Habraum reached his hand out to her, forcing a smile on his face. "It's me."

His eyes began welling up. Habraum wiped the tears away with the cuff of his sleeves. When he attempted to speak again, his voice failed him. This had sapped more of his energy than he realized. For several nanoclics Jennica stood there like a statue, turning paler still. Then, slowly at first, Jennica rounded the bed and came towards him. Her face was unreadable when she stopped about a metrid in front of Habraum. Warily, Jennica raised her arm, pointing her fingers in Habraum's direction.

Habraum stared down at her arm in confusion—just a moment—before he understood. He raised his arm as well, extending his fingers until they touched the tips of hers. On the slightest contact he felt her tremble, heard her gasp. Jennica squeezed her eyes shut and a fresh wave of tears streamed down her cheeks. When she finally opened her eyes, she beamed with the purest joy. Habraum's heart sang. He took a guarded step toward her. But she ran to him without pause, sweeping her arms around him in an amorous embrace. Habraum held onto her petite frame, almost afraid that if he let go, she would disappear again. "I've missed you so much, Jen!" he gushed.

Jennica snuggled fiercely into his chest, her tears soaking his uniform. "Thought I'd lost you."

"You'll never lose me. *Ever.*" Habraum dotingly tucked her hair behind her ears before leaning in and kissing her passionately.

T-1
(Deleted Chapter from Star Brigade: Resurgent)

Ever since Habraum was little and tagged along with his dad on freighter runs, zoning out on the shimmering blue of luminal space always helped him sort out his thoughts. Luminal space—or L-space as it is called—set him straight even on a bad day. That much hadn't changed since returning to the Galactic Union. He enjoyed the stillness within his SR-23 V-wing fighter, traversing from Cercidale to Terra Sollus at faster-than-light speed. The only sound serenading his ears was the rhythmic hum of the L-Drive as it pushed the limits of its 8.1-speed multiplier. He rubbed the back of his bald head as he scanned the naviconsole readings. Much to his own surprise, he still didn't miss his curly Afro. It was for a different Habraum Nwosu, one who lacked humility; not for the man he was nowadays.

Moreover, once Habraum regained all of his muscle weight, Jennica simply loved the clean-shaven look—definitely an incentive to keep it. After scanning over the ship's readings, Habraum hugged his bare arms around the blue cut-off hoody he wore, staring off at his viewport. The privacy of piloting a single-being vessel was refreshing, privacy he truly enjoyed for the first time in weeks. As he began to zone out on the glowing lines making up L-space, Habraum couldn't help but notice how the speed of those lines was parallel to the speed his life had moved at the past few months.

So much had happened during his first few days back. Jennica had all his belongings stored up in his bedroom closet and was actually going to send them to his parents. But with Habraum back in her life, the couple unpacked the boxes together and put all his belongings back to where they originally were in their apartment before his alleged demise. After that, he got himself reacquainted with the taste of real non-synthetic food, enjoyed the sound of music, and went through holos of his friends and family. He basically overdosed on every material thing he had been denied while in the Cybernarr's captivity. Cybernarr had no furniture or other amenities, so after five months, even a toothpick looked amazing. Jennica was visibly amused by his candid curiosity for everything that was commonplace to her.

From there Habraum threw on some real clothes and the young couple traveled to the Parallel Mesas, a vast expanse of grasslands and flattened mesa formations in Northern Cercidale. The skies couldn't have been more perfect, cloudless and dazzling with the golden noonlight of Kyshrielle, Cercidale's sun. For the next few orvs, he and Jennica walked hand in hand through the Mesas' plains, relishing in the aromatic crush of baby quillgrass under their bare feet. They talked about everything that happened during the last five months: the war, Habraum's captivity, even Marguliese. The whole time Habraum couldn't keep his eyes off Jennica. How much he had missed the way that stunning smile lit up her face. His heart skipped a beat when Kyshrielle's noonlight caught the full luster of her black hair and the way her azure lace summer dress hugged her trim figure like skin.

By late afternoon, Habraum felt ready to go see his parents. But Jennica smartly suggested contacting them via TransNet first before stopping by their ranch. As he expected, the call was emotional and tearful, ending with both his mother and father demanding that he come over immediately.

In the early evening, he and Jennica arrived at his parents' sizeable kurokoos ranch near the base of the Corde Vedriis Mountains. The snowy peaks painted quite a picture behind the ranch as they jutted into the billowing clouds. His father Samuel, an Earth human who was as tall as Habraum and twice as hefty, didn't even wait for him to get off the transport. He howled with joy as he ran to meet his second eldest son, picking Habraum up and whirling him in the air as if he were a small child.

His mother Vara, refined and elegant like most native-born Cercidalean humans, was a little less dramatic in her show of affection. But to Habraum, it was still as potent and meaningful as his father's. Vara silently wrapped her arms around the much taller Habraum in a long, warm embrace.

Within a few orvs the whole Nwosu clan joined in the celebration: his five siblings and aunts and uncles from both sides of the family. How they all got there so fast boggled Habraum's mind, but he could not have cared less at the time. No one asked about his time with the Cybernarr, a blessing he thanked the Maker for.

Hugs, kisses, many praises to the Maker of Cercidale and plenty of tears swelled throughout the get-together, along with more delicious real food. Seeing how scrawny he looked, everyone plopped more food onto Habraum's plates—it got to the point where he needed three to hold all the food. The reunion with his family was magical, lasting until the early morning. He wished that it had never ended.

After spending the night at the ranch, Habraum knew he couldn't delay the inevitable. He had to report to the Cercidalean Union Command headquarters outside of Medillius. So in the late morning he left his parents and Jennica after a delicious three-course breakfast and headed to the UComm HQ.

As he expected, there was an inordinate amount of disbelief among the UComm brass once they did an ID scan. Habraum was then grilled with a battery of physical and mental tests to verify if he was indeed Habraum Nwosu and if the Cybernarr had altered his physiology by any means. The Cerc maintained his patience during all the tests. This newfound tolerance was definitely something Habraum felt proud about, because in the past he would not have sat still for more than 10 nanoclics.

After they confirmed that it was him and his physiology type was fine, then came a tedious debriefing. He told them everything he could remember about the Cybernarr and their technology, though he made sure to leave out the communication device that Marguliese gave him. Habraum actually meant to keep his promise of staying in touch with the Cybernarr who freed him.

Thankfully, the debriefing only lasted a few orvs, and then he was free to go. By that time it was the early evening. Habraum returned home to his apartment and found Jennica there, who gave him a message from the UComm AeroFleet to "get his arse to Terra Sollus HQ immediately."

He left for Terra Sollus the next day with Jennica in tow and met back up with his SR-21 squad for another emotional reunion—mainly with his longtime chum and fellow Cerc, Rukk Rigeff. Within the week, he received three medals of merit for his actions in the Ferronos Sector War. As honored as Habraum was by his awards from his peers, he felt uncomfortable receiving all this attention. In his mind the real heroes won the war while he, the genius that he was, got captured and just happened to get a lucky break. Jennica was there, his pillar of strength as always. When Habraum and Jennica finally traveled back to Cercidale, the young pilot was actually looking forward to spending some time on the ground and reacquainting himself with his life entirely. Or so he thought.

Habraum was not only deemed a war hero, but also an intergalactic luminary. Within the span of that week, word spread like wildfire throughout the Union about Habraum's return from Cybernarr space. Holozines dubbed him "The Fearless Navigator of Cercidale."

Just weeks after his return he met the Viceroy of Cercidale, the Magistrate of the Cercidalean Sector and even J'Kyver Leon-Greyse, the Chouncilor of the Galactic Union. But that was just the beginning.

Habraum became the subject of countless news stream stories on all the local IPNN™ and GBC™ affiliates around the Union. Holojournalists fought tooth and nail to get an interview with him. Holodocumentaries and biographies were mass-produced for holoview detailing his bravery and courage during the Ferronos Sector War, along with ludicrous imitations of the Cybernarr who held him captive. Most were so unspeakably awful that Habraum found them more comical than offensive.

At first Habraum rather enjoyed the attention, just a little, and did some interviews for the more credible holozines like the Union Tribune. And since his commanding officer at UComm AeroFleet had given him an indefinite leave to get back into the flow of things, Habraum had the chance to help train any new AeroFleet recruits. The fame and press were joined quickly by charity functions, sporting events and super posh parties. He only attended maybe five or six gatherings of the latter category because of the mob of sentients trying to meet him and Jen.

And of course, there was free stuff from the megacorporations. And not useless stuff either. How else would Habraum have gotten the new SR-23 V-wing he currently flew months before its release date?

But after a month, the luminary lifestyle got tiresome. He couldn't go anywhere in Cercidale, Terra Sollus or any other GUPR memberworld without attracting a crowd. The same went for Jennica, who had to take a special covert transport just to get to and from her teaching job on Terra Sollus. The Union Command had to create fake IDs for him just so he could get on and off GUPR memberworlds discreetly.

Now he sat in the solitude of his SR-23, dreading the moment it broke out of luminal space. He felt more trapped now than he did with the Cybernarr. Habraum shuddered at the thought.

"Trajectory to Terra Sollus completed. Preparing to break from L-Space."

Habraum jerked forward, the computerized voice jolting him out of his reminiscence. He glanced at his navicomputer's multicolored array to confirm. "Ah *hazik!*" Habraum fumed. Had it been two and a half orvs already? The lowered hum of the stellar drive engine kicked in, and he felt the ship vibrate for an instant as it reverted back to normal space. Habraum watched as the shimmering smear of light beyond his viewport broke into separate star lines, and then as those shrank into bright, distant dots. And there, at the midpoint of this starry vista lay his destination: a bluish-green sphere swaddled in feathery white.

It still wowed Habraum at how much it resembled Terra Firma, or Earth. With the exception of the higher land-to-water ratio and the shape of the continents, this planet was virtually identical. The similarities between the two worlds, coupled with Earth's overcrowding and polluted environment, was why the Terra Firma humans had declared this planet their new homeworld almost 150 years ago. The mass relocation inspired the Terra Firma humans to rename it Terra Sollus.

As the capitalworld for the Galactic Union of Planetary Republics, Terra Sollus was a melting pot of politics, commerce, magnificent landmarks and diversity. The Union Bicameral and the GUPR Chouncilor were situated on this planet, making it the most orbital-defense heavy world in the Union.

Habraum always regarded the planet with cynical ambivalence. Despite all of Terra Sollus's beauty and opportunity, the Cerc couldn't get past how Earth humans basically stole the planet from its natives, the Korvenites. That was part of the reason his family chose to live on Cercidale. He only tolerated Terra Sollus due to its importance in the Galactic Union and because Jennica's family was there.

Terra Sollus now filled up his viewport, its greenish continents looking more defined. He eased his fingers onto the flight console and shot the ship past the countless spacelanes to the planet's surface. Every lane was back-to-back traffic, a variety of different space vessels in each trying to reach the planet.

"Ha, amateurs," he laughed, rolling to port and rocketing toward the very edge of Terra Sollus's nightside. This was a useful military shortcut just over the continent of Onisus that he learned about in the AeroFleet. As he expected, the space lanes over in that area were moving along rather quickly.

"Transmit your GU ID." Habraum tapped on his comm transceiver, broadcasting the ship's Galactic Union ID to the traffic controller station floating somewhere above orbit. The response was immediate.

"Thank You. Welcome to Terra Sollus, *Wilbur Troubadour.*" Habraum gritted his teeth and punched the throttle forward without a word. Wilbur Troubadour, his horrid fake ID name, was a necessary evil so he wouldn't be stopped and extolled by traffic controllers.

Shooting through the billowy clouds, a myriad of city lights shot past several thousand pentametrids beneath him. Since he had a military-issue jet, normal speed laws were relaxed on him. The inky night bled away into lighter gold pastels of daylight. Habraum smirked, giving the ship an extra kick of speed as he approached Vesspuccia. The SR-23's flight controls were so responsive it was scary.

Because it was Terra Firma Memorial Week, Habraum volunteered to speak for Jennica's second-level class at Lincoln Elementary School in Conuropolis, the capital city of Vesspuccia. Because of the potential bulrush of media, Jennica tried to keep it quiet and made sure Habraum only spoke to her class. But she warned him to park in a corona wood forest about one pentametrid from the school and take his hovercycle, another free gift from Mekaal Ship Yards, and ride it the rest of the way.

"Are you sure the Union Intelligence Bureau isn't your calling?" he had quipped with her last night when they discussed this overly meticulous plan. Presently, Habraum soared over the sprawling cityscape of Conuropolis, heading south to the city's more suburban Corowood District, where Lincoln Elementary was. Even though Corowood was less metropolitan than the rest of Conuropolis, one could still see a similar congestion of residences spread out below, worming up the bases of the distant hills.

Once he found the corona wood forest, Habraum hit the landing thrusters (the roar was much quieter with the SR-23) and parked in the open patch surrounded by the towering, gold-leaved corona wood trees, which is how Corowood got its name. He popped open the cockpit and hopped out, taking in the vast flora around him. The noonlight sparkled off the blossoming corona wood leaves, so much so that their reflections cascaded down on the surrounding forest soil. He then unloaded his hovercycle from his jet's underbelly storage section and blasted through the forest toward Lincoln Elementary.

Upon arriving at the school's rear, he saw Jennica waiting for him. "Hi, you," she ran forward and gave him a quick firm kiss on the lips. Even though it was supposed to be professional teacher's attire, Habraum audibly marveled at how sexy she looked in a caramel pant suit with her hair in a classy twist.

"Oh relax, you walking hormone," Jennica laughed. "My students are watching a holovid that's about to finish, so let's hurry." She took Habraum by the hand, and the duo dashed inside with as much stealth as they could manage. Lincoln Elementary, a spread-out building made of azure and gold-colored ferroment, held pre-level through six-level student classes. After jogging through the empty hallways and then taking a two-flight translifter trip upstairs, they were at the entrance of her class.

"We're here," she turned to Habraum, clear concern in her eyes. "You sure you're ready for this?"

He pulled her close and grinned roguishly. "I was born ready. You more than anyone should know."

"I'm serious, Braum," Jennica smacked his chest in frustration. She tried her best not to return his smile, but just a glance into the Cerc's hazel-gold eyes and all her resolve went out the door. "These are second-level kids. They can be rambunctious when we have guests."

"Sounds like the egomaniac space jockeys in my flight group," Habraum shrugged. "So what's the problem?" Peering through the room door's viewport, Habraum saw the only light source coming from a large ovular holoscreen in the center of the room. It cast a pale illumination over the sixteen students inside. But what really held Habraum's attention was the picture on the holoscreen. This imagery had been burned into his memory since he was five years old. "Let me ballpark on what they're watching?"

"Yep, it's the Terra Firma Massacre documentary produced by IPNN™," Jennica said quietly. "The one the school shows every year during this week, with occasional updates." Both fell silent as they snuck into the classroom. Jennica's desk was in the back, while the children's desks circled around the holoscreen in the room's middle. Habraum moved behind Jennica's desk, but could not take his eyes off the blue and green image of Earth on the holoscreen. The holodocumentary's narrator became background noise as memories of that planet came rushing back with a clarity that surprised him.

Habraum had been to Earth twice as a child: once to the USA and another time to his father's home country Nigeria. Of all the planets he had seen, the Earth visits were among his favorites.

The tragedy happened 19 years and two months ago on Avril 8th, 2375. Earth, the original homeworld of Terran humans, was already suffocating under its own overpopulation and pollution. Ever since Earth humans had declared Terra Sollus their new homeworld 150 years prior, the telepathic Korvenites—native race to the planet—had been repeatedly kicked off their lands in favor of the expanding human and GUPR citizenry. It got to the point where the near-13 billion GUPR populace totally outnumbered the 700 million Korvenites on the planet.

By the mid-2300s, the Korvenites had had enough. The reasons were simple. Since day one, Korvenites were never given fair representation in the Galactic Union Bicameral, and the planet they once called home was no longer their own. Their acts of insurgence began with small riots on Terra Sollus. But given that this was the capitalworld of the Galactic Union, the UComm and local Regulat forces promptly contained any disorder. And then the Korvenites were given the large island country of Korvanland just so they would be silenced. Yet the land of their ancestors was no longer theirs, no longer even recognizable. Terra Sollus had been altered into the image that the GUPR wanted it to be. Rolling grasslands were now covered by megacorp plants and sprawling city-states that wormed up into the feet of the mountains. The once clear skies were now littered with arriving and departing space vessels, and an endless crawl of crisscrossing hovercar traffic made sure that one could never fully see a Rynn duskset.

This led to that one fateful morning when a dozen Korvenites sabotaged Earth's planetary shields, accidentally filling the planet's CO_2-rich atmosphere with thaelarite in its gas state. CO_2 and thaelarite gas created a toxic combustion that scorched the atmosphere and sent a poisonous inferno raining onto the surface. Over half of Earth's populace died, the highest non-war death toll in Galactic Union history.

Because of the massacre, Earth was rendered uninhabitable. What remained of its atmosphere was now comprised of lethal toxins. Despite his young age at the time of this tragedy, Habraum never forgot what it did to his father. The relatives, the birthplace, the culture lost to him were blows that Samuel Nwosu never fully recovered from. No one found the actual Korvenites responsible, but that didn't matter. The entire Galactic Union demanded vengeance for Earth. Within a few months, the whole Korvenite race became public enemy number one, hunted down with extreme prejudice.

Any Korvenite captured alive was whisked away to an unknown conjunction of internment camps. Habraum remembered the Union Chouncilor at the time saying, *"The containment of the Korvenites is for the greater good of the Union. If just twelve can murder so many, imagine what this entire race can do."*

"Hey, are you awake there, Habraum?" A soft hand rubbed against his forearm, jolting Habraum out of his recollections. He blinked in the darkness and turned to see Jennica staring at him.

"Just thinking, Jen," he turned away hastily. Jennica, still skeptical, thankfully didn't push the issue.

"Lights," she stood up as she spoke. The room lights came back on and the holoscreen completely vanished. The sixteen students in the room painted a diverse picture of what the Union represented. A pair of marooned-scaled reptoid twins that had to be Rothorids sat in the middle of the circle. Closest to Jennica's desk was a Nnaxan girl with two writhing craniowhisks branching out of her forehead. Next to her sat a snowy-white Kintarian kitten-male scratching his arm out of boredom.

Murmurs and whispers rippled among the students. They all pointed curious glances and fingers at Habraum. "Now class, attention please," Jennica raised her voice, adding some firmness to its tone. "I have a special guest today to speak with you about Earth Memorial Week. Say hello to Lieutenant Commander Habraum Nwosu from the Union Command AeroFleet."

Habraum rose to his feet and strode into the circle of desks. "Hullo," the Cerc glanced around and waved modestly at the class. The classroom went dead silent. All the students just sat there and stared.

"Class," Jennica prodded. "Say hello to Mr. Nwosu, please."

The students continued to sit there and stare at him. Just as Habraum looked to Jennica for some help, his eardrums practically exploded. The room erupted in joyous shrieks as the children leaped out of their desks and literally threw themselves at Habraum. He was almost knocked off his feet at the throng of children trying to embrace him, tugging at his hooded sweatshirt.

"Now, class!" Jennica darted forward, already prying some of the more enthusiastic students off her boyfriend. "Back to your seats! That's it, keep going." She dragged the young Kintarian kitten-male away before his flailing, prepubescent claws scratched anyone. She blew a stray lock of hair from her face while stuffing the furry boy back into his seat. When she turned to Habraum, her expression said, "I'm sorry, they're usually better than this." But Jennica's surprise was clear upon seeing Habraum's reaction.

Amid the swelling sea of children tugging at him, yelling with joy, the more undersized kids hugging his ankles since the horde of their peers prevented a hug around the waist, Habraum felt genuinely happy. It wasn't an ambush of narrow-minded holojournalists or random bystanders invading his privacy. These were just children showing gratitude as best as they knew how. And it totally warmed Habraum's heart.

After five or more macroms of cajoling from Jennica, her pupils finally settled back into their seats. But their animated energy still buzzed throughout the classroom. Habraum sat in front of Jennica's desk so he could see the entire class and began the tale of how he became an AeroFleet pilot.

He started simply enough with his life as a youth on Cercidale, briefly speaking on the various planets he visited and the influences of his parents; his mother Vara, a Cercidalean kurokoos breeder and his father Samuel, a Nigerian freighter merchant. Habraum's deep, Cercidalean lilt was captivating to the children's ears, causing a small titter among the female younglings.

Then Habraum touched key parts of his teenage years, like the moment when he knew he wanted to make his dream of joining the AeroFleet a reality, and by then the younglings were hooked. Several students gasped in wonder and others whispered "super galactic" as Habraum described his first space dogfight in detail. By the time Habraum got to the abridged version of the Ferronos Sector War and his capture, he glanced around and was pleasantly surprised at the wide-eyed interest on the children's faces. When he leaned back in his seat and left the story hanging, quite a few disgruntled cries rang out.

"You all want to know what happens next?" Habraum glanced around the room. The answer was unanimous and loud. The children fell silent again as he finished off the story in earnest. Habraum added an urgency to his voice as he breezed through meeting Marguliese (only calling her "a Cybernarr") to returning to Cercidale and seeing Jennica again. Every student erupted with applause after he finished.

By the beaming look on Jennica's face, Habraum could see why she loved teaching so much. He returned her smile eagerly and calmness spread through his heart. Jennica's smile quickly faded when she glanced up at the elliptical chronometer on the other side of the room. "Wow, time flew. Okay class," she rounded her desk and went to Habraum's side. "There are only fifteen macroms left in class (loud groans from the students). So you can ask Lt. Commander Nwosu any questions you want."

All hands shot up in unison. Most questions were the girls asking when he and Ms. Hoang were getting married, while the boys asked about flying or if his AeroFleet shoulder tattoo hurt when he got it. Habraum answered all the questions as best as he could manage, but laughed at the marriage question. He only said that they hadn't set a date yet. Jennica, despite her professionalism, turned bright pink when the kids yelled out teasingly, "Oooh!" But the last two questions stood out in Habraum's mind the most.

"Lieutenant Commander," hissed Vogohnor, one of the Rothorid twins. "Sssince you have achieved ssso much in the AeroFleet, are you going to ssstay or begin another profession?"

That inquiry from one so young caught him totally off guard. "Good question, Vogohnor," Habraum replied, nervously fingering one of his small hoop earrings. "At this point I'm weighing my options." The truth was Habraum, despite loving AeroFleet, did want to try something new. Shooting a glance at Jennica, the Cerc knew it was something he had to consider for their future together.

"Mr. Nwosu," it was now the Nnaxan girl. "On the news streams, I've seen humans get angry and say bad things about the Korvenites each year during Earth Memorial week. Do you do the same thing?"

"Not at all," Habraum shook his head. "I'd rather remember Earth's wonders, not its tragedies."

"Don't you hate the Korvenites for what they did?" asked a human boy, a frown on his pudgy face.

"Of course not," Habraum said quietly. "It's exhausting. My father hated the Korvenites for years."

Habraum leaned forward and looked each student in the eye. "I blame those individuals responsible for Earth's demise. Do any of you think it was right to imprison an entire race for the crimes of a few?"

There were several headshakes and murmurs of, "No." Only a few, mainly the humans, nodded.

An electronic klaxon signaled the end of the school day, jolting many to their feet in a discordant shuffle of shoes. "That's all for the day, class. Say, 'thank you' to Mr. Nwosu for visiting us." The classroom rippled with an enthusiastic, "Thank you!" as they began to scamper out the door. Some came up to Habraum and shook his massive hands with as much adult-like gravity as they could muster. "Don't forget the writing assignments about an ethnicity from Earth, due tomorrow," Jennica called after them.

She turned to face Habraum after the last student left. "You were amazing!" Jennica squeaked in joy as she bounded up and wrapped her arms around his waist. "That went better than I could have hoped."

"Hey, I had fun," he shrugged, stroking her hair. "Got me thinking about having our own sprouts."

Jennica snapped her head up from Habraum's broad chest and looked at him dubiously. "You're serious? This coming from the same man who said 'No kids, no crying, no thank you?'"

"Yes, but that was then," Habraum laughed, cupping Jennica's face in his hands. "I want to start planning for *our* future." As he gazed at her, Habraum saw the shock on her face, felt her trembling.

Jennica composed herself with a smile and clasped her hands around his own. "I like this new you, Mr. Nwosu. He better stay around awhile. Especially while I have some classwork to do," she pulled away and moved to her desk. "This should take about half an orv, and then we can get out of here."

"Of course, Jen." Habraum walked toward the classroom viewport left of Jennica's desk. "Take your time." She sat at her desk and settled into her work, but with this broad smile on her face that Habraum had never seen before. Smirking to himself, he folded his arms and turned to the semi-dusty viewport, watching the swarming traffic of children below exiting the school building. He wondered then what kind of father would he be? And what future beyond being a fighter pilot could he build for his offspring?

The hiss of the classroom door opening caught his ear. Habraum turned his head to see an adult Rothorid standing in the entrance, trailed by the much smaller twins from Jennica's class. Given the thickness of the long, muscular tail swishing feverishly from behind, it was obviously a male Rothorid. His sinewy physique was evident, even under the blue-and-yellow Union Command uniform he wore.

The male, like his children, had scaly maroon skin, but his was darker and much more leathered with age. Those large ginger eyes, the triangular thin-lipped maw and wrinkled brow folds betrayed nothing, only a stoicism that brooked no tolerance for waywardness.

"Mr. Ishiliba," Jennica was on her feet. "How nice to see you! Is there something I can do for you?"

"No thank you, Msss. Hoang," the Rothorid spoke in a raspy voice. His s-words sounded like hisses, and not welcoming ones. He then turned to Habraum. "I wanted to ssspeak with your classss guessst." The Rothorid turned his narrow gaze on Habraum. "Sso my offspring tell me that you are filling their headsss with ssstoriess about the Korvenitesss," the Rothorid prowled into the room, past Jennica's desk and into Habraum's face at disquieting speed. "How they aren't culpable for the sssinss of their brethren." His twins, who hung back outside the classroom, went into fits of sissing that loosely resembled laughter.

Habraum straightened up and stared back at the Rothorid's reptilian face, not the least bit intimidated. He stood at least three inches taller than the Rothorid. "Someone has to, because the parents sure as hazik aren't," Habraum said with a biting edge, his tolerance for slipshod parenting non-existent.

"Okay," Jennica rose from her desk to stop the clash. "I'm sure there's a better way to settle this—"

"It'sss okay, Msss. Hoang," the Rothorid smiled, displaying long, needle-like teeth. Habraum recoiled. He preferred it when the other just glared at him.

"I'm jussst glad that your guest actually thinkss rationally about the Korvenite matter," he continued, holding out a clawed hand. "Pleasssure to meet you, Habraum. I'm 2nd Lt. Honaa Ishiliba."

"Same on this side," Habraum cautiously returned the handshake, seeing Jennica relax visibly from the corner of his eye. He then saw the strange insignia on the upper-left torso of Honaa's uniform.

"Uh, excuse me for asking," Habraum stared at the insignia. "But you're a 2nd Lieutenant of…?"

"The Sstar Brigade Ssspecial Forcesss," Honaa rasped, stepping back a little.

Habraum frowned. He had heard a bit about this 'Star Brigade.' Some specialized branch of the UComm full of super-powered beings that battled against terrorist threats to the Galactic Union.

"Thisss is why I came when my offsssspring told me of your presssence. You're a maximum, yesss?"

Honaa hissed it so coolly, Habraum felt his jaw drop. "That's not public knowledge," he stammered.

"I know, but you are on Section M's dossssier of regisssstered maximums, which isss how I know."

Habraum didn't like where this was headed. He didn't like discussing this subject. "Look, Honaa…"

"Don't fear Habraum, for I am one assss well. Observe." The Rothorid snatched up an e-marker from Jennica's desk before she could protest. He stared at it in his hand, his orbs narrowing into mere ginger slits. Then the e-marker began to warp and twist, the very air around Honaa's hand rippling with some unknown energy field. Habraum's eyes became saucers. Jennica gasped. More sissing giggles from the twins, who had probably seen their father do this many times. The sissing died with a glare from Honaa.

"My abilitiesss are matter dissstortion." Once a writing device, the e-marker now looked more like a pretzel. "Becaussse of the sssuperior training program within the Star Brigade, I can do far more than that." Honaa casually placed the misshapen e-marker back on Jennica's desk as if he had done nothing amazing. It rolled off and clinked oddly onto the ground, bringing Habraum's attention back to Honaa.

"There are many maximumsss that are recruited to the Ssstar Brigade. We work hard to uphold the idealsss of the GUPR while guarding it from any terrorissst threat that may present itssself."

"But why are you telling me this?" Habraum asked.

Honaa flopped his tail from side to side, which was a Rothorid shrug. "Becaussse many in the Star Brigade feel that you, with your exceptional piloting, are a perfect candidate for our organization."

Jennica had heard enough. "I think I speak for both of us when I say that Habraum is happy just to be on solid ground right now," she stood up from her desk, her voice with a permanence that caught both males' attention. "Joining another military organization is not on our list of priorities."

"I'm not recruiting him, Msss. Hoang," Honaa snapped his head back to Habraum. "But I will asssk you to consider coming to a preview of what we do, Mr. Nwosssu." He held out his hand; this time it held a white comcard. Habraum cautiously took it. "Give me a call if you desssire to hear more about the Ssstar Brigade. Good day, Msss. Hoang, keep up the good work in teaching my offspring."

He pivoted and hissed at the twins in his native tongue of Wuiroth. The twins stood up at attention when their father passed them and stalked out the door, his tail swishing lazily in his wake. The small Rothorids stared at Habraum with twin pairs of ginger eyes for a few moments before scampering after Honaa. The classroom door promptly hissed shut. Habraum stared at the ivory comcard in his palm, the Star Brigade logo shimmering on either side. "Me, in a team of elite maximum commandos?" he thought out loud. It sounded even more absurd then. So why was the idea of it still stuck in his mind?

"Well, that's one offer we won't be taking." Jennica was busily sweeping her datapads into a sleek grey satchel. "Come on, let go before any of my other students' parents come with even stranger offers."

Habraum absently nodded and stuffed the comcard in his pocket. Jennica watched him while slinging the satchel over her shoulder. "You're not actually considering his offer, are you?"

The Cerc shrugged. "I'm not sure yet."

She froze, her features hardening. "You *are* considering Honaa's offer."

"Jen—"

"After all that you've gone through," Jennica cut him off, looking down at her desk in barely controlled fury. "I cannot believe that you would even consider putting your life in danger again."

Habraum felt his cheeks warm. "And I said that I hadn't made any type of decision yet, Jen. It is just an option at this point. Besides, it would be better than sitting at home, barricading myself from nosy holojournalists and the whole galaxy!" The frustration of not doing anything useful burst out before he could stop it. "*Rogguts,* Jen, I can't live my life standing still just because it's the safe thing to do!"

Immediately Habraum saw the way Jennica stared back, staggered from the gusto of Habraum's argument. The sight of it struck his heart with a pang of embarrassment. "I'm sorry, Jen. That was so uncalled for," he said quietly, idly scratching at the back of his head.

"No, *I* should apologize," she walked back toward Habraum. "I won't become a nag like my mom."

"Thank the Maker for *that!*" Habraum wrapped his arms around Jennica's small frame and held her tightly, relishing her sweet fragrance under his nostrils. Life had become too short for petty arguments.

"Let's just go home, okay?" Jennica kissed him firmly on the lips and pulled back a little with a renewed smile. "You can cook us some of those scrumptious kurokoos strips for dinner tonight."

That brought a grin to Habraum's face. "Definitely, and you get to ride home in style today." He waved his SR-23 keys in Jennica's face. As they walked out of the classroom to the translifter, Habraum threw a burly arm around her and pulled her in close. He could feel the shameless stares of teachers and students alike that were still in the hallways after school, but ignored them.

Once inside the translifter, Jennica cuddled against him and stared blankly at the smooth doors of the lifter, obviously lost in her own thoughts. "Ground Level," Habraum said, feeling the translifter descend. He glanced at the floor, and still that insignia lingered on his mindscape.

So the Star Brigade was always hard at work upholding the ideals of the GUPR? Habraum had already done that and then some with the AeroFleet. But since returning from Cybernarr Space, the Cerc realized how small his world was as a fighter pilot. What used to be exhilarating was now mundane. Habraum even interacted with his sophomoric pilotmates differently, almost embarrassed with how they carried themselves. Something needed to change. He remembered another job offer he had received from a holofilm director. As a holovid actor! Habraum cringed, fiddling with the comcard in his pocket.

I should at least give this Star Brigade a brief check, he said to himself.

Exiting the translifter, Habraum and Jennica walked through the near-empty halls of Lincoln Elementary and into the bright noonlight. *Me, a Star Brigadier?* Habraum chuckled at the thought as he and Jennica saddled onto his hovercycle. In his twenty-four years he had seen stranger things happen.

Inside the Galactic Union

Despite being a young star-spanning government, the Galactic Union of Planetary Republics has quickly established itself as a force to be reckoned with. Its promotion of equality and diversity amongst its members has made the Union one of the most prominent and fastest growing hyperpowers in the known galaxy.

Formation

The Beginning

The early seeds of the Union were planted in 2068 when Earth first achieved FLT space flight outside the Sol System. A decade or so afterward, humanity was welcomed into the interplanetary community by other spacefaring races like the aquatic Galdorians, the pacifist Kudobans, the energy-based Voton and the squid-like Rhomerans. For the next half a century, the five species became key trading partners and allies.

During this period there were quarrels that nearly destroyed this early accord, like the Half-Year War (2093-2094) between the Voton and the Rhomerans, as well as the Voton Civil War or The Radiance War (2115) that nearly tore Aurealis apart. Talks began to create a more formal merger of affairs during the Interstellar Boom of the 2120s and 2130s. But these discussions became actionable after aggressive encounters with the Kedri Imperium and the Ttaunz Supremacy.

The first incarnation of the Galactic Union was the Coalition of Free Worlds formed in 2148. This government ends in disaster a year later due to a weak central government with next to no power over the five members' independent governments. The Voton and Rhomerans almost doomed any future attempts at a unified government due to their timeworn feud reigniting.

Two years later in 2151, cooler heads prevailed and another effort toward a star-spanning government came in the form of the Galactic Union of Planetary Republics. Many mistakes from the Coalition of Free Worlds were corrected, per the Articles of Unification, with the formation of a stronger central government holding authority over the memberworlds' independent governments and sharing authority between the Five Founder Races.

At this point, the Galactic Union comprised of Earth (earthborn human), Aurealis (Voton), Rhomera (Rhomeran) Bal-Dobra (Kudoban) and Galdor (Galdorian) along with each planets' respective colony worlds and territories. The capital world was Galdor.

The Union at the time was led by the Executive Council, which appointed two Chief Executives from each memberworld. Each of the five memberworlds had equal voting power, so no one race could overrule another on their own. As the ultimate authority in the Union, the Council was responsible for maintaining law and order between Union worlds, colonies and territories.

The High Tribunal Court, established on Galdor in 2152, was the head of the government's judicial branch and the ultimate authority to punish those who violated Union law.

A rumor amongst Union citizens was that just before the Frontier Wars with the Ttaunz Supremacy, the Executive Council created and employed a secret agency of elite combat operatives known as **C**overt **R**econnaissance and **O**perations (CRONOS). The agency's alleged mandate was to keep the Union stable by any means necessary. The agency's existence has been neither confirmed nor denied by the Executive Council.

Every year since 2151, Unification Day celebrates the historic date the Galactic Union officially formed.

The Frontier Wars

The much larger hyperpower known as the Ttaunz Supremacy had been a threat to the Union memberworlds dating as far back as the late 21st century. The Ttaunz had been long been interested in adding Galdor to its dependencies, which the oceanic world always rebuffed. The Supremacy attacked a new Union colony, claiming that the settlement had encroached on its borders, even though the Ttaunz had no claim to the territory. This 'blatant affront' gave the Ttaunz an excuse to declare war on the fledgling Union in the year 2153.

The Union knew it couldn't win a fair fight against the Ttaunz Supremacy's larger, cohesive military fleet. And the Ttaunz, overconfident in an easy victory, deployed only a small portion of its fleet to engage the Union. But thanks to intel gathering by Rhomera's spy network, the unconfirmed infiltration efforts of CRONOS and devastating guerrilla tactics from Galdorian, Earth and Voton forces, the Union took the fight to Supremacy forces. Less than a month later, the Ttaunz retreated in humiliation.

After that, the Union memberworlds combined their military forces and the Union Command Armada was born.

Union Command's first true test came in 2155 when the Ttaunz Supremacy attacked again in an attempt to conquer the *entire* Galactic Union. The war lasted over a year and almost ended in the Union's defeat, after the Supremacy launched orbital strikes on Galdor and Rhomera – briefly conquering the former planet. The Union repelled the Supremacy with a combination of guerrilla tactics and the new unified might of their nascent armed forces, but couldn't fully drive the Supremacy out of Union Space. The Ttaunz's military had size and firepower superiority.

But AeroFleet Admiral Odin Tayal's daring gambit changed the course of the war. Tayal took a small fleet of ships to attack the Supremacy's core worlds and outposts, disguised as Vorn attack cruisers, causing Supremacy forces to turn back toward their own aerospace. As the Supremacy made their way through asteroid fields, the UComm forces sandwiched them in a devastating sneak attack that lasted for two days. The Ttaunz were decimated while the Union barely lost any ships.

What remained of the Supremacy forces surrendered in late 2156, leading to the Accord of Terra Sollus (then an Earth colony), effectively ending the Second Frontier War. A key component in the Terra Sollus Accord was the creation of definitive borders between Ttaunz and Union Space to prevent future warfare. These conflicts, dubbed the **Frontier Wars**, were also known as the **Supremacy Wars** or the **Borderland Crisis**.

The aftermath of the war led to the Union's continuing military buildup in order to prepare for another Ttaunz attack, as well as any other hyperpower that might attack. Also, to protect the branches of the Union government, the Executive Council's center of operations was moved to Bal-Dobra.

The Age of Expansion

Sometime after the second Frontier War in the year 2157, a magnetar destroyed all of the Ttaunz Supremacy's core planets in the cataclysmic event known as the Supremacy's Ruin. This left a graveyard of dead worlds and a number of the Supremacy's far-flung colony worlds that remained untouched by the devastation. Free now from the yoke of the Supremacy, the natives of these planets kicked any remaining Ttaunz out. This left the imperiled Ttaunz homeless and at the mercy of the many enemies they had made over the centuries.

Surprisingly enough, it was their old enemy the Galactic Union who came to the displaced Ttaunz's aid, ferrying them to safety and finding a home for them on the planet Faroor.

The Union's actions in regards to the displaced Ttaunz refugees garnered much praise and respect from the galactic community, causing many planets to request membership. The influx of new members over the next several decades was welcomed by most Founder Races.

However, unease over having to share power caused some growing pains when new members took issue with only the five Founder Races being eligible for the Executive Council. These growing pains led to the creation of the Union Bicameral in 2173 and office of Chouncilor in 2174.

Membership guidelines were established in order to weed out candidates who could not contribute economically to the Union. Some of those worlds deemed ineligible became colonies or territories depending on their potential for growth.

As of 2403, the Galactic Union now had up to eighty-seven full memberworlds, along with hundreds of colony worlds and territories in at least seven designated sectors of space.

Government Structure

The Chouncilor of the Galactic Union

The Galactic Union's elected leader and head of its executive branch is the Chouncilor. The position is voted in by the Chamber of Delegates, which in turn receive votes from the memberworlds, colony world and territories they represent. The Chouncilor and the Executive Branch reside on the Union capital world, which is currently Terra Sollus.

The Chouncilor presides over meetings with the Executive Ministry, which are the leaders of the Union's Executive Branch. The Chouncilor can serve a maximum of two five-year terms, but every two and a half years they receive an approval review from the High Tribunal, based on anonymous members of the Bicameral and their track record (a form of checks and balances). There have only been two instances in Union history where a Chouncilor has been ousted due to a below average job performance.

One of the Chouncilor's most important roles is being the Supreme Commander of the Union Command Armada. In matters of extreme urgency or during war, the Chouncilor can make immediate, unilateral decisions without the approval or the High Tribunal or the Union Bicameral.

The Chouncilor's second in command is the Vice Chouncilor, the first person in the line of succession to the Chouncilorship upon the death, resignation, or removal of the sitting Chouncilor.

The Honor Guard, an interplanetary law enforcement agency within the Ministry of Homeworld Security, is tasked with the safety of current and former Chouncilors and their families. They also provide protection details for Vice Chouncilors, Chouncilor candidates and visiting foreign Heads of State.

The Executive Ministry

After the Executive Council was dissolved, the Executive Ministry was formed to assist the Chouncilor in governing the various needs of the Galactic Union. The 15 supervising officials of each ministry hold a position in the Executive Ministry, as stated below:

- Minister of Union Affairs
- Minister of Defense
- Minister of Homeworld Security
- Minister of Commerce
- Minister of Finance

- Minister of Education

- Minister of Interior Development

- Minister of Expansion and Exploration

- Minister of Interstellar Relations

- Minister of Justice

- Minister of Transport

- Minister of Energy

- Minister of the Proletariat

- Minister of Agriculture

- Minister of Health Services

High Tribunal

The High Tribunal is the head of the Union's judicial branch, and the highest court with the Galactic Union. The rulings are handed down by eleven Chief Magistrates. The High Tribunal Court remains on Galdor, even though it is no longer the Union capital world.

The Union Bicameral

When the Union was founded, the Executive Council served as both the Union's legislative and executive branch. But once so many new members began streaming in, the Executive Council was dissolved in 2173. A two-chamber legislative branch was then formed to represent every memberworlds in the Galactic Union.

The Chamber of Delegates consists of Delegates from all areas of the Union, including territories and colony worlds. A memberworld's number of delegates depends on the planet's population and influence. The Union Senate is comprised of three Senators from each memberworld, which brings the current Senate up to 261 members.

Delegates and Senators represent the interests of their planets in the Union legislative process, but they aren't constitutionally authorized to execute the laws. Various parties are represented in the Congress, chief amongst them are Populist (favoring a less centralized government), Temperate (moderate/middle of the road), Imperialist (favoring a more centralized government), Technocrat (technology-leaning) and Theocrat (religious/spiritually leaning).

Union Memberworld governments

Each memberworld's government is a microcosm of the GUPR's government. A memberworld's executive branch is ruled by a Viceroy, with a World Court heading the judicial branch and a Global Congress for the legislative branch. The main Union government usually doesn't interfere with day-to-day governance of their memberworlds, particularly their interior affairs.

But in a number of domains such as warfare, communication with other star-spanning governments and resolving disputes between memberworlds, Union mandates always supersede individual memberworlds' law.

Military

The **Union Command Armada (UComm)** falls under the Ministry of Defense's jurisdiction. Since its formal creation in 2153, the UComm's size, capabilities and responsibility for protecting the Union from any interior or exterior threats has grown exponentially. The four military branches subordinate to the Ministry of Defense include UComm PLADECO, UComm AeroFleet, UComm Space Marines and UComm Border Patrol.

The **UComm Planetary Defense Corps (UComm PLADECO)** deal directly with the protection of all Union memberworlds, colony worlds and territories. This includes aerial, terrestrial, nautical, and suborbital armed forces.

UComm Space Marine Corps (UCSMC) provides outerspacial force projection, utilizing the mobility of UComm's AeroFleet to deploy its units. Subdivisions include Space Marine All-Terrain Operations Command (SMATOC), UComm Fleet Space Marine Force (FSMF), and Space Marines Consulate Security Command (CSC).

Union Command Aerospace Defense Fleet (UComm AeroFleet) represents the Galactic Union's military space fleet. This ranges from fighter jets and massive battle command cruise ships in AeroFleet Combat Command to deep space exploration vessels in AeroFleet

Exploration Corps (shared between the Ministries of Defense and Expansion & Exploration). AeroFleet Academy, where the next generation of aerospace officers is trained, also falls under AeroFleet's umbrella.

The primary mission of **UComm Border Patrol (UCBP)** is ensuring the safekeeping of borders between neighboring races and unclaimed space. Vessels and personnel in this agency are tasked with patrolling Union borders as well as conducting health and security inspections for ships suspected of violating Galactic Union laws. Other Border Patrol duties include preventing terrorists and terrorist weapons from entering the Union, stopping individuals attempting to enter the Union illegally and ensuring the safety of travelers entering and exiting Union Space.

UComm Joint Special Operations Group (JSOG) oversee all special operations elements, even those within the other UComm branches. Star Brigade, PLADECO's Omega Group, and the Space Marines' TROJANs fall under JSOG's authority.

The **Union Command Joint Medical Division (UCJMD)** create joint oversight between all areas of the UComm in four key areas: medical research, medical education and training, health care delivery, and shared support services.

Another key division is **UComm Installation Operations (UCIO)**, which manages all military border outposts, deep-space stations, mining stations, shipyards and starbases.

Other military subdivisions include Military Advocate General (MAG), UComm Corps of Engineers (UCCE), and UComm Military Intelligence Directorate (UCMI or Military Intelligence)

Noteworthy Chouncilors

- **Vut'guios'ajjus** (2174 – 2179), aka 'Sajjus', was an esteemed Kudoban diplomat and mediator who helped extensively with the Great Migration of displaced Ttaunz refugees, was elected as the first Chouncilor of the Union.

While many believed his pacifist nature would make him a weak choice for Chouncilor, Vut'guios'ajjus in the end defined the role for future Chouncilors, which included setting the balance of power between the High Tribunal and newly created Bicameral. He held the

Union together during the First Terminus War (then called the Separatist War) between 2176-2178, eventually reaching a truce with the separatist leaders. Sajjus served just one term, which was heralded as a major success.

Unfortunately, certain policy decisions made during his tenure were blamed for the Economic Slump of 2180.

- **Gulthresh'Gishroo 'Gult'** (2264 – 2267), a Voton male, was a lackluster Chouncilor renowned more for his carnal indulgences than his policies. In 2264 he approved a mandate for Terra Sollus to become the official homeworld for earthborn humans 150 years after it became a colony world for Earth. The move was seen as a slight to the indigenous Korvenites who were losing more and more acreage to immigrating humans. Gult's push for Cantalese's full membership, where he spent an excessive amount of time, was unsuccessful. It was rumored that he wanted to make the Vacation Planet the new capital world of the Union.

But Chouncilor Gult is mainly remembered as the first Chouncilor to be assassinated. The culprit behind Gult's death was a radical sect of Rhomerans. This renewed hostilities between Rhomera and Aurealis for many years.

- **K'Lyrrid Varo-Kata** (2374 – 2383), a Kintarian female, was a former AeroFleet Admiral and Defense Minister who rode the wave of her 'war hero' status after the Second Terminus War into the Chouncilor's office. Her combat prowess served her little in her tenure's first few years, but helped after a series of tragedies. The first was the Earth Holocaust in 2377. Varo-Kata rose to the occasion, holding the Union together and ordering the capture of all Korvenites. It was under Varo-Kata's tenure that the secret internment camps were built to contain the Korvenites.

The second tragedy happened when the Terminus Cluster rebelled again after two of their planets, Ysaeld and Shrall, applied for full Union membership. The mutinous species in the Terminus Cluster declared these planets to be traitors and seeing the Earth Massacre as a sign of weakness, obliterated Shrall. They threatened to destroy Ysaeld as well unless the Union left the Terminus Cluster and abdicated all claims to it.

Varo-Kata refused to bend, and once all Union personnel had been evacuated from Terminus Cluster worlds behind the uprising, Varo-Kata struck. She ordered the destructions of all rebellious worlds— seven in total—completely eradicating these species. Many in the Bicameral wanted Varo-Kata tried for multiple counts of xenocide, but a trial was rejected by the High Tribunal in light of Varo-Kata effectively ending the Third Terminus War and any future rebellions.

Varo-Kata's actions made testimony to any memberworld or star-spanning government doubting the power of the Galactic Union. This earned Varo-Kata the nicknames of 'L'Kyrrod the Destroyer' and 'World Breaker.'

- **Aristotle 'Ari' Bogosian** (2396 – 2403) was a former Chamber Delegate and Union Senator elected to office of the Chouncilor in late 2396, a year after the Ferronos Sector War. Bogosian was a shrewd politician and conciliator, finding ways to bring even his staunchest detractors to the table and reaching a middle ground that appeased most parties. He successfully put down the first incarnation of the Korvenite Independence Front as well as averting a near-war with the Juunthra Accord over long disputed borders.

A major triumph during his tenure was capitalizing on the goodwill between the Kedri Imperium and the Union after the Ferronos Sector War to move toward a historic interstellar trade merger, which would've been the largest in recorded history.

Unfortunately, the actions of the Korvenite Independence Front terrorist group turned the merger into a disaster and the Union's relationship with the Imperium is now in disrepair. Shortly afterwards, Bogosian resigned from office in disgrace in the middle of his second term and now dedicates himself to philanthropy.

WANT TO HEAR ABOUT NEW RELEASES?

Join My Mailing List at ccekeke.com!

Members get release announcements, sneak peeks of future books and other bonuses during the year. Plus, emails are **never** shared or used for any other purpose.

Feel free to contact me on Facebook, Twitter and email (ccekeke.com/connect)

***

OTHER BOOKS BY C.C. EKEKE

STAR BRIGADE SERIES

Star Brigade: Resurgent (Book 1)
Star Brigade: Maelstrom (Book 2)
Star Brigade: The Supremacy (Book 3)
Star Brigade: Ascendant (Book 4)

About the Author

Born in 1979, C.C. Ekeke spent much of his childhood on a steady diet of science fiction movies and television shows, as well as superhero comic books like the X-Men and the Avengers. It was in college studying for a degree in advertising that he stumbled across a desire to write books. Some of his heaviest influences include authors J.K. Rowling, Michael A. Stackpole, Peter David, Timothy Zahn, and most recently George R.R. Martin (both TV show and books). Currenly living in LA's San Fernando Valley, he's hard at work on the next Star Brigade novels and short stories.